ILMAR PENNA MARINHO JR.

The beast of a thousand years

ILMAR PENNA MARINHO JR.

The beast of a thousand years

Title: The beast of a thousand years
Author: Ilmar Penna Marinho Jr.

publisher Paula Cajaty
design 54 Design
cover design Aline Martins
revised Fabiana Colasanti, Louisa Lopes
translation Fabiana Colasanti

Issued in electronic and printed format.
Print run by Ingram.

ISBN 978-989-8938-83-1
E-ISBN 978-989-8938-84-8

rua de Xabregas 12, lote A, 276-289
1900-440 Lisboa, Portugal
tel. [+351] 308 803 682
editoragatobravo@gmail.com
editoragatobravo.pt

Content

About the Author

ILMAR PENNA MARINHO JUNIOR was born in Rio de Janeiro. He spent his childhood and teenage years in Europe, where he learned to appreciate the French culture. He is a journalist and has graduated in Law at PUC-RIO, and in Master of Comparative Law at Georgetown University, Washington, DC. He has been Secretary of Administration of the State of Rio de Janeiro, with relevant management and advisory functions at PETROBRAS, and studied at the Military Academy (ESG – Escola Superior de Guerra). He has published seven books, and today dedicates his life to literature, historical researches, and traveling.

*To my solar muse and
unrelenting proofreader
Solange Maria de Castro
Barbosa Cordeiro da Silva,
who inspired me to visit
the Apocalypse Tapestry
in Château D'Angers.*

Chapter 1

THE LARGEST AND MOST IMPRESSIVE TAPESTRY in the world was the topic of the lecture given by the curator of Château D'Angers at the 21st edition of the Journalism Festival, promoted annually by the municipal administration of the historical capital of Anjou, located in the Loire Valley, France, with its majestic castles and delicious rosé wines.

"My friends, I have the honor to be here, at the Palais des Arts, to talk to you about the magnificent tapestry inspired by the last book of the Gospel, or better yet, by the Apocalypse, according to Saint John. A stunning work of art that transcends the feudal values and the imagination and that was only displayed during the big festive events of the royalty to show the power and the luxury of the princes of Anjou. I'm also proud to tell you about Château D'Angers, this impregnable military fortress, built by a woman with a fighting spirit, ruler Blanche de Castille. Currently, the castle houses the Apocalypse Tapestry and the Museum of Medieval Weapons, which gathers the most complete collection of war crossbows in France, this blessed land of François Villon, Pierre de Ronsard, and Joachim du Bellay..."

From then on, it begins, on the night of October 13th, 2006, a long journey through time made by renowned historian and curator Ferdinand Rochemont de Sailly, assisted by priest Antoine Duvert, both speakers at the auditorium of the Palais des Arts. Initially, there was an explanation about how the province of Anjou was annexed to the kingdom of France in 1204, and how the ruler Blanche de Castille, who reigned from 1221 to 1244, mother of ten children, had a colossal fortress built, with seventeen towers, to fend off the threats and ambitions of the then king of England, Henry

III. The curator sang praises to the beauty and wisdom of the ruler, celebrated in medieval songs and verses, as she had the same sovereign authority and determination of Catherine II of Russia, known as Catherine, the Great.

Then, the curator, wearing a blazer and a bowtie, revived the tumultuous life of Louis I of Valois, Duke of Anjou and Touraine, king of Naples (Napoli), Italy, and Count of Provence, France, the second son of King John II, the Good, and brother of Charles V, the Wise, both kings of France, of the Valois dynasty. He told that, during the time of English domination and the Hundred Year's War, Louis I, even residing only for a brief period in Château D'Angers, commissioned, in 1373, the famous Apocalypse Tapestry to the Parisian workshop of Nicolas Bataille, who took nine years to complete it. He then projected several texts and photos to illustrate the saga of the origin, and the destruction and resurrection from the ashes of the most famous French medieval tapestry. He didn't shy away from reproaching Louis II's son, René, the last Duke of Anjou who lived in the castle, also known as René I of Anjou, Duke of Lorraine, France, and king of Naples, the Good King René (*Le Bon Roi René*), who donated the tapestry, in his will, to the ecclesiastical dignitaries of the Angers Cathedral, dedicated to Saint Maurice, patron of the city.

"It was a real sacrilege what they did to the *haute lisse* tapestry donated to the cathedral. As a consequence of this thoughtless act, it was cut into pieces and offered for sale."

After the remark, in a heartfelt tone, Ferdinand de Sailly explained that, during the French Revolution, the sacred objects were destroyed. In the case of the tapestry, something extraordinary happened. Instead of disappearing, the dismembered pieces were miraculously reassembled at Saint-Serge Abbey.

The curator, noticing that Father Antoine couldn't sit still, showing evident impatience, authorized him, with a nod, to read a document from 1806 that he had just taken out of his briefcase and described the terrible state of the tapestry, thrown in "a damp place, where it would break and tear apart at the mere touch of a hand." But the priest wasn't satisfied just reading, and also expressed his opinion about the chromatic vitality of the religious oeuvre.

"It's very important to point out that the tapestry maintains to this day, on the reverse side, all the power of its original colors: hot reds, deep blues, golden oranges, and stunning greens. These colors blend into the splendid images of the twenty-four elders, the Four Horsemen of the Apocalypse, the trumpeting angels of the Annunciation, the worshipers of the Antichrist, the formidable beasts with seven heads, the chosen ones, the baldachins, and the gothic churches."

Taking the floor once more, the curator pointed out that the results, especially of the most recent restorations, were not always successful, because modern chemical dyes would prove, over time, to be inappropriate for the restoration of masterpieces woven by master medieval craftsmen, who used natural dyes, extracted from plants.

When the conference was over, an avalanche of questions ensued, some of them misplaced, like the first one, from a young woman, that caused the audience to burst into laughter.

"I would like to know, Mr. Curator, if the ruler Blanche reviewed the troops like Queen Catherine used to do?"

This was the curator's answer to the trick question:

"*Mademoiselle*, since the walls of the castle were thick, deaf and blind to their owners' affections, there are no records of what the ruler Blanche, widow of Louis VIII, deceased in 1226, did with her spare time after reviewing her guard of honor. Oddly enough, your question makes me remember the famous episode, told by the minstrel of Reims, in which an extravagant gesture of this queen was able to silence the slanders of the Bishop of Beauvais and other vassals. The ruler went to the Parliament, where she had a stand. She went in, wearing a long coat, demanded silence and attention, climbed on a table in the center of the room, and yelled to the bishop: 'Look closely and see if I'm pregnant', while she dropped the coat to her feet. She spun around, naked, in all directions under the captivated stares of the audience, all to prove that the accusation that she was expecting another child was false. They all rushed to her with respect and admiration, covered her with her coat, and led her to the royal chambers. To this day, no one knows whether they acted this way out of devotion to her beauty or her courage."

"Could you explain the reason for the sale?" asked a lady in the back of the auditorium.

"Father Antoine Duvert, who knows well this nefarious period of the tapestry, will answer you."

"Well, after the donation in 1474, the tapestry was on display in the cathedral's nave on Saint Maurice Day, Christmas, Easter, and Pentecost Sunday. As much as they considered it 'absolutely magnificent', the priests complained about the hard work of lifting it from the vault and the expenses to keep it intact. They also complained that it drowned out the songs and made the sermons inaudible. They decided to put it up for sale in 1783, right before the Revolution. No one wanted to buy it! But the worse was yet to come. Since its conservation had become a nuisance, it was cut up and began to have the most unexpected uses. It served as protection in greenhouses, curtains, saddle hides, and even doormats. It was an insult what they did to this great work of sacred art."

"Could you tell us when the restoration works began?" asked a young lady, moved by the description.

"It was Canon Louis-François Joubert, named guardian of the cathedral, who had the brilliant idea of creating a workshop to restore the tapestry. The work began on February 1st, 1849, and continues to this day. They have recovered the six pieces which contain fourteen tableaus each, plus the scenes with the 'great characters'. Altogether, it is 338 feet long and 14.8 feet high. It's impossible not to be impressed with the four huge restored images in the middle of the canopy supported by columns, in which we are invited to contemplate and ponder about the biblical scenes."

The panelists were subjected to several questions about the missing scenes.

"Well, gentlemen", the curator explained, "I have a lot of hope that we will recover some of the missing tableaus. It's a dream I nurture with religious faith. I count on the help of the students of the *Lycée* Saint-Serge; we've launched an international warning through the internet to all the art centers, historians, museum directors, antique dealers, and religious art researchers, as well as to the famous auction houses, trying to locate the oeuvre. This excellent work has been coordinated by our dear Father Antoine Duvert, from the Abbey and the *Lycée* Saint-Serge. He has helped me correct misconceptions and dismantle fraudulent tips that always come up when it comes to works of art."

"It's true, I'm a great fan of virtual communication", Father Antoine confirmed, still fidgeting on the uncomfortable chair, after being praised by the curator. "I've been developing a tracking system with a group of young students who work with computer science at the *lycée*. The boys have been helping me a lot with the researches all around the world."

"Have you had any results?" asked a bearded young man who looked like a college student, had a tattoo on his neck, and was seated on the second row.

"Unfortunately, nothing significant until now. There are rumors that one scene of the tapestry might be in Poland," remarked the curator. "The information is being analyzed. Where there's any evidence, I will use all the means at my disposal to recover at least one of the lost tableaus. I won't give up."

Having no further questions to answer, after running his hand through his frontal bald spot, the curator concluded the lecture:

"My friends, you're all invited to visit Château D'Angers, one of the most important museums of France's great historic heritage. Visit the Museum of Weapons and the tapestry that reveals the Apocalypse, which brings hopes of a world without poverty and violence when New Jerusalem descends from Heaven. Marvel at the beauty of the biggest tapestry in the world before the gallery's renovation work to install the new lighting, scheduled for the beginning of the summer, starts."

Very pleased with the ovation they had grown used to share, the two old friends left, smiling, the remodeled building at Michel Debré Square, a few yards from city hall. They saw all the lights on the white façade of the Palais des Arts on, just like the mayor had demanded it to be during the 21st Journalism Festival. He wanted the greatest socio-cultural event of that municipal election year to be intensely lit by the lights of knowledge to a French audience always eager to learn the greatness of their history.

"What most impresses me in this festival is how these people want to breathe culture", praised Father Antoine, smiling. "This is great."

"Soon they'll be rewarded. The gallery is getting beautiful! I've decided to put the tableaus closer together and get rid of the huge empty spaces between them. There won't be the negative impact caused by the missing scenes anymore. I left only one empty space, so the dream can go on."

"Where did you leave it?" Father Antoine asked, curious.

"You'll see, my friend, when we make the final inspection for the reopening of the gallery together", teased curator Ferdinand, smiling and offering his hand to say goodbye.

"I'll wait. I'll find out everything you've been hiding from me", said the priest, as if, behind the curator's wry smile, he suspected something evil the mysterious gap on the wall wanted to hide.

Suddenly, Father Antoine Duvert fell silent, and his face got serious, distressed, like someone about to pray. He recognized the castle curator's ambition to recover at least one of the seven lost tableaus of the Divine Revelation sequence as legitimate and healthy; in particular, the recovery, at any cost, of the unknown scene of the *Caged devil for a thousand years*. Actually, he feared that this missing tableau meant that the seven-headed dragon was free and responsible for the current mayhem of the world. Wherever it was, it would be spreading discord, AIDS, encouraging abortion and human cloning, pedophilia, inciting violence, greed, and corruption. It all suggested that men had lost the battle between good and evil. This was the terrifying vision his mind had, hovering under the huge round towers of Château D'Angers. More than ever, he believed it was crucial, from the religious or cultural point of view, to find this missing tableau of the Apocalypse Tapestry, whose images illustrated the visions St. John received from Jesus Christ through an angel.

The search for the tableau of the beast should be intensified anywhere in the world. Therefore, get down to business, Mr. Curator.

Chapter 2

CURATOR FERDINAND ROCHEMONT DE SAILLY had never imagined what was about to happen, especially in Brazil. The curator had been sincere in his profession of faith before the audience in the auditorium at the 21st Festival when he said he would do everything to recover any of the tapestry's missing scenes, even if they weren't the most famous of them. He had never imagined that it would intertwine, in a mysterious and fortunate way, with the fate of Leonardo and an astrologer, famous unknowns from overseas.

On that October 13th, 2006, the same day of curator Ferdinand de Sailly's lecture, Leonardo Marcondes had received, in the morning, in Rio de Janeiro, the good news from the American banker. Everything was evolving as predicted in his first consultation with astrologer Lisa.

"Congratulations, Mr. Leonardo, the board of directors has authorized an increase in your line of credit. The bank has never granted such a high amount to a Brazilian client."

The morning phone call had left no doubt about the international recognition that Leonard had become a powerful member of the privileged international financial society, above the law of ordinary men. The occasion would certainly deserve a celebration when he got home.

As predicted, it was already very late at night when Leonardo, lying on the bed in Lisa's apartment, all of a sudden decided to get up and solemnly invite her, with no romance whatsoever.

There was nothing unusual in the invitation, as it was always him who took the initiative, since that remarkable first time.

Lisa continued with her *Sudoku*, majestic, until she concluded the right sequence. After marking the page with her

Mont Blanc pen, she closed the booklet and put it below the lamp on the nightstand. Her almond eyes were fixed on Leonardo's already naked body. She began to release the tiny buttons on her nightgown, and her beautiful lap appeared with her generous breasts. She pulled the hem of her nightgown above her waist, showing her bellybutton. She pulled it even higher. The protruding aureolas of her breasts were exposed in all their sensuality.

But that night he didn't want to take long. After the first thrust, there were moans, sighs, obscene words, gasping, increasingly uncontrolled breathing. Five, seven, twelve, who knows how many minutes, until Leonardo lost control and let the torrent flow, untamed. Then came the restorative silence of those floating in nirvana. They cuddled until their breathing calmed down. After a deep sigh, Leo rose still lazily, turned on his side, and resumed his place on the left of the bed. Next to him, on the nightstand, the two cell phones, temporarily turned off, lay.

"It's good, it's very good", Lisa sighed, her eyes sleepy with a delicious languor.

Leonardo liked to hear her thankful voice. Sometimes he lay sprawled on the bed, sort of facedown, staring at the closed shutters, through which, through two small slits in the window, a cool breeze, conducive to sleep, came in. But on that night of celebration, it was different. It took him a long time to fall asleep. His thoughts, muddied by dates, numbers, deaths, counted anxieties and fears. They only quieted down again when they were replaced by good memories and the emotions of that memorable afternoon when he met Lisa in her intimacy with the stars. Diffuse memories of prophetic visions and of the Milky Way outlined on her tanned shoulder. He recognized his life had changed after she read his astrological chart, when he was taken by a love spell.

Leonardo was suddenly surprised to see the "entities" arising from the mysterious cosmic light being incorporated by the unknown woman in the almost dim light of the room.

"Mr. Leonardo, I'm going to talk a little bit about astrology. When men began to look at the sky, more than ten thousand years ago, they realized they were integrated with the world. They began to notice that the course of life, the gifts and talents, and even the mood are influenced by the movement of the stars."

Leonard watched the harmonious movements of her hands.

"It was when they discovered that it was possible to know their fate through their natal chart, which is a photograph of the sky at the exact time, on the day and place of birth. It's the cosmic birth certificate of the person who comes into existence for the universe."

At this moment, dog barking grew louder in the next room, but the astrologer went on without losing her concentration, raising her voice.

"Let's start reading the twelve houses of the zodiac on your chart, each representing an area of your life. Here, on the top of the mandala, is the tenth house, which is the place of your professional life. From what you've told me when you called, this is your biggest concern right now. Well, you have four planets in this house: a *stellium* formed by Uranus, the Sun, Pluto, and Mercury. With these energies gathered, you have all the tools to be successful and achieve your goals."

Completely entranced by Lisa's words and beauty, Leonardo watched the complex dance of her fingers above the chart of the planets.

"See this big quadrature here on your map? It represents the challenges you must break through to get what you want. No one can escape their fate."

The astrologer paused. She took a sip of Coca-Cola, looked deeply in the consultant's green eyes, and went on:

"This Moon in the fourth house, in Aquarius, indicates that you are someone who cares deeply about family. But the many challenging aspects of your chart indicate that you may have been separated from them."

Lisa took another sip from the soda and resumed the reading, in a trance with her deities.

"I did the transits in your chart back and forth, studied what happened during some stages of your life. It's all there: the first hurdle you had was around when you were twenty-five years old, when Uranus made exact conjunction with your Sun. Then you lost someone very dear to you, right?"

Leonardo shivered and agreed, nodding. He wanted to say something, but she waved her hand, signaling that he should not interrupt her, and read the chart with an emotional tone.

"The chart shows that your father didn't die of natural causes. This caused a profound impact on you, especially because it was something sudden and unexpected. The astrological transit shows that everything collapsed around your father and, when he departed from this life, you were taken by an extraordinary rage against the world. Your mother died sometime later. It's here, in Neptune's quadrature with your Moon. It was from an incurable disease."

Lisa saw his eyes turn grey, fraught with pain and suffering. She then decided to dismiss the formal treatment.

"Your father was everything to you. No one understood your anger against the world! Then you married the girl who you were dating. When the first Saturn return happened, you had a son. There's a Moon in the fourth house. This is very good. It means that even with all your duties, you'll always find time to take care of him. You two have a lot of affinities. What's his name?"

"Lucca", he answered, lowering his head slightly.

"It's a beautiful name. You'll always have an ally at home in him." Lisa took another sip from the soda and went on. "Your solar revolution shows that this year will be very hectic, because when Pluto forms aspects with the personal planets, it comes with an amazing transformative power. Those things that are no longer useful are eliminated to make way to new things. Pluto is entering your twelfth house. It will take out all the things that were repressed. It's like an earthquake."

Leonardo kept listening for another half hour, his eyes fixed on the colored symbols of his chart.

"Everything indicates that the time to learn how to deal with the things that are blocking this decisive moment in your life has come. You are an ambitious person and will know how to use all the means you have to achieve your goals. The prediction is that you'll get everything that you wish for. The power you'll have in your hands is amazing, if you know how to use the transformative energy of Pluto, the god of darkness, to evolve. Be very careful with the underground and fire."

They heard scratching and more intense barks from the dogs, maybe hungry. Lisa wasn't disturbed by it and went on.

"Many good, promising things are about to happen. I may be wrong but, in this year of transformations, you have everything to become a great boss. There's even a specific time for them to be fulfilled. You're going to pay a price that only you can say if it's high or fair. Well, this is all I can read from your chart."

"Ms. Lisa, I'm sorry, but I feel that you're hiding something from my current life", he complained, noticing some embarrassment after an hour of consultation, thus ending a session that seemed vaguely based on astrology and seduction.

"I didn't hide anything. Reading a chart is not fortune-telling. Please, Mr. Leonardo, your consultation is over."

After the warning, he saw her tilt her thin neck and her breasts, outlined in her thin blouse, heave, before a long, mysterious sigh.

"Excuse me", muttered the astrologer, standing up as if she wanted to cheat time with a strategic pause. From the kitchen door, she asked, "Would you like a glass of water? Tonic?"

"No, thank you. I would like to continue with the consultation, please."

Lisa didn't return immediately, but when she came nearer, she was bringing more soda on the silver tray, a sign that she was willing to resume the reading with more information, and that was what she did for another thirty minutes with other revelations, concluding:

"Understand, Mr. Leonardo: I cannot change your chart. You will be dealing with very profound things in your inner self. If you make the right decisions, things will flow and your life will be transformed for the better. You'll experience very tense moments because you'll go through a phase of many changes."

"I promise I won't stay still."

"Here's Jupiter, the planet of optimism, signaling a period of great expansion. Your life will be transformed. Of course, you will be tested to become the wealthy man your father wanted to be."

He stared at her, gritting his teeth at the mention of his father.

"It's not a coincidence that you're here today to rethink your life. You'll have the help of powerful forces. All these energies will act in your favor. A former Brazilian president, in an adverse political context, disregarded them, calling them 'hidden forces'. In your case, they are going to help you to get where you want. It's only a matter of time."

She paused, staring at a point in the solar revolution chart as if she had discovered something astonishing.

"There's something weird showing up right here."

"What do you mean?" asked Leonardo, curious.

"It's as if there's a shadow, someone with whom you're going to make a pact. You'll have a lot of money, much more than you imagine. You can lose everything, but not the money. This shadow is associated with a situation of many surprises. It will force you to live on the edge from now on. Never forget that!"

A gust of air came through the window. There was something mysterious, evil, in the spontaneity with which the gust blew the charts.

"I'm going to act, Lisa, I promise", he replied, using for the first time the name of the astrologer with a surprising intimacy.

At that very moment, totally seduced by her looks, he asked something about her tan and lightly felt the skin on Lisa's bare shoulder, who did not react to his bold touch. She just closed the eyelids of her hazel eyes. Leonardo's fingertips then went on. They reached the back of her neck. His arm wrapped around her neck to then pull it gently and kiss her on her half-open lips without lipstick.

On the way down, in the elevator, after the happy ending of the astrological consultation, Leonardo was totally convinced:

"I'm living on the edge."

What surprised him the most were the wild twists of fate and passion. They were always unpredictable. Lisa's final words came to his mind. He would not forget the omens of the stars, let alone the abundance of money spilling over the edge of his chart.

*

Something weird had made Lisa get interested in studying that chart, where death and greed teemed. This only made her curiosity grow. After she'd typed the data, day, month, year, time and place of birth, she saw the path of his planetary cycles appear on the computer screen. And, very shaken, she saw that his chart was the complement to her own. The degrees of the ascendant were identical, planetary twins, and equal in the matters of soul and body. The most astonishing revelation would come later, when she put his solar revolution on top of her own chart. She was able to identify the arrival of a new man, nameless in her chart, about to bring major changes to her quiet day-to-day life.

After Leonardo's fiery touch and a kiss, Lisa threw herself in his arms. She felt all the heat and the smell of lavender of his manly body. They let their tongues linger on the craving of the kisses, with no beginning or end, as if it was the first time they had ever been kissed. The mutual caresses intensified wildly between the woman and the man of perfect astral conjunction. They could no longer hear the dogs bark jealously. Lisa let her shirt fall to the floor. The mouth of that man out of his mind went down to her breasts. The living room carpet was present so as not to delay the surrender. Wearing only her skirt and kissing his ear, she whispered to him that she had her period. The trespasser didn't seem disturbed by the detail. On the contrary, that man, as unknown as he was known, hurried to pull off her lacy panties and penetrate her. And after the exaltation of the passionate bodies and the bright conjunction of the planets, they would never be the same again.

When the earthquake was over, nothing moved on the earth and the sky. Not a whisper, just the silence of the blessed. Lisa thought about the power of passion, what He must have felt when He created man. It was late already. There was no way of not communicating that a consultant from Petrópolis would arrive at any moment. Leonardo sympathized with her professional integrity. He rose quickly from the carpet and standing, naked, regained that unique look, one she had never seen from any other man. He asked if he could take a shower. Completely dizzy with everything that had happened, she tried to put things back in their place while she was alone in the room, realigning the couch and chairs. She realized how unlikely it was to return to her former calmness with the scent of him pervading her hands, down the pores of her neck, breasts, arms, hands, buttocks, legs, pubis, all over her body, in delicious indolence. She wanted to wrap her long legs around him on her flowery sheets.

Later, during a long bath, she recalled some of the things she's read on Leonardo's solar chart. Some tragic events. She relived the moment when she shuddered upon hearing form his sexy mouth the confession that he had entertained the thought of committing the same foolishness as his father. The revelation left her livid and speechless as she continued the reading. She thought it was advisable to pause and invoke the deities to help her in counseling the imponderable of astrology.

When they were saying goodbye, with a long kiss by the elevator door, Lisa made him swear that he would never again think about his father's outrageous anger, which had led her to a panic she had never felt before. And, before leaving, he, with an ardently seductive smile, made her promise that they would meet later at a motel, since his wife and son were absent from Rio in Itaipava and would not arrive until the following day. He was adamant that it had to be in a motel. Lisa accepted the offer, not knowing where she had found the courage to accept the great challenge of fate.

Chapter 3

LONG BEFORE HE MET LISA on the first consultation, Leonardo had already chosen to live in the shadows and duplicity. It wasn't easy to maintain a seeming composure as an honest accountant. Those who knew him for his discreet looks, walking hurriedly on the streets, wouldn't believe that, behind those steps, there was another man with secret things happening in his clandestine life. But this other identity, well hidden, hadn't come up overnight, nor did it stem from the environment in which he had been raised, in the comfort of an upper-middle-class home, with a pampered childhood and good schools. He had always attributed to "circumstances" the fact that he did not follow his father's politically correct example — a good man who died in ruin because he committed suicide.

As much as he liked Math and the magic of numbers, his father wanted him to be a lawyer. Not wanting to upset him, Leo got into Law School, but he also attended Accounting Sciences at night. At first, his father frowned upon this, but then accepted his adult son's wish to fulfill his dream of registering the flow of money. At that time, he was unhappy, working as an intern at a law firm of a friend of the old man. He hated going to the forum.

After his father died and he graduated as an accountant, he decided to open an accounting office on the sixth floor of a shopping mall near Saens Peña Square. His clients were some condos managements and small shops in Tijuca. But, before that, Leonardo had already gotten involved in "petty crimes" and had things facilitated by chance, by the unavoidable, which made him interact with the worst kind of people. Through that scum, he embraced the unusual opportunities that made him powerful and respected for the simple fact that he made a lot of money, although he began to live on the razor's edge.

He would give helpful aid on the accounting schemes, and then began to accept well-paid, unscrupulous "small tasks" from his close friend, the head of a drug-dealing group in the state of Rio de Janeiro. He had met him at a dive bar, which had a hidden room where people played *truco*. They soon got along when they won a hand in the game. When he realized it, he was up to his neck in the bookkeeping of the drug dealing ledger. That was not what he wanted from fate. He dreamt about being a corporate accountant who would give his father a lot of pride. The so-called "circumstances" and the bad influences gave life to the other Leo.

He walked on the street, wearing, as usual, a blue sweatshirt, white t-shirt, loose pants, and sneakers with six shock absorbers. No one suspected the quiet intern who had taken a leave of absence on the fourth year of Law School. After his father's death, Leonardo would become known as "Big Head" on the sidelines of the gang run by the man also known as "Skull".

In all those years, no one suspected the hard-working, skilled gang accountant. And, unlikely as it may seem, neither his family nor his girlfriend Ana, knew about his criminal activities and how he had become such close friends with one of the leaders of the drug dealing, whose longitudinal and cadaverous face did justice to the dreaded nickname, "Skull".

The fact is that Leonard became the drug lord's partner for the card game on Fridays. Throughout this gambling experience, he met his future mates: a killer called Runner, men who ran illegal gambling, drug dealers, gunmen, "friendly" policemen and military outsourced from the payroll, gigolos, prostitutes. The skinny Skull, who wore size 14 shoes, knew how to reward him for rendered services for the traffic bookkeeping and, even more royally, for perfectly executing the bribes to inspectors and authorities. Truth be told, it had been Leonardo, at a time when he was not yet taking huge amounts of aspirin, who organized the main "tip jars" for the bribes and "deals" that explained how Skull kept working without being arrested or exposed by law enforcement, coincidentally when the generalized impunity and urban violence in the city were widespread.

Leonardo never forgot how the definitive friendship between them was sealed. He kept the decisive dialogue in his memory.

"I've been wanting someone like you for a long time, man."

"Hey, I'm not the only one around. There's a shitload of guys."

"It's been hard to find an honest white dude. The dopeheads of the gang weren't born rich, didn't go to school and haven't learned shit in life. They were born looking like trash. You have a good head on your shoulders, you're cool. You command respect. You were already born different, prepared for thug life, you know?

"Different? What do you mean, different?"

"You know what you want from life, brother. You're the only one I can trust", said Skull, taking a drag from his cigarette.

He really could trust the helpful Leonardo, who hadn't come from the streets, had always refused to distribute any kind of drug and considered it something that only "crazy" or "insane" people did. The tasks he agreed to do, a little reluctantly at first, but that he would later do with pleasure and talent, were being the gang's accountant and the distributor of the "dough" in police stations, government departments, and "to the men on the top", at a time when drug trafficking was taking over the slums in Rio, and Brazil became definitively a route for drugs as a distribution point to Europe.

Ana Magalhães Castro, whom Leonardo dated, came from a traditional family of Rio de Janeiro politicians. He won her over with the most childish of smiles, used to declare that only she existed in his solitary life. She believed so much in this that, after dating for a short period, she got married wearing white and a veil in the church where she would always go to pray. And on the walk down the aisle, her father whispered to her, saying he was sure that he was giving her to a "lucky man" to make her very happy, despite him being "a sad lad". The girl was twenty-years-old when she dropped out of her Literature studies because she got pregnant. She never wrote her poems again; she traded them, during her pregnancy, for the embroidery on the baby's layette.

Ana only learned about the office at Saens Peña Square on the day her son Lucca was born. She thought Leo was still a rookie lawyer. The accountant justified it saying that he hadn't told her anything because it was a surprise. Nobody knew he had graduated in Accounting Sciences. At that time, Leonardo already had his underground secrets well-hidden. So much so that it was normal for him to become glum and vent with his wife during dinner, when his son Lucca was still a baby.

"I need money, a lot of money, to keep fighting."

She never suspected this obsession, nor did she suspect the "circumstances", the harmful friendships, let alone the demonic "hidden forces" that enthralled the greedy, vengeful Big Head.

Ana embroidered flowery pillowcases and tablecloths, delicate works of art, with patience and taste. She got used to seeing her husband, year in and year out, earning more and more money, thanks to his supposedly total dedication to Accounting Sciences. Their son Lucca grew up living in Andaraí, then in Grajaú, and, when he was already a teenager, he lived in Flamengo with a view to the park.

Now they had just moved to a four-bedroom apartment in Barra. Oddly enough, Ana never had the curiosity to visit her husband in the old nor in the new office at Downtown Shopping Mall.

"I don't want to be in your way now that you're surrounded by important people", she would apologize for her lack of curiosity regarding her husband's business. She trusted him.

However, things began to become very muddy. Ana was the first to recognize that Leo had changed a lot. He was always tense. He had crossed the line of the conventional husband and became a man full of secrets and habits. He would give her increasingly evasive answers about his routine outside the house. In the ten years they've been married, that hadn't bothered her. Lately, things had taken a contentious turn. This new, unknown Leonardo distressed her more and more. Rude words and attitudes in front of the neighbors or strangers became a usual thing. This would upset her and make her sad. She also didn't accept the fact that her husband, despite having three cell phones, wouldn't take her calls and called her less and less to tell her what was going on. The simple "hellos" were going up in smoke. He would justify himself, always saying he was busy with bloodsucker clients. It had never been like this before.

She didn't like to question, as she had been doing lately, why had Leonardo changed so much, and why she put up with the man's behavior without reacting.

On the long balcony, images of the waves crashing on the sand and the clouds tacked over the monolithic buildings of Barra were obscured by dark thoughts and painful reminiscences. She went back to the time when she nurtured the maternal and almost merciful feeling of comforting him from the absence of his parents, like the wet nurse who takes in her arms the fragile creature to feed her with the will to live. Since her marriage, she had created this kind of devotion with extreme compassion for this suffering, outraged man who, before the change of habits occurred, which included the torment of the cell phones at night, lovingly accepted her directions and advice. As time passed, he barely listened to her questions, let alone had the courtesy of answering them. This indifference was slowly killing her inside.

"How about leaving the cell phones off? Have dinner in peace at least today. Is it hard?" asked the woman sitting at the table, after serving the usual pea soup.

Leonardo was surprised by her tone of voice. It was the first time he heard his wife complaining at the table, in front of their son. *For her to be irritable like this… it must be menstrual problems*, he thought without much concern.

"Can we do that, darling?" reiterated the woman, with an even more nerve-wracking tone of voice that showed her annoyance for not being heard.

"I can't. It's the best moment to talk to people," answered Leonardo, after the second quick dialogue on the phone, not audible at the table, except for a distinct "go ahead" at the end of the call. It was only possible to hear that because he answered the call standing in the dining room, without stepping on the marble floor of the balcony.

"Can you tell me why?" she insisted, not resigning.

"Just because people want to talk to me or they'll do things wrong and I'll have to work like a mule to fix the shit they did. Did you understand now?"

"Can't you talk to me nicely at the table? Lucca is here. At least respect the boy."

The son saw his father's face tighten nervously, shutting up without replying. The cell phones kept ringing continuously throughout dinner. Leonard would stop eating and get up from the table. He would answer all the calls, without hesitation. His wife and son remained in an almost religious silence.

"How about a trip to Itaipava?" asked Ana, trying to compromise, even if she had to forget her annoyance with the cell phones. "It's been so long since I've gone to my parents' farm."

"What for?" asked Leonardo, immediately showing his lack of interest in spending the weekend out of Rio with Ana's family at the Magalhães Castro's farm.

Ana knew that the "what for?" was his way of saying "no". This made her think more seriously. The old Leonardo was predictable and trustworthy. He had a right time to leave and come back home. As soon as he arrived, he would kiss her lightly on the cheek and go buy bread. Now he lived like a *nephelibata* — she used the strange term after she checked its meaning on the dictionary and liked to use it to define her husband's indifference toward his family world, full of sun and love. To her anguish, her husband was always on the clouds and, lately, would lock himself in the home den and ordered everything on the phone. After all, she didn't want a lot from him: attention to his family, the tenderness from when they were dating, and silent cell phones during meals. She thought of the numerous times when she was concerned about his nervous cough. She wanted him to see a specialist. He never did. And Ana had to face, alone, the long silences of the words not spoken by a husband connected to some other place of the planet, oblivious to the earth cord connected to his home, which was always invaded by strange voices.

She decided to take action and expel the unknown enemies and clear things up, after so many repressed heartaches about to explode.

"Do you know that there's a world waiting for us outside, Leo?" she suggested during dessert.

Leonardo was silent. Instead of looking at his wife's face, he stared at the colorful *kilim* rug, very different from the soft red *boukaras* at his parents' mansion in Botafogo. He kept his unapproachable silence for quite a while. He didn't utter a word, just diverted his gaze to the dark night that framed the window and the outside world. In it, it wasn't admissible to lose anything, much less time and money — thus thought Big Head, sitting at the head of the dining room table surrounded by his family.

Well, it was from this sovereign silence that Ana Magalhães — still young for her age, soft-spoken, musical in her long syllables, with faint wrinkles, enhanced by the fact that lately her countenance was always tense — decided to rebel and learn more about her husband's life away from home. A shiver suddenly electrified her body; fear ran through her spinal cord when she thought about the bold gesture. She dreaded the fallout caused by female intuition. She reconsidered giving her husband more time to mend his ways. But she decided to go ahead with her fight; after all, there's always a first time in life.

Chapter 4

ON THE MONTH OF MAY, at 6 PM in Angers, the sun still touches the walls of thin layers of shale and limestone blocks of the imposing fortress. Its light shines and reflects on the seventeen towers and also on the helmets, shields, swords, spears, and crossbows of the Museum of Medieval Weapons. In the long eleven-thousand-square-feet gallery going through renovations, when the workers and the engineers left the site, at the lack of construction work and voices, in the silence of the nave of an empty church, the only thing left were the lights being tested for the approval of the new lighting system and the modern ventilation system that would be able to keep the environment controlled at a constant temperature of 68 degrees Fahrenheit.

Father Antoine Duvert was, as usual, late, this time by fifteen minutes. Curator Ferdinand de Sailly's wrinkles looked more prominent on behalf of the inconvenience of his pudgy cleric friend's tardiness. He arrived breathless, with his cheekbones on fire, ashamed for being late for such an important meeting. Ferdinand knew that the chubby, cheerful character liked to chat on the narrow streets, bistros, and flowery parks with no concern for his watch, already a few minutes forward to avoid the usual tardiness. Father Antoine Duvert had promised to himself to arrive in time for the honorable invitation to see the new forty-lux lighting before the official opening to the public. That would be a privilege for few, to attend a sneak preview of the reopening of the famous gallery. This was announced with a big fuss by the city, through billboards scattered throughout Touraine and ads on the internet — although the priest considered this "a tool of the devil" that corrupts men.

The priest immediately gave a huge smile to greet his friend, who waited for him on the castle's drawbridge, frowning.

"Hurry up, I'm dying of curiosity. You know that God tends to forgive the careless and punish the grumpy" Antoine apologized jokingly.

The keeper of the castle, of the high nobility of Anjou, impeccable in his blazer and bowtie, went down the slippery stone stairway in hurried footsteps, followed by the sweaty priest.

"Be careful! Don't stumble and fall down these medieval stairs! They are very steep, watch your step."

"Oh, dear! These steps are still horrible," complained father Antoine. "I almost fell, with your haste, like the world is coming to an end."

They finally crossed the limestone portal, the boutique, the closed box office and, after going through the two doors, with a space between them to keep the acclimatization, they entered the long, lit hall of the gallery, which housed the tapestry.

Antoine took one step forward and stopped in front of the tableau of the first major character, sitting beneath a canopy, depicting St. John on the island of Patmos. He was in awe, silent, suspended in the contained admiring reverence before the embossed masterpiece woven by the magical hands of wonderful craftsmen. He shifted his eyes to the *Seven Churches* scene. He felt like he was walking on clouds with the new lighting. As if it was the first time he saw those biblical scenes of the canonical book and the four great characters, urging the viewer to be amazed by the contemplation and the allure of the exceptional masterpiece.

"Wow, it looks wonderful! It's like the tableaus speak! This new lighting recovers the forgotten values of the Middle Ages. My eyes are thankful for being here" said Antoine, moved by the breathtaking longitudinal vision of the tapestry, completely restored and with its colors totally rejuvenated, that went on as far as the eyes could see on the large wall. The scenes came one after the other in six big tableaus, each one more dramatic and exceptional than the other. It became difficult for him to choose which one was more beautiful and illustrative, some abstract, others figurative.

"There have been several restorations on the seventy-seven scenes after the tapestry returned to the castle in 1906, because of the law of Separation Between Church and State. Although it remained linked to Catholicism's worship, it was declared property of the State. It came back to Chateau D'Angers after a six-century absence. This time, for the gallery's modernization, we've used cutting-edge technology" the administrator clarified while they slowly entered the perfect semidarkness of the room. This was guaranteed by the two-thousand diffusing lamps, powered by optical fibers, on the sequence of impressive images hung by thick Velcro strips, avoiding the use of nails that could damage the tapestry.

"You did it. The visitor feels blessed by God for being here, at the heart of Christendom and the renewal of faith."

"We just have to tweak the placement of the tableaus."

"It looks very good like this. Why mess with it? Leave it like that."

"Look at this tableau of Christ and the sword, how the blues were enhanced," said Ferdinand, slowly moving forward.

Antoine passed by the fifth scene, the one with St. John in tears, and thought of the miracle of the representation of the divine scenes, based on the saint's apocalyptical visions. He squeezed his hands behind his body and stood before the sixth scene of the incredible vision of the world disfigured by the earthquake. He kept on walking in silence. He saw the grandiose scenes of the battlefields, of the terrible fight between good and evil, the land devastated by the seven plagues and the Four Horsemen of the Apocalypse, the assault of the beasts sent by the devil, the beast from the Earth, the one from the sea, the frogs, the locusts. He contemplated the war of fire and the trembling of the earth. He took a few more steps and watched the fall of Babylon and, a little further on, with a hallowed eye, he saw the suspended New Jerusalem, triumphant, in the glory of eternal salvation.

"No one can imagine the work that has to be done to keep this masterpiece intact in the grandeur of its biblical dimension," said Ferdinand, touched. "There's been an immense effort in order to increasingly improve the state of preservation of this work of art so that the public could appreciate the prophetic vision of the Apocalypse and understand its message of hope."

"These are paintings that explain the permanent struggle between humanity and evil. Look at this tableau, number 52," said the priest. "It's the scene of the *Sleep of the Seven Righteous*, who managed to resist the words of the Antichrist. They rest in their mortuary berths with their souls saved before ascending to the starry sky, taken by two angels."

"Beautiful! The lighting canonized this image of the ascension to Heaven."

"Look at this scene of New Jerusalem," the curator pointed with his index finger. "It's one of my favorites. It's a shame we weren't able to recover all the missing pieces of the tapestry. I'm heartbroken when I see, at the gallery's exit, the frustration on the visitors' expressions caused by the absence of the images of the *Sixth Great Character*, of the *Horseman with the Horse the Color of Fire and War*, of the *Earthquake*, of the *Four Winds*, of the *Condemned Prostitute*, of the *Wedding of the Lamb*, of *God's Verb*, of the *Birds Devouring the Ungodly* and of the *Final Judgment*. I'll never accept the fact that they've disappeared without trace. I won't lose hope that one day they may find all the scenes and that they can come here, to complete the Revelation."

"You didn't mention the most important loss," Antoine pointed out.

"Which one? I think I've mentioned all of them. Did I miss one?"

"You've skipped the scene of the *Devil Caged for a Thousand Years.*"

"You are right, Antoine. Forgive me. It's so obvious I forgot! The visitors always leave frustrated because they haven't seen the caged devil. Without a doubt, tableau 75 is the great absence in the gallery. Maybe the greatest one, because of its symbolism."

"Do you have any idea of how the original scene looked?" asked the priest.

"Specialists have researched and came to the conclusion, based on the rigor of the color alternation throughout the tapestry, that the missing tableau 75 had a red background, since tableaus 74 and 76 have a blue background. And the devil was represented by a seven-headed dragon, the classic figure used as a representation of the Beast," answered the curator.

"To the Catholics, it's not the tableau itself that is important, but its message. The scene would show the insistence and the survival of faith. We imagine that, if the scene from the tapestry is traveling the world, with the devil on the loose, this explains so much crime, lust, perversion, and pornography, and the worst thing is that it may have worshipers all around the Earth…"

Father Antoine continued, as if preaching at the altar, and was totally taken by his pious, rapt inspiration before the curator's admiring gaze, who saw him go from the state of artistic grace to that of divine grace.

"Then Satan would symbolically win the battle against faith if the scene is roaming free around the world, as he would also be. That's why we, men of faith, preach to our believers to not use condoms, because sex is meant for procreation, never for pleasure and lust. They don't understand that. The plague of AIDS is nothing but the victory of lust and degradation! They don't want to hear us when we are against abortion and researches with stem cells from human beings who didn't have the right to be born. They don't understand that they are killing the embryos because life exists since conception, the soul is already present. They don't understand why we are against human cloning, because only God can give and take life. They don't want to hear God's voice anymore in the Babylon of our time. Enough! I don't want to talk any further. "

"I've tried to recreate the lighting so that the visitors can find the hope of New Jerusalem again," explained the curator, emphasizing his interest in the renovations.

"You definitely did it. Congratulations on the beautiful work of renewing the message of faith and hope in today's frantic world. But this is not enough. We need to show the defeated devil. We have to lock up Satan for another thousand years."

The curator didn't immediately agree. He took the priest by the arm and led him to a spot where he'd left a blank space.

"Look at this, Antoine. Do you know why I left this space empty, between tableaus 74 and 76?"

The priest was silent. His eyes stared at the throne of God's emerging river, which irrigates the hills of fruit trees.

"About six months ago there were news that the tableau with the caged devil had been seen," confided the curator, whispering.

"Why did you wait until now to tell me this, you snake in the grass?"

"What good would it do to tell you if the Ministry of Culture wasn't willing to finance its search, acquisition, and restoring? Now I can tell you because they have accepted to finance everything. I'm very hopeful. My intuition tells me that we'll have the tableau back very soon. Our only problem is that we cannot have the police involved in the case as long as we are not sure about the authenticity of the tableau."

"Where did this happy news come from? Can you tell me?"

"From Brazil," answered the curator, raising his tone of voice.

"My God! From that far! You know, my nephew Aurélien was there during Carnival. He had his passport stolen."

"Your sister's son?"

"Yes. He liked it so much that he stayed for months. He told me he made good friends. He only came back because he didn't want to lose his job at the Library of Historic Monuments in Paris. He graduated in Saint-Cyr, but decided not to become a *gendarme.*"

"Is he the researcher?"

"That's the one. He's a researcher and a police officer. Do you remember the case of the theft at the "Tiger's" house in Paris? He was hired by the Clemenceau Museum and solved everything by himself. A fanatic had stolen the personal items and the manuscripts of the collection."

"Of course, I remember it well. The case was in every newspaper."

"He was here in October, spent hours visiting the halls in the Museum of Weapons. He praised the perfect state of conservation of the medieval crossbows. You know, he's a crossbow champion, which is commonly known as bow and arrow, and has even won several medals as an archer in championships."

"You gave me an idea. I'll tell you later. Now I have to run home, or my wife will throw me in the lake of fire where the devil drowned. She has invited the mayor for dinner," confided Ferdinand, nervous, walking quickly on the stone steps at the exit of the gallery toward the manor courtyard of the castle.

"Don't tell me that coward is going to eat those delicious *quenelles* at your house?" teased father Antoine in the face of his exclusion from the gastronomic honor of the Rochemont de Sailly.

"We are very invested in the mayor's reelection. He deserves it."

"No, he doesn't," protested Antoine, looking at his watch. "My Goodness! It's so late already… The boys must be worried about my delay. I'm late again."

The curator made a sudden pause in his walk to ask the priest, still breathless as he climbed the stairs.

"Can you give me your nephew's phone number in Paris?"

"Sure, I'll send it to you by e-mail later," the flustered priest said as goodbye.

Smoothing the folds of his bowtie, the curator took one last look at the twenty-four species of rose bushes planted in the garden facing the gallery's outer wall. A refreshing wind hit his face when he crossed the castle's draw bridge. In the silence, his lips smiled at the results achieved with the new lighting, which added to the biblical imagination a touch of the unimaginable, the halftone of the eternal temporality of the Apocalypse, as if the tapestry called for an exegesis, left hanging in the air. Or as if it wanted that the visitors always returned, as they return with tortured souls to the church masses or to the prayer before God's altar so He can renew our certainty and the beauty of faith. Now the curator's thoughts focused on the dream of bringing tableau 75 back to the gallery: nothing that a good sum of money couldn't do — he laughed to himself.

Chapter 5

EVEN THOUGH HE KNEW THAT the world turns and fate brings people from different continents together, curator Ferdinand could never had thought that besides Leonardo, a stranger, and Aurélien, Father Antoine's nephew, the contemporary history of the tapestry would also count with the participation of Júlia, Baudoin's daughter, born in Visconde de Mauá, a city located at an altitude of four-thousand feet on the Mantiqueira Mountains, a region consisting of villages and valleys, waterfalls and hiking trails.

The word "Mantiqueira", in Tupi-Guarani, means "where the waters spring". A perfect definition for a region exuberant in its hydrological richness and beauty that enthralled Júlia's father, a Belgian tourist with a fancy name: Baudoin Fontenoy Werhofen. He was a botanist and had decided to go on vacation to the country famous for being "the country of the future". But, besides being in awe with its forests and birds, he found himself also in awe with Brazilian women; a tourist on vacation in the country of the future, in awe with Brazilian forests, birds, and women.

On the way up the mountain, the Belgian was already impressed by the Harpy Eagle that followed the car on the bumpy road to Mauá. Being superstitious, he believed it was a good omen for a weekend ride. But he liked the virgin nature so much, the crystal-clear, unpolluted rivers, that he decided to extend the days of his stay, turning them into months, years, and his whole life. A few months after meeting the sexy Maria Tereza, with whom he bathed in the Slide Waterfall, they got married in an ecological ceremony at the Bridal Veil Waterfall, before Belgian and Brazilian friends.

In love with Maria Tereza and with nature, it's easy to understand what led this man of proud carriage and a slightly angular chin to sell his hardware shop in Belgium and his furniture to build an inn on the Mantiqueira Mountains and opt definitively for the pleasure of living a healthy and loving life in the woods. In time, he became familiar with the geography and the history of the area, and found himself to be a self-taught guide because of his wise decision to come to live in Mauá, where he started his small family.

"I stopped taking medication and didn't go to the doctors anymore. This region is miraculous," he used to say to the visitors, recalling the time when he used to resort to decongestants to breathe.

From the union of the hot Maria Tereza Gusmão with the adventurous Walloon traveler with a Francophile soul, better known in the area by the nickname "Baldo", was born the lovely Júlia, who would become a fan of photography and adventure books. And, once he was well established with his inn, named "Blue Angel" as suggested by Maria Tereza in honor of her husband, it didn't take long for Baudoin to realize that, with his knowledge of languages and the forest, he could register in a book the perception and emotions of a European botanist apprentice who loved the woods. Thus the work *Know the Tourist Region of Visconde de Mauá and Its History* was born.

"Coming to live here was the best decision of my life. The people and nature gave me the support to stay in Mauá. I never want to go back to Brussels," the happy Belgian, passionate about Brazilian things, used to say to everyone.

Little Júlia grew up amidst nature and a lot of reading. When she turned fifteen, Baudoin gave his daughter a camera and a new pair of glasses with a thinner rim and lenses. He saw his daughter go into the woods among native pines, *quaresmeiras*, and robles, to click bromeliads and orchids. He liked to see her climbing trees to catch the sun hitting the river or the glow of the rays scattered through the translucent waters caused by the waterfalls. The photos were developed in postcard format, for sale in the arts and crafts shops and the restaurants of Mauá. He saw his daughter, more grown-up and experienced, cover local events with stories or journalistic texts for magazines that had tourism supplements, published weekly in Rio and São Paulo, and in the monthly magazine *Nature.*

From her beloved father, Júlia had gotten her blue eyes and the curiosity for mysteries. Despite her farsightedness, in her teenage years her aquamarine eyes already tried to find the whereabouts of a cougar or an armadillo in the woods. This instinctive curiosity was strengthened with the reading of the *Tintin* books in their original version. She knew by heart the names of all the characters, the countries visited, the criminals' nicknames, and Captain Haddock's weird curse words.

At first, her father translated the text in the illustrations shyly and with the few words he knew in Portuguese, but then he learned to find a way with bolder and bolder sentences until he could speak fluently. He would make up funny words that made his daughter laugh. The fact of the matter is that, in the hide-and-seek language game in search of hidden words, Júlia studied French as a second language, as her father learned Portuguese as a very useful, fun activity that evoked a lot of laughter.

For Júlia, born in the small world in which her father had reinvented himself, there wasn't anything more affective than sharing with him the simple, direct language of the comic books. For Baldo, the comics allowed his daughter to assimilate an infinite range of information about known cultural, social, and political environments, without having to leave Mauá. He told her that "Brussels breathed the atmosphere of the books, present in every bookstore", the same passion that Júlia had felt in Mauá, always showing enthusiasm for the travels and adventures of reporter Tintin (pronounced "Tantan"), that delighted her so much.

Júlia listened closely to her father Baudoin explaining the extraordinary power of influence of the comics that "opened their minds to the imagination" and went way beyond mere fun. She never forgot the lesson.

"You know, Dad, what I want most in life is to be a reporter. Will you let me go to Rio? I'm already eighteen."

"Your life is here, darling. You have everything you need here. That city down there doesn't need your sensibility. Urban violence despises your beautiful pictures of nature, full of flowers and love. You belong in Mauá, Júlia."

"What if I run away some day?"

"I would be forever sad, baby. You'll hurt me deeply, because you'll convince me that all that I've taught you was a bunch of crap. It didn't make you happy."

"Happy, without me choosing my own life? Why can't I be like Tintin, by a thousand lightning and thunder?" asked Júlia, using the same expression as Captain Haddock, the famous character from the books, who her father liked so much and who made Baldo laugh.

"Baby, Tintin never had a family. That's why."

"Hervé, Tintin's creator, experienced this conflict when he lived in a city where he didn't feel free anymore. Suddenly, all his dreams and drawings became white. He drew the Tibetan book without colors. He even had a consultation with a famous psychiatrist in Switzerland. You told me that, Dad. Do you remember? He only got rid of his white demon when he ran away from Brussels. I have to leave Mauá, or I'll begin to dream all in white. Let me do it, Dad, please, let me..."

*

The more the clientele of the inn hidden in the mountains grew, more beautiful the flower gardens became, and the number of accommodations increased, and the kitchen was modernized. Júlia saw her mother, on weekends and extended holidays, tie her apron around her waist and the white scarf over her head and take the position of chef. She didn't miss the timing of preparation of the dishes, each tastier than the other. Among the house specialties, the simplest was the dry, crunchy French-fries, a Belgian secret shared by her husband: the potatoes were cut and put for a few minutes in boiling water, then in cold water with ice; after being drained, they were deep-fried and dried up in paper towels.

Júlia also knew that the breakfast was unbeatable, with the refinement of Belgian royalty, flavorfully buttered by the happy morning smile of the inn's owner. Those who stayed at the Blue Angel didn't regret going, nor did they forget to come back.

Since she was a kid, Júlia was interested in the inn's administrative and commercial tasks and in helping her father with the eco-tours. She avoided the kitchen like the plague. She had never peeled a potato, made coffee, or stir-fried rice. But what she lacked in the ability to deal with pots and pans, she had to spare in the competence to organize papers and deal with the mail. She also liked to talk with the guests at the front desk. She was very skilled in convincing hesitant guests on the internet and was the guarantee of a stay of total rest and many pleasures, that only her family hospitality business, and the good climate and the charms of the mountains, could offer.

Júlia had always been curious about the lives of mature couples, newlyweds, lovers, male and female homosexuals, increasingly out and frequent. In these meetings, she didn't speak a lot, but she would hear many things about the stories of the big city. She only became talkative when the guests spoke French. It was her opportunity to practice the foreign language and reap the progress she had made with her father's teaching, who, whenever he could and there were no guests around, communicated with her in his mother tongue. Her face radiated an *inouïe* happiness if the foreigners congratulated her for her ease in the idiom of Baudelaire, her favorite poet. The things the guests told her about the daily life in Rio grew into fantasy thoughts that lazily traveled through the yellow ceiling of the room. It was her way of daydreaming about the big city.

"Mom, the magazine that published Dad's guide asked me to write about you. The editors want to know how he ended up here and how you two met. They think that the differences in origin and culture would make a very interesting piece."

"Not now, darling. I'm very busy."

"Please. Love encounters set up by fate make good texts. Come on, help me. Could you at least tell me how did my father end up in Mauá?" insisted Júlia, frowning her forehead.

"You know, baby, I think that differences are attracted to one another in love. That's what happened with us," explained her mother, holding the wooden spoon. "I still don't know exactly how everything happened. I just know that a hurricane passed through my life."

"It's understandable. You were young, in a place like Mauá, and a foreigner comes and says in your ear that love overcomes the differences. It was impossible not to fall in love. Tell me a little bit about him, Mom," insisted Júlia, curious to know more about the stranger.

"The first time I saw him standing at the square with his backpack, I went crazy. He was a gorgeous man smiling at me with his blue eyes, who didn't want to go back to his country because of me. Look, I still get goose bumps," said her mother with a sweet smile.

Maria Tereza was silent, with an ethereal look while she handled the pots. An enigmatic smile gave way to a triumphant one.

"I'll tell you this, baby: he was going to stay for a weekend, and he stayed a month. He had to go back to Belgium, but he didn't even stay for two months there. He left his wife, left everything behind, and came back to be with me. He came to live here for good, and a year later my little nuisance was born."

"Did you know he was coming back? You were sure of it, weren't you?"

"Baby, I prayed every night to Saint Thérèse of the Child Jesus. When he left, he told me in his best "Brazilian": 'I'll come back, I'll protect our love, because I've learned at the *waterfell* that the souls are only soulmates if they have the same heart.' You know, baby, I love my Belgian king like I've loved him from the first day."

"King? Where did that come from?" exclaimed Júlia.

Mother and daughter laughed and hugged, moved.

"I just hope you find someone who makes you a queen."

"Here in this Godforsaken place? Not even by a miracle"

"It's not the place that matters. It's the line of fate that is written on our hands and the stars. You'll eventually find him, wherever he is, my love. Have faith in this."

"Then help me, Mom, so I don't have to run away from here."

"Don't even think about that. You're still my little girl."

"Little girl? Mom, I'm already twenty-years-old. It's time to live in Rio," she argued, wiggling the stem of her eyeglasses with the tip of her fingers. "I can't stand being in Mauá any longer."

"Aren't you happy here with us?"

"Of course I am, very much so. But I don't have a future here, Mom. I want to go to college. Work in a newspaper. Have my life as a woman. Talk to him, Mom. I can't listen to other people's stories anymore. I want to write my own story."

"I'll try, my love. Things are not that simple. No one can open your father's thick skull. I'll plot something, baby. I'll grab the Belgian by the stomach on his birthday. You'll see."

Maria Tereza was not laughing anymore. Her daughter

could go away any minute now, without permission. She knew that her daughter's absence from the inn would open a painful wound in her father's heart. But she couldn't disappoint Júlia. Time had come not to frustrate her dream of being a journalist in Rio de Janeiro and find love. Saddened and resigned, she asked herself: *How could Júlia follow her destiny if she didn't help her a bit, huh?*

*

"*Wonderful! Wonderful!*" repeated the king's friends.

Maria Tereza had prepared a dinner worthy of the *Ordre des Agathopédes*, a famous Belgian gastronomic coterie. In the art and the pleasure of good cuisine, she had outdone herself with the *quiche royale*, accompanied by a green salad and *fruit rouges*, as a first course; the roasted boar with *marron glacé* and potatoes *au gratin*, and the dessert, never served before. They even had the tasty *bleu de Bresse* cheese[1], which her husband loved and that now was also being produced in Minas Gerais, where mornings and nights were usually cold, and the pastures were rich in nutrients, like in the Rhône-Alpes region, where Bresse is located.

When the lights in the room were out and he went to blow the candles on the cake, the birthday boy began to cry copiously. And it was no wonder. The cake had the colors of the Walloon flag, red and yellow around the lit volcano, with incandescent, molten *bleu* lava. Baldo didn't feel guilty for accepting several pieces of the cake. *Chef* Maria let him and his Belgian friends who lived in Rio have seconds and thirds of the delicious dessert. The next morning, solemnly, like King Leopold III, who had to renounce his throne in 1951 in favor of his son Baudoin, father Baldo, although grumpy and upset,

---

1 A sort of blue cheese produced in the region of Bresse, France (*N.R.*)

finally allowed his daughter to travel in search of her destiny.

The vigorous mountain dweller did not resist the celebrations and, for the first time in many, many years, fell ill. Perhaps it was too much emotion for a quiet Belgian, or just for a father who was heartbroken by the terrifying event of his beloved daughter leaving the Blue Angel Inn for the very first time.

"Go, baby girl, take Saint Thérèse of the Child Jesus's medal. I asked your father to bring me one if he decided to come to live here. Keep it, my love, to light your path," said Maria Tereza, very moved, crying while she said goodbye and put her daughter on a bus and the medal around her neck.

Her father was so emotional he could barely speak.

"Remember the first words in French that I taught you? From the first scene in the book *Tintin in the Land of the Soviets*?"

"Of course I remember, Dad. It was *bon voyage*. You made me repeat the word *voyage* a thousand times, until I got the pronunciation right."

"Then I wish you *bon voyage*, my love, and stay away from violence," her father whispered, looking crestfallen, as if he had not had much sleep and had had a piece of his heart ripped off at a single stroke.

It wasn't easy for Júlia to leave Mauá. To leave behind her childhood of rag dolls, animals and woods, her teenage years of many books, memories of laughing, happy, bouncy times in the flowery gardens of the inn. To stop having her father's company, who had encouraged her to see the world. Maybe if she hadn't read so many stories and had so many conversations with so many guests she wouldn't have this urge to venture out in a big city and be a reporter like the fearless Tintin.

"What did you tell him, Mom, to let me go?"

Her mother told her about the terrible argument. He didn't want to let her leave Mauá at all. He got to the point of screaming. He only lowered his voice when she challenged him to answer something like this:

"Don't you understand, you stubborn man, that Mauá has become too small for her? Do you want your daughter to be miserable for the rest of her life? Do you want your daughter to get old without finding the destiny of happiness as a woman as she deserves? You'll never forgive yourself for this cruelty. When I met you, right after you came from Belgium to be happy here, you weren't that selfish."

Chapter 6

AURÉLIEN KLÉBER, SON OF A FRENCH SOLDIER, during all his childhood and teenage years had to follow his father's footsteps on all displacements on French territory. Although *le petit* continuously reinvented his love for the French soul and culture, these constant travels, in which he got acquainted with cities and people, in time became a burden because of the frequency in which they were made. He had to change schools several times. At each return, Aurélien would complain about not being able to keep the memories from the places and the people. He gained life experience, but the images and memories were so fleeting that they had faded in an invisible chamber.

"It's just a matter of adapting," his father François would sum up to justify the changing of houses, cities, and temperatures.

His maternal grandparents would always protest, in discontent:

"Why the hell can't the boy have a permanent home, friends, and a normal education in Strasbourg?"

"No and no!" hollered the father, zealous, and, more than that, stubborn on giving continuity to the military tradition of his family.

The concern of his grandfather Jean-Philippe, known as Jojo for his lovable bulldog face, and his grandmother Michelle, a sexagenarian marathon runner, didn't matter.

"You don't understand. It's *le petit* that worries us."

"What about him?" his mother Dominique would ask.

"He'll have to attend a different school? Poor boy!" the grandmother would say in anguish, distraught by her grandson's wails.

"Well, Mom, he's big enough to know that this is the way it has to be. Think on the positive side. He must be enjoying meeting new friends and the change of scenery. To have adventures to tell!" praised the mother, still young and happy with the nomadic life, not realizing how much the travels and changing schools bothered *le petit*. He was always huffing in a bad mood, outraged at each transfer.

It was only after the visit of his grandfather, a retired divisional general who lived in Marseille that things got better. The lieutenant colonel received a long letter in which the concerns about his son's lack of military vocation were conveyed. A letter full of concern about the future of cadet Aurélien.

The father took the grandfather's alarmist letter seriously, but he didn't know how to reverse the situation. Luckily, everything was solved after the phone call from the High Command, notifying François of his relocation to Nancy, less than sixty miles from Strasbourg. When he determined that his son should move to his maternal grandparents' house, his father's only concern was that Aurélien received the best possible curricular preparation to be accepted to the Saint-Cyr Military School or the École des Officiers de la *Gendarmerie*, known as EOGN – the famous national security academy.

After living in so many cities, Aurélien had stopped believing that, one day, he would be able to get settled in one city. For him, returning to Strasbourg, the city where he was born, was cause for great happiness. Besides, because it had been designated one of the European capitals that housed the Parliament's headquarters, the capital of Alsace had — unlike Nancy, in the Vosges — a flawless educational system. It had become the ideal place for someone who, according to his father's wishes, would attend the strict French military schools.

His father had requested Grandpa Jojo's involvement to

supervise his son's studies, so that there would be no obstacles to be accepted to the great military École, where the "action and reflection officers were trained in positions of command to be able to act in difficult situations to keep public safety." His father's request was a military order, although Jojo had other educational plans for *le petit*.

When he arrived in Strasbourg, Aurélien already had a solid background in Computer Science, Nichiren Daishonin's practice of Buddhism, and a great curiosity for historical documents and monuments. He couldn't tell since when he had been able to be interested in such different universes and things at the same time. He didn't have any special feeling of affection except for his computer. Wherever his father was transferred to, he would carry with him his faithful companion, including to his new home. However, despite the short time he lived there, the é added a little human content to his cyber world. In Strasbourg, without letting go of the internet and the contacts of his virtual community, he made a loving connection with the owners of the house, in particular with his restless grandfather, a retired politician, former member of the Resistance, who had literature as his favorite pastime.

So, besides his dedication to his studies to get in EOGN, he was motivated and encouraged by his grandfather to research rare books, especially those on historical monuments, Gothic architecture, old fortifications, as well as famous manuscripts. He read the originals of the love letters from Napoleon to Joséphine de Beauharnais. Similarly, in Jojo's beloved company, his grandson paid tribute, during his free time, to the great classics, permanent residents of the house. They were commented readings of the works of Stendhal, Flaubert, Balzac, Proust, Anatole France, Romain Rolland, read with the emotion of the celestial rapture that only reading bestows on the privileged literature lovers. In the gallery of classics, his grandfather also collected Aristophane's comedies. They laughed a lot reading Pluto. Nothing more contemporary to portray the scenes of French politics and corruption, controlled by the evil power of money, the corrupting vile metal, in all times, since ancient Greece until today's globalized world.

The texts that Aurélien read flowed gently to his ears, like the flowing stream of the River ill, a tributary of the Rhine that, with its five arms, bathed the center of the city of Strasbourg — a scenery that was always evoked when the two travelers of imagination, grandson and grandfather, rambled and savored the delicious buttery cookies lovingly prepared by his grandmother Michelle, and thus felt enraptured in the peace of mind that followed a good night's reading, after dinner.

Aurélien started to be always in a good humor, he had even ceased to huff. Unfortunately, he resumed his addiction when he enlisted at the recruitment center number 17 D, at Molsheim Street. After the usual interviews, he was finally accepted to the EOGN military academy, all as the rules of procedure dictated and his father's stubbornness had ordered. He did all the operational exercises, carrying his frustrations in his backpack and his weapons at the waist through French territory. Fortunately, France had not engaged in the Iraq war, or, by his father's wishes, he would be riding a camel in the desert.

The time in the army only increased his existential anguish in search of his true calling and his personal choices. He then got into the habit of practicing crossbow shooting — a bow-and-arrow weapon like the one used by the legendary Swiss William Tell. He particularly liked the name of the weapon, which alluded to the old papal ban on using it against other Christians, although it was allowed to shoot at the infidels and at the vampires. "Aurélien, the Archer" — as he became known in school — won several shooting competitions, and joined the Royale Arbalète Brainoise.

However, this time fate decided to go against the family's military tradition and give the archer a big scare. When he was a sophomore in military school, during training in Saint-Astier, something uncanny happened. Suddenly, Aurélien's face showed a rigidness and a waxy paleness that made everyone around him certain that the cadet had abruptly died. The stern chief of the battalion, Lucien Beauchamp, in charge of the command, declared, without a shadow of a doubt, that he was clinically "dead", and panicked. Only at the hospital, moments before the funeral home was called, the doctor on duty found out that Aurélien suffered from a severe neurological disorder, which caused the temporary loss of organic functions due to voluntary contraction of the muscles. The disease was then diagnosed as a rare case of an unknown etiology, a variation of the Gélineau syndrome. After the serious incident, the EOGN school allowed Aurélien to graduate as a police officer, but soon retired him prematurely from the *gendarmerie* due to his "unreliable" state of health face his operational requirements, in which he would have to deal with "difficult situations to maintain the public order."

Relieved, Aurelien welcomed the goodbye to arms and complied with the daily medication for the rest of his life so as not to be ill again and maybe fall into a deep sleep with no return. He decided to enroll in the public tender for the position of librarian. The exams were held in Strasbourg. The approved candidates would be distributed through the libraries and media centers in French territory. Henceforth, he intended to travel to great capitals and exotic places only for leisure. And finally fulfill his dream of being a qualified librarian, not just a dilettante researcher.

After lunch with the entire family, in which he told them he had passed the librarian exams, Aurélien saw his father for the last time at the station. He thought he looked troubled, feverish. He realized that the cause probably wasn't due only to the disappointment with the fact that *le petit* hadn't pursued a military career and was leaving for Paris. Aurelien had become a practicing Buddhist who prayed the Nam-Myoho-Renge-Kyo every morning. And, during that visit to Strasbourg, he thought his father was going through the six bad paths, which are states of life in which people are pulled by negative external influences. He was perplexed to be asked when his father, recently promoted colonel, became interested in his opinion for the first time in his life:

"How's your Buddhism, son? Have you been practicing?"

However, his father, maintaining his habits, didn't wait for an answer. He apologized for having received higher orders to return immediately to Nancy. He sneaked a kiss on *le petit*'s cheek and left running, not waiting for the departure of the train. What was his father's intention in creating a rapport with his Buddhist faith, after all? *What was so weird about that?* wondered Aurélien. He sensed that the silent goodbye was rooted in something personal, which unfortunately remained unacknowledged.

When the train departed, without his father's presence, the only things left were the affectionate goodbyes of his grandparents and his mother, who was crying, sad, holding her handkerchief on the platform of the Strasbourg station, full of waits, people getting in and out, crowded with nervous voices. Amidst them, her last words stood out:

"Go and live life, *mon petit*."

On the fast train ride, his father's worried, pale face lingered in his thoughts for a good while and was projected on the window pane during the high-speed trip. Suddenly, the wistful image became fluid, gave way to the magnificent scenery of the flowering fields and productive plains of northeastern France. A clear sign that he had freed himself from the past, like a pressed champagne cork hitting the ceiling, and the hopes of a happy, fulfilled life as a librarian arose.

Aurélien Kléber was first on the public tender for librarian in Paris, thanks to his knowledge in computer science and History books. He was assigned to a *mediathèque* of the Ministry of Culture and Communications near Place des Voges. Thus, in the City of Lights, in addition to becoming an influential mediator between readers and books, he could choose to wander the Seine River or go to Notre-Dame Cathedral or Sainte-Chapelle and listen to their magnificent organ concerts. Possibilities that would open up for him in Paris, at only a good walk from his new work location. Little by little, Aurélien gained, inside, a growing conscience that life is a journey full of mysteries and surprises, connected to the great adventure of being in the world, that marked man's evolution on Earth.

Chapter 7

AMELINHA, A DEAR FRIEND OF ANA'S, Leonardo's wife, used to encourage her to consult with an astrologer she knew to discover the omens of her destiny.

"You have to go there, Ana. She's wonderful! She knows how to restore hope in the midst of disillusions!"

But Ana kept postponing it and postponing it, and in the end quit the idea of going to see the astrologer, Lisa. Without telling his wife, it was Leonardo who ended up going to see the astrologer, because he felt haunted by the doubts about his involvement with the drug traffic.

After his father's death, feeling less controlled in his life, Leo allowed himself to quit the law firm, which was imposed on him by his father, and commit exclusively to his occupation as an accountant and negotiator of the bribery connected to the drug traffic. He continued to expand his professional services to the organized crime, with no one ever finding out that, behind that cordial, low profile man who complained about urban violence, at the bottom of his heart there was a calculating Leo, thirsty for revenge. He'd never gone to a single *favela* to relay messages nor had he ever handled weapons or dealt drugs. He was happy to stay concealed in the background, in a minor role as an accessory, bestowed with the privilege of being the man of trust and the protégé of the thug Skull. But he expected a lot more from destiny and the mysterious "occult powers".

Everyone recognized his competence and mathematical mind. Thus the nickname Big Head — as he was known in the criminal underworld. He became friends and performed small services for all the members of the gang. And, as if to prove that opposites attract, his closest friend was the boss' "muscle", the feared exterminator Runner, nicknamed with this nice sporting alias for his habit of entering the slums running and shooting to kill.

He was happy to be welcomed and called Mr. Leonardo. He thought the astrologer would refuse to open the door if she knew she had "Big Head" in front of her, although he had never been directly involved with drugs, larceny, robberies, and serial murders, typical of large urban concentrations. He would hate not to be allowed in the party of the stars or have his natal chart read like this: "Do you understand, Mr. Thug Helper, that you're going down if you keep this double life as a criminal?" He laughed at the difficulty people have understanding that not every offender is a criminal. For the astrologer, the important thing was — whoever he might be — to not allow him to hinder the complicated reading of his solar progression.

"Do not interrupt me, please, or I won't be able to read. Everything is in your favor. You'll be rational and unemotional in order to achieve your goals, but first you'll have to break connections with the past. There's a vengeance here. It's a double-edged sword. Be careful not to let everything go down the drain and ruin your life"

It was worth to be forewarned and not lose his mind with everything good that was yet to come — he told himself after the consultation, in which the woman of the stars picked from the past the deaths of his parents and warned him not to spoil his son too much. And she also told him, during the extra time of the consultation, several truths about his marriage of over fifteen years with Ana. However, what left him most sad and shaken was to remember his father's death.

His head throbbed when he returned to the scene of the past. It was as if, all of a sudden, he'd heard the bang of that fatal shot in the den. He'd never forgotten that damned year. The shot was fired in the mahogany library. The upholstered couches, the valuable paintings, the lavish collection of secret books from the Inquisition, the beautiful china, the luxuriant ferns, everything was shaken by the deafening blast. There, death was inescapable — in the company of books and so many memories — disturbing the cozy place in which his father's friends used to come to talk or sip a twelve-year-old whiskey, with the traditional five ice cubes.

When his mother opened the door, she was desperate with what she saw, unable to believe the classic suicide scene before her: his father's head fallen on the blotter, blood still spilling on the table and dripping over the edges. A dark stain spreading through the silky Persian rug. His mother had burst into a convulsive cry, leaning on the back of the leather armchair, and soon began to yell hysterically. She just got silent when she was dragged from the library. Leonardo never forgot his mother's petrified eyes and her last look of infinite affection toward his father's lacerated head. His mother had named him Leonardo because she was very devoted to Saint Leonardo Murialdo, a saint nobody knew, but that she had heard Pope Paul VI pontificate as "excellent in the ordinary". She never got over the suicide. She also suffered with the absence of her friends and the bad company of the white walls of the hospital, where she died months later, victim of an incurable cancer.

"How's everything, sonny boy?" was the way his father always greeted him when he arrived at the landscaped manor on São Clemente Street.

He'd told the astrologer, when he scheduled the interview over the phone, that he was born on August 25, 1961, at 11 AM. Right on the day President Jânio Quadros renounced. It was a turbulent day for the country.

"How's everything, sonny boy?" echoed the voice of nostalgia.

The dictatorship period was over and everything promised to go politically well, while economically everything was going bad. The first civil government elected after twenty years of repression had inherited the problems of the economic development model practiced by the military regime and worsened by successive international crises. On February 28, 1986, the government decreed Plano Cruzado, whose failed general price freeze and adoption of a "wage trigger" only contributed to an environment of economic recession, uncontrolled financial speculation and the threat of hyperinflation. Foreign exchange reserves were quickly exhausted and the confidence in the democratic country failed. Brazil went bankrupt.

"How's everything, sonny boy?" echoed the voice of tragedy.

In that damn year of 1986, Leonardo's family world crumbled. Until his last breath, his father had concealed from everyone the buildup of unpayable debts with banks and loan sharks, leaving a lot of bitterness within the disunited family. After bitter meetings with his uncles and with his father's oldest sister, with whom they barely had any relationship, they went to live in São Paulo, ashamed by their relative's bankruptcy, once so cheerful and unconcerned, whose picture stayed like this for a while on the grand piano in the living room. Leonardo was the only one who remained in Rio and witnessed the declaration of bankruptcy. He saw his father's pictures vanish from the piano as well as from the memory of his family and friends. He watched, by himself, the bush take over the gardens, the dust collecting on the furniture, the silverware disappear from the manor, sold in an auction. He was sure that the most important reference in his life, his father, was gone forever.

"You're the only one who believes in this corrupt government!" warned his father's friend.

"We have to invest in the democratization," replied his father, full of civic enthusiasm.

Leonardo recalled that, during the time his father was working on the stock exchange, he was interning at the law firm. His father's friends were getting rich, benefited by the good times of millionaire public constructions and the boom of the stock market. And his father insisted with the hesitant, greedy investor:

"Don't tell me you want to limit your profits. You don't understand that if you don't by the stocks now you won't be able to double your capital!"

It was with the sale of the beautiful properties he had inherited that his father bought the brokerage firm. The first year was wonderful and he made great friends. But it was all a big roller-coaster ride! When the times of euphoria were over, he woke up in the middle of the night with no friends, struggling with the nightmare of debts as a consequence of the bank's crippling interests. Boom! A shot right on the temple, in an unbelievable cold act. He lost his head along with the family's fortune.

The honk of a car on the street made Leonardo's thoughts return to Lisa's house. He recalled that, on one of his trips to the kitchen, during the first consultation, she had turned off the stove, but a delicious smell of white beans came through the door and entered his nostrils. Oddly enough, he was taken by the nice memory of his father's culinary refinement: the sophisticated French *feijoada*, with a well-known name, *cassoulet.*

Then he recalled the first time he had made love, when he was sixteen. His father had planned the whole spree without the knowledge of his mother. He had financed his son's date with an experienced older woman from another country. He became an *habitué*, as he would spell, pursing his lips to the madam. He got to know the best working girls and the most modern motels in Barra, all sponsored by his proud father. He became picky and, with the experience he had gained, he began to prefer older, more enigmatic women, who knew how to give everything they had and were grateful for having sex with an insatiable beast.

"How's everything, sonny boy?" always echoed the distant voice.

After his father's death, the more he read the papers, the more he felt indignant about the cases of corruption. The more he remembered his great dad, who believed until the end in the vitality of the stock market as an essential leverage for the growth of national companies. He believed in the purity of the good intentions of the government of civilists, who had come from the dungeons and the revoking of political tenures during the dictatorship. This filled him with anger, or worse, with vengeful hatred.

Poor guy, he thought. His father had always been a nationalist moron. He had never even thought of opening a bank account in a tax haven. If he had done like his clever friends, who got rich, he would be safe and sound, him and his respectable family. He spoke with the ghosts of the past: it's crazy how we miss those we really love. He liked the old man since he was a little child, on the lazy Sunday mornings when he would go to his father's bed before having breakfast on the terrace. It was good to feel protected, loved, under his mother's jealous stare, who would rather have the company of his well-behaved sister than that of the rebellious brat. Fuck! Money, always money! — Leonardo exploded angrily. His father lost everything. He died saying that in the old days being poor was an unfortunate situation, and today being poor is a social injustice. His biggest dream was to buy his father's manor back one day, to live in it.

It was Lisa, the astrologer, as in a whispered prayer, who revived the pain of those wounds by evoking Uranus in exact conjunction with his Sun. To go through what he did at the age of 25 was too much suffering. Because he couldn't count on a past of poverty to succeed, but he soon realized that he didn't need a bachelor's degree in law to be rich. He just had to have trust in himself — as he thought astrologically — convinced that the stars go around the sky many times and play tricks on people, like him falling in love with Lisa, who made him have faith in the future and love. He had never forgotten what he'd hear before scheduling the consultation, like a hand break he would use not to lose everything in his life.

"Be patient, Mr. Leonardo. All in good time."

Ana, Leonardo's wife, had already decided to satisfy her curiosity and find out what her husband was up to when he was not home. She recalled what her friend Amelinha had read to her when they were leaving the gym, in an introductory text of the weekly Kabbalistic conscience: "Nothing is set in stone, you can always change your destiny". Then Amelinha had forced her to run her finger over the page, going from left to right, until she stopped at a number. It was the seventh of the seventy-two names of God, the DNA of the Soul. This was the message: "I receive the full impact of the forces of Creation. I return meaning to lives that seem meaningless and without purpose to a world that often seems to have no resolution. The order returns. The structure emerges. Everything will be fixed."

As soon as her husband went to the bathroom, Ana didn't hesitate and went to his den to check the three cell phones on the table. She went to see if her husband was still in the shower. He was. She then made the automatic calls to the last numbers in the log, without fearing that the times of the calls would be identified. She was shaking with fear from Leo's unknown world.

"What's up, boss?" answered a hoarse, vulgar voice.

"Who's this? Ana said shyly.

"Who do you want to talk to, bitch?"

She called other numbers. Everyone hung up abruptly, without identifying themselves. All of the voices were from rude people, who abused her with curse words before turning their phones off.

Since it was impossible to identify the calls, they didn't

mince their words. Not a single civilized voice answered her calls.

On the sixth or seventh call she heard something curious.

"The toys arrived yesterday, man. Top of the line," said the anxious voice. "Everything is in the warehouse. The bosses haven't seen it yet." And then, without receiving an answer, the voice shouted: "Who the fuck is this?"

Before putting Leonardo's three phones back in their places, the woman deleted all the calls so as not to leave a trace, erasing the records. She went back to the kitchen thinking about her husband's life when he was not at home. If being an accountant meant dealing with this kind of low-lifes, she had to feel more sympathy for her husband now than she did shortly after his parents died, she reasoned. However, at the same time, everything seemed very suspicious and weird. Starting with the repetition of a certain dialed number, apparently residential, which felt a bit familiar. She didn't want to take any chances. She wrote down the number and decided to call it later from a payphone.

That night, at the dinner table, she tried to learn more to put things in order and focus on what she had to find out to give, Kabbalistically, "mean and purpose".

"Hand me the bread knife, please," asked Leonardo to cut the fresh bread from the bakery, now delivered at their door.

"How was your day, darling?" Ana asked sweetly, trying the shaky ground of unknown calls and numbers.

"As always," Leonardo replied curtly.

"Anything new?" the woman provoked, staring.

"All normal. The usual problems."

The cell phones started ringing with urgency. Leonardo would stand up and answer immediately, after checking the origin of the call. A police informant had warned him that they were setting up an operation to arrest Skull. From the distance Ana and his son were seated, they couldn't hear his words. Once in a while, and only when he raised his voice, they could hear curse words, the only thing distinct.

"I don't know why men swear so much," said Ana provocatively, waiting for her husband's reaction.

Leonardo kept silent, focused only on cutting a smaller piece of baloney to fit in the small piece of bread. She hated baloney, but Leonardo and their son stuffed themselves.

"This one came directly from Bologna, son. It was an Italian friend of mine who brought it. It's very spicy, you'll like it."

His son nodded, giving it an approving look. Leonardo then smiled affectionately, generously, offering the piece of bread stuffed with baloney that he had prepared.

"Try it!" ordered Leonard, as if he was a general.

His wife watched closely the loving scene, like so many others that always happened in the playful relationship between father and son.

"Do you like it, son?" asked Leonardo, watching his son avidly chew the bread with his mouth full.

"All your clients curse. Is this normal?"

Leonardo laughed, a cynical, provocative laugh.

"What do you want, darling? That, in the computer age, men say *bonjour*?" answered Leonardo pouting with his lips pursed, making his son, who soon began to mimic him, laugh. They laughed a lot and Ana had no alternative except to join them and dissipate the bad mood with which she had come to the table, caused by the suspicions she had about her husband's phones.

"Have you decided if your son will join the Army?" asked the woman, changing the subject after the half-hearted smiles.

"Yes, he will. When time comes, he'll join."

"I think it's good. He'll learn some discipline and to obey his mother."

"What, doesn't he obey you?" Leonardo asked, surprised.

He didn't have the chance to hear his wife's answer,

because his cell phone rang and he left the table to answer the insistent call.

"Boss, Rainstorm tracked the private call he received and identified it as being this number. There's no mistake."

"What the fuck? I haven't called him!"

"Oops! This phone is tapped, boss!"

Leonardo was thoughtful, stroking his belly, which had gotten more evident during this frantic last year, full of worries outside his home. The other phone rang. He checked the number and answered it.

"Is everything OK, man? The battery was dead, so I couldn't answer."

"I didn't call you. Well, it doesn't matter. Can you tell me at what time was the call?" asked Big Head in a low voice.

After hastily closing the lid of the last cell phone, the smile on Leonardo's face was completely gone. His face was now one of pure tension, something that made the furrows of his forehead protrude. Leonardo didn't return to the table. He went straight to his bedroom to look for an aspirin on the nightstand, before the pangs in his head killed him with the pain. He had to be patient, as Lisa had said.

"What's up, Major?'

The phone had rung very late after dinner. It was the last call Leonardo answered. It was the Major, with news.

Chapter 8

AT FIRST SIGHT, ONE OF THE MAIN REASONS why organized crime emerged, broadened, and reached the current stage of violence, was quite simple: the uncontrolled growth of the cities. In them, peripheral neighborhoods, slums, and rogue territories arise and, from inside the penitentiaries, criminal groups that keep commanding and perpetrating crimes. Hiring labor for crime abounds due to the poverty and lack of education of the economic minorities. And the criminal organizations grow because they make a lot of money with the business. This illicit wealth resulted in the widespread notion in Brazil that crime pays off, because there's no punishment and it brings lots and lots of money. With time, this eventually created a ripple effect, increasingly stimulating other criminal networks, like the traffic of weapons.

In one particular night, just like Zé do Bigode, one of the founders of Comando Vermelho (a Brazilian criminal organization engaged primarily in arms and drug trafficking), a criminal gang emerged at the "Devil's Cauldron", in Ilha Grande and, according to the legend, fought against four hundred police officers; the thug Skull also resisted bravely for hours against all the attempts of catching him alive. He killed and injured several officers. However, with the reinforcement of five police units, unlike Zé do Bigode, who died, he finally surrendered, seriously wounded. From the hospital, he was transferred to a maximum-security federal prison, still in an ambulance, followed by a convoy of police cars.

When a leader dies or is arrested, there's a void of power in the *favelas* while the natural shifting occurs, that is, a war between criminal organizations. Those who live in the *favelas* have to live with this reality, doing what they can to survive the tragic stories of murders of women, old and innocent people, and the heavy gunfights that include even children holding weapons. This reality, as shocking as it may seem, is accepted as a common, normal fact by the dwellers of the *favelas,* who are forced to endure this fate in silence, victims of an omitted society, and of usually unprepared governments, powerless to deal with the traffic.

"It's all going to start again," complained the housewife when she heard the sound of the first shots at the entrance of the Dona Marta slum, right on São Clemente Street and that has a strategic position for the sale of narcotics in the South area of Rio.

But this time it wasn't only ordinary gunshots. The scene was a war of proportions never seen before between rival groups. The unusual thing about this shooting was that the actions were marked by the extreme barbarity of the invaders to take over Skull's territories, which stretched from Dona Marta Hill, to Ladeira dos Tabajaras and Favela da Rocinha, however distant these places might be from one another.

Dona Marta Hill is not different from other slums built on the hills in Rio, which have their own independence. They are full of mazes and, in general, have few, difficult steep accesses. Each slum has its reality and its owner, due to the armed conflicts. They are the ideal places to use as a base camp for selling drugs and defend the territories, as they naturally offer the protection of the physical space against rival groups and the police. And the residents, coerced by the cohabitation codes and the lack of presence from society's legal power, end up cooperating with the drug dealers, helping them and hiding them from the invasions of the "strangers", that is, anyone who doesn't belong to that environment is regarded as an enemy.

After many deaths, the rival gang took over Dona Marta Hill. The domination was visible through the graffiti on the walls of the *favela* exalting the victors. The residents revered the new leadership, who had a lot of plans for their cocaine empire to expand on the circuit of poverty and human misery. With the cease-fire, the points of sales resumed their operation, and the "ant traffic" — moving small amounts of drugs and guns — was replaced by the "convoys", as the big shipments are called. As it always happened in the slum, the voices silenced with the drug money going around the narrow streets and alleys again.

Skull, who'd started in the lowest position in his career as a drug dealer, thought he could control traffic from prison, through cell phones, because crime's greatest power in Rio de Janeiro is not on the streets, but inside the penitentiary system. But the new "owner" of Dona Marta Hill had come to stay. He wasn't from that "community" (as the *favelas* are called) or from Rio de Janeiro. He was the nephew of the criminal known as "Marcola", a former bank robber who became the leader of the criminal organization Primeiro Comando da Capital (PCC)[2] in São Paulo and had chosen Dona Marta because he thought that it wouldn't resist the attack with the new weapons imported from Paraguay. Marcola's nephew's invasion of the *favela* prophesied that the CPP had accepted the challenge of direct confrontation with one of the three criminal groups that dominated the sale points of drugs in the state of Rio de Janeiro. Uncle Marcola was proud of having had read three hundred books, his favorites being *The Art of War*, by Sun Tzu, and *The Prince*, by Machiavelli. The invasion was a practical lesson.

The new chief of the *favela*, Alcides Pinto da Silva, simply known as Pimpão, had showed a talent for crime since his teenage years, robbing shops and gas stations. He was arrested and escaped several times, until he quickly "changed

2   First Command of the Capital, one of the largest criminal organizations in Brazil (TN)

careers". He chose the drug traffic because profits were higher and it only required dexterity to use a Kalashnikov AK-47. In his first armed actions, he proved to be a natural leader: ambitious, pragmatic, and very cruel, the basic requirements that led him to take over Dona Marta Hill and occupy Skull's other territories.

Leonardo's cell phone went silent. He received very few calls during the invasion. He had already thought about running away if things got ugly. But the phone rang repeatedly after dinner. He couldn't ignore it.

"What's up, Major?"

"Everything's cool. You bet, man."

"Really, Runner?" asked Leonardo, although the reassuring and commanding voice of the former captain of Skull's assault troop left no doubt that his friend had joined the enemy and it would be no surprise if he wasn't already the new general manager.

"They want to talk to you," he said in an authoritarian tone.

"Are you crazy? I'm gonna die. I know too much, man. I'm getting out of here."

"It's all right, Big Head. You can come, no need to worry. I assure you there'll be no trouble. I'm waiting for you at Antonio's bar."

"I've never gone to a *favela*, Runner. I don't even know where it is."

"Figure it out, man. The boss doesn't like to wait," advised his friend, relaying the message as if caressing a gun in its holster.

On the terrace of the shack, after the massacre, the survivors of the group, with their hands tied behind their backs, were watched by Pimpão's inquisitive gaze and his neck stretched out. The winners counted their earnings. After the accounts and the smile of approval of the new boss, the manager of the black (marijuana), the manager of the white (cocaine), the manager of the soldiers, and those of the sales point left. The only one who remained was Runner who, during the war between the groups, was surrounded by rival soldiers and forced to face the general manager in a saber fight. He was spared after he killed his enemy with a saber strike, in a duel in front of the new boss. The rival's decapitated head that rolled on the floor terrified everyone. The new boss was impressed by the feat and immediately hired the other man.

"He died like a pussy. You're gonna be my major, get it?"

"I've never seen an Army major in my life, Boss."

"But now you will. Are we clear?" summarized Pimpão, arrogant, confident in the command of the *favela*, just like his uncle Marcola, who ruled everything from prison, acting as a "wholesaler", buying the cocaine abroad, refining it in São Paulo, and then distributing it to the urban centers.

"You smashed it with the guns, Boss," confirmed the Major, omitting the participation of child-soldiers, trained by military police, who, when they changed sides, made the difference in the war between the criminals.

"Now, let's think big, Major," Pimpão reacted to the compliment, happy with the betrayal of the kids and for having used more modern weapons than the ones of the official police forces.

"Why change it, Boss? Everything is fine the way it is!"

"No, it's not!" Pimpão objected. "I'm gonna increase sales and the delivery on bikes. Where's the accountant?"

Leonardo met the Major on Francisco de Moura Street and, from there, they went up to the headquarters. From the questions made by the new boss, he quickly realized that he didn't like to talk, unlike Skull. He was more interested in the money he would make in the *favela* than in bragging about the tragic casualties of partners and innocent people, considered to be "natural". He implied that he would command Dona Marta Hill without giving assistance to the residents and terrifying them. He was going to focus on a strategy that would guarantee a constant supply of drugs and the defense of the sales points against invasions from rival gangs and police raids, while training and arming soldiers to invade the territories of other criminal groups.

Pimpão explained that he was going to take over other *favelas* with advanced guerilla techniques and that he wanted to see the income of money grow. He would use violence as a big business tool. He listened carefully while Big Head explained how the "fund" worked. Many top-notch companies didn't have this reserve fund. It was like an emergency fund for the accounting, capitalized with the collection of approximately five percent of the revenue of each of the group's sales points. It was an avalanche of numbers. He heard Leonardo's many ideas and plans, and how he intended to increase the profitability of their earnings, as long as he could count on two more assistants, computerize the accounting, and hire an expert in finances and money laundering, things that Skull also refused to do.

It was clear that the new boss was impressed by the accountant. Although everything was written down, he had all the numbers in his head. Everything he wanted to know about the ledger, Leonardo knew by heart. He was explanatory and precise, without being tiresome. He had no more doubts. Side by side with the Major, who commanded the soldiers and the managers like no one else, Big Head was the other essential piece. He would strengthen the traffic's financial power, avoiding losses, and increasing profits. His uncle, in prison, would also like to have a guy like this on his side — reasoned Pimpão, before making the final adjustments to the deal.

"We're gonna increase the drug money a hell of a lot."

"For sure, money is gonna flow in like crazy," replied Leonardo, getting the new boss excited enough that he could ask for what he so badly needed. "I'll need qualified people. Can I hire them?"

"I gave you your life back, Big Head. Instead of going six feet under, you're working for me. You're gonna do what I say. We're gonna modernize everything. The drug operation will become a first-world company, just like Petrobrás[3]. You can hire them. Are you calmer now?"

"Yes. Your factory will make money like hot bread from the bakery. You can bet on it."

Without the Major's presence, the boss got pensive before surprising Leonardo, sealing the trust that had been spontaneously created, just like it had happened with Skull in the card game.

"You'll be my Minister of Finance."

"What do you mean?" asked Leonardo, a little pale.

"Exactly what you heard. You'll be my Minister of Finance and Bribes. Are we clear?" he sentenced, convinced he couldn't do without that man who knew everything and made the deals with the police and the "people upstairs".

Leonardo didn't think twice. There was no point in arguing. The man had this childish habit of giving titles to men he trusted. First it was with Major Runner and now with him, appointing him Minister of Finance. *What a stupid idea!* he thought, repeating, with mocking gargles, the position with all his might. Better being a plenipotentiary minister than being six feet under.

Leonardo saw the smile on his boss' face with the plans he shared to increase the profits after the carte blanche was granted. He felt like Joseph Fouché, from Stefan Zweig's book, which he had enjoyed so much. The plenipotentiary French minister known as "provider for the winners". Everyone owed him favors and used his secret, questionable services. He served Robespierre, Napoleon Bonaparte, and Louis XVIII with the same efficiency and shrewdness, having betrayed all of them, not without getting rich and being

3   Brazilian Petroleum Corporation (TN)

cruel in his own way first. When they sent him to "clean" the area, from Nantes to Lyon", of the counterrevolutionaries, Fouché became known as "the Executioner of Lyon", for having ordered 1906 executions. He was also very good at what he skillfully did: pay bribes and create an efficient network of informants. He controlled many people through bribery and corruption.

Leonardo read that Fouché had never touched a firearm. He — who hadn't come from the streets — wouldn't have the need to touch one either, because he would use the best thing he had — his head — feeling confident that the drug consumption would be the tip of the iceberg of great businesses, in a scale never seen before, if he were able to modernize the finances of the traffic organization. Being the new boss of the *favela* the most capitalist and brutal of the drug dealers he had met, he had everything to turn the traffic business in a profitable and productive enterprise. And he would make a fortune controlling the traffic's accounts, since he had made a deal to get a generous percentage of the profits and have the Major's help. He couldn't go back anymore, now that the "hidden forces" were in his favor.

Before saying goodbye to Leonardo, Pimpão called Major Runner and asked them both a strange question:

"I'll have a black and white yin-yang tattooed on the kids," said the boss, omitting that is was a suggestion from his uncle, whose diagram represented "the way to wisely balance good and evil".

"What do you think?" and he showed them the drawing.

While the Major limited himself to express his opinion with a quite conventional "cool", Leonardo felt he had enough prestige to dare and give his honest opinion. It was as if the "forces of evil", in Lisa's version, had whispered it to him.

"It would be cool in Japan. But nobody will understand it here."

"Right. I like it. Do you have any suggestions, Minister?

How about tattooing Satan? It will show that he's on our side to turn the lives of our enemies into hell."

"Good, Major! We'll tattoo Satan on their arms and a 666 on their foreheads. I want all the guys to get tattoos. All of them!"

"I'm on it, boss," said Major Runner, immediately pointing to the spot on the arm where the mandatory tattoos would be.

Pimpão laughed. Then his eyes got somber when he recalled what he said to his uncle before he chose "the only path" he had to succeed in life and dream about being the boss in one of Rio's *favelas*:

Fuck, there are children that, fuck, starve... I won't starve... I won't stay on the streets begging people for food, fuck it, I'd rather get a gun, be in a favela *shooting guns, selling drugs every day than to starve with my mother.*

The following weeks were filled with excitement. The phones rang non-stop, interrupting dinner at home. Ana was furious. "What can I do?" Leonardo asked himself. He couldn't tell her that now he was Minister of Finance for Pìmpão from PCC, and that, at night, the private channels of corruption were more accessible and communicative.

Leonardo saw his son hesitantly approach him to say goodbye.

"How's everything, sonny boy?" asked Leonardo, smiling.

Lucca looked over his shoulder to make sure his mother wasn't following him. He got near his father's face as if to kiss him, and whispered in his ear:

"Are you aware that Mom has been going through your things, Dad?"

"I have nothing to hide, son. Trust me."

"I don't know, Dad. I've seen Mom messing with your phones."

"Thank you for the tip, buddy," said Leonardo, opening the elevator door, not without kissing him on the forehead and hugging him first. "Next week, I'll start to drive you to school."

As the elevator slowly went down, Leonardo was taken by the memory of his protest at the end of his chart's reading, so that the astrologer would give him another half hour of consultation. It was then that his marriage was mentioned. He recalled the pause Lisa took, drinking her soda in slow gulps to dose the embarrassing revelations.

"Well, then I took your wife's chart, a very intelligent person, I'd say smart, and also seductive, because she has Venus in her first house. Ah! You felt a great physical attraction since the first time you've met, haven't you?"

Lisa even changed her tone of voice before she continued:

"You were afraid you were going to make the wrong decision, but ended up getting married during Saturn's return. At first, everything was wonderful. She was very protective, helpful, encouraged you to move up in life. But now that you're going to make a lot of money, she wants to interfere in your goals. You won't like to hear the things I'm going to say now."

"Say it," said Leonardo, holding back a hidden annoyance.

"Your wife doesn't accept your way of prospering through ambition. Her way of thinking is different from yours. With the Moon in her fourth house, she'll use emotional blackmail and will do everything in her power to change the way you think and act. I'm not talking about if she loves you or not, if she's right or wrong. I'm just reading her chart, right?"

"Yes. Do you really think it can't be solved?"

"It depends. I don't see any problems. But look at this: Pluto is entering her seventh house. It's the house that rules marriage. This aspect concerns me. Never forget Pluto's transformation power."

Leonardo nodded, agreeing.

"Then I studied your chart until 2 AM and compared it to hers. I did the synastry and everything fell into place. Pay close attention to what I'm going to ask: do you think your wife would be capable of hindering your life in a sea of wrath?"

"I don't know, honestly. I've never thought about that. I think that…"

"Whether you think or not, be very careful, because I was stunned with both of your charts. They show an intense, tragic story in previous lives. The curious thing is that, in this incarnation, you had the opportunity to make your karmic rescue and forgive each other, ridding yourselves of this incompatibility connection. But you didn't do it. Now you can't avoid confrontation anymore. Your Sun in conjunction with Pluto forms the aspect of a powerful man who wants to reach his goals at any cost and having to face other people's anger. I would double my attention on her from your birthday on. No! It would be better if you started today. Right?"

"Do you really think that confrontation is inevitable?"

"Pluto doesn't rest. Be careful! Use your mathematic coolness to calculate the best path and carry on."

Leonardo was still thinking about his son's warning when he stepped on the gas and left the garage. He only relaxed when he remembered the magical moment when his gaze locked on Lisa's tan lines and he felt the swelling of the need for sex. Something that couldn't be postponed by someone who would follow his destiny as plenipotentiary minister, about to receive the famous "Relic" from the hands of a *babalorishá*[4] from Bahia. Thankfully, he could count with the help of the killer Major to speed up delivery and be able to hang it on the wall of the office at Downtown Shopping Mall soon.

4 A male priest of Umbanda, Candomblé and Quimbanda, the Afro-Brazilian religions (*TN*)

Chapter 9

NOT HEARING THE CONTINUOUS SOUND of water from her husband's shower, Ana hurried and put the cell phones lined in the right order, just like Leonardo had left them, with no traces that they had been used, and sought shelter in the kitchen.

So that the maid wouldn't notice her nervousness, she started making a cake. As she melted the chocolate bar, her thoughts remained absent from the bowl smeared with butter. At first, she was taken by a feeling of compassion when she thought about how Leo had to deal with the riff-raff from the cell phones and fight like a lion every day to support their family and give them a home with the comfort she recognized they had. Then, many doubts and dilemmas arose about what she should do.

She had never heard such angry voices or such an avalanche of profanity. From the list, she hadn't dialed just one number, the one her husband had called, because apparently it was a landline and not a cell phone. She would have plenty of time to call that one later from a payphone, without taking any risks. It must be a very important, very special number, perhaps the boss'.

Ana finished baking the cake and called her husband and her son to dinner. And while her husband's phones let them eat in peace, her suspicious eyes saw something strange happening at the table. During dinner, she noticed, in silence, the change in the way her husband treated their son, starting with the kiss on the top of their son's head, before Leonardo sat at the head of the table. He had never made this loving gesture before. A bit of jealousy sprung in Lucca's mother and the woman who had baked the chocolate cake for the men of the house.

Because the cell phones were quiet that night compared to the previous days, Ana noticed how moving it was to see this father, heartless up until recently, playing with his son, who returned the attention with laughter sprinkled with slangs. This was part of the male jokes which she resigned herself for not being able to take part. *Where's the Leonardo I knew?* was what she would like to know, because in the last year her husband surprised her every day. He had changed dramatically.

She was willing to find out at any cost what was happening. She intended on asking her best friend, since she had no talent to play detective. Her friend had caught her husband having an affair with a slut. The cheater was forgiven and everyone forgot the "hiccup", and the family remained together to this day. It wasn't her case, which she recognized to be way simpler, because there was no "other woman".

As a Roman apostolic Catholic, she just wanted her husband and her marriage to return to their former peaceful normality, without cell phones, when her husband rarely received phone calls at night and was not so restless and irascible at the table.

It was in one of those rare phone calls, a while ago, that she'd heard the word "Skull", said by Leonardo. She thought she had heard it wrong, or that it was one of these masculine poor taste jokes. It was from this mysterious call on that everything went upside down in her husband's life. The phones started ringing and they never stopped harassing him. One time, they called him in the middle of the night. Leo answered it in the bedroom and then locked himself in the bathroom.

"Who was it?" asked his wife, very worried.

"A client."

"It's past midnight. That's crazy!"

"It was a client that ran over a guy in São Conrado. He just wanted to know to whom he should talk at the police station."

"And did you know somebody?" asked Ana.

"Of course, every accountant needs to have good contacts. Well, let's go to sleep now," Leonardo ordered dryly.

For the first time, Ana heard an enlightening clue about accountant work. Her husband new people in police stations, to the point that someone remembered to call him in the middle of the night to know who to look for. It was comforting to know that her husband was well connected and knew the men of the law - she thought, relieved by the discovery, before falling asleep and dreaming of angels and pets.

She always went to the mass in the neighborhood on Sundays. It seemed to be a sin to snoop her husband's life like that and examine his special phone on her own. But the seduction of the mystery of getting to the bottom of the situation had already gotten to her. She felt drawn to the forbidden adventure of following her husband after he dropped their son off at school — a habit recently acquired in this period where the cell phones had become unbearable at night. But she was still hesitant about her audacity.

"Do I call or do I wait a little bit longer?" she asked herself when she left the mass. Undecided, she only called the mysterious number on Monday, changing her voice on purpose.

"Is this from the drugstore?"

"No. Which number did you dial?" said the woman.

Ana was surprised by the polite female voice. She didn't hang up immediately. She could hear her panting.

"Who is calling? Who is this?" There was a brief pause. "Is it you, honey?" the voice whispered before hanging up the phone.

She called again from the payphone, but nobody answered.

It wasn't the curse words that concerned her anymore;

what unsettled Ana was this landline number on the list of calls in her husband's phone. It was a very special voice.

The next morning, she didn't hesitate. She took a cab and followed her husband's car. She saw him drop off their son at school and then take Avenida das Americas to number 500. She followed her husband's car through the internal streets of Downtown Shopping Mall, in Barra. From a distance, she saw her husband park his car in a private area, presumably near the office she had never been to. She dismissed the cab, watching from a store opposite the low commercial building. She waited for over an hour in a small bar and got tired. She decided to repeat the stake out the next day. She saw her husband, before he went up to his office, go through the balcony of an empty pizzeria. Soon there was a small crowd around her husband. Everyone greeted him. No pat on the back, but a lot of cursing — she deduced from seeing the guys' informal language and ostentatious mocking gestures. A few got in the elevator with him.

Only this day he didn't stay very long at the office. He left in high speed and parked his car in Lagoa, on the sidewalk of Epitácio Pessoa Avenue. He went in an imposing building with a white marble façade. She waited for approximately two hours, reading a magazine under a tree on the opposite side of the avenue until her husband left smiling and returned to Barra. On the following days she didn't have to stalk him, she already knew the fixed addresses. She went straight there. All she needed was to see her husband's car parked at Downtown Shopping Mall or Lagoa. One afternoon she waited for so long that she saw the beautiful early afternoon blue sky change, until the clouds got thicker behind Dois Irmãos Hill and rain began pouring on Epitácio Pessoa Avenue. This day, she arrived home, in Barra, long after Leonardo, because traffic was awful. Leo, busy with the voices on the cell phones, didn't even notice his wife's extravagance; she always waited for him sitting on the living room couch, watching her soap opera on TV.

At dinner, Ana couldn't help herself and spitted the questions out:

"Where exactly is your office located at Downtown Shopping Mall?"

"Block 6, right in front Banco do Brasil. Can you tell me why are you asking?" asked Leonardo, not hiding his concern.

"I felt like going there to visit you. Did you handle a lot of annoying clients there today?"

"A lot. Give me a heads-up first, so I can clean the mess."

"Do all your clients go to see you at Downtown Shopping Mall?"

"Those who don't live in Barra don't want to go there. It's too far. It's complicated. I have to go to downtown or to their house. Why? Is there a problem?" asked Leonardo, showing annoyance.

"There was a terrible bank robbery downtown today," lied Ana. "I thought you were near at that time."

"Shootings are common downtown. What time was that?"

"In the afternoon. You're telling me you were there?"

"Of course I was. But what difference does it make, if I'm here in one piece?" asked Leonardo, laughing and winking at Lucca. "Say, son, what's the game going to be like today?"

"Mengão is gonna thrash the other team, Dad. Wanna bet?"

"I don't know, I don't know…"

Ana was silent but happy to see them both laughing and having fun. Her husband had lied. Mr. "In One Piece" hadn't gone downtown. He'd spent the afternoon at Lagoa. She saw it first hand. Her police-like mind began to think: now, more than ever, she would need help to find out who her husband was. She got a bitter taste in her mouth.

*

During the first reading of his solar revolution, Leonardo promised that he would never think about suicide again, given his father's tragic death. In return, and because she let herself be seduced far beyond her usual intimacy with the stars, Lisa fulfilled her promise to go to a motel, knowing that Leo's wife was in Itaipava with their son and would only return the next morning.

That night, she left the motel feeling satiated but confused. She wanted to forget what Leo had said about being a happily married man with a solid marriage who, somehow, regretted what happened when the consultation was over. She feared he wouldn't call her for consultations or better things. But, even though this seemed true, she wasn't totally convinced with the confession, because solar revolutions don't lie and Leonardo knew how to manipulate the words at his will to keep his true feelings hidden.

It had been three days since the first consultation and the night at the motel, when Lisa woke up that morning hearing the birds singing happily on the trees. She slowly opened her eyes and could follow the trajectory of the sun's rays settling on her legs and untidy pillows. And soon the preposterous doubt came to her mind: what if the readings and the fit of the astral charts were wrong? Everything was still vivid, lucid. The careful preparation of Leonardo's chart, how she feared him, the provocative birth mark on her shoulder, the explosion of desire on the rug and at the motel and, finally, the appeasement of satiated sex. She knew that this had only happened because the natal charts and the lunar nodes were complementary. Besides, you don't need to be an astrologer to know that it's impossible to stop the rhythm of the planets and the course of fate.

Lisa heard the dogs barking. It was the doorman leaving the mail under the door. The body lying on the bed didn't move. The phone suddenly rang. It was Leonardo. At first, he was extremely formal and confused. He gave a pathetic speech to then ask her if he could schedule a consultation for the following month. He couldn't justify why he wanted to schedule it so far in advance. Lisa recalled smiling at the Virgo distraught by the changing nature of his Gemini ascendant.

Less than ten minutes later, Leonardo called again. It was the unpredictable Leonardo with whom she had fallen in love:

"Is tomorrow OK? I still have many doubts regarding what you told me about the money."

"Why can't it be here?" Lisa interrupted to know if it was a reading of his chart or her birthmark that Leo wanted.

As much as she tried to dissuade him, Leo did not budge from the idea of the motel. Lisa had not forgotten the poor taste of the room she ended up in compared to her own room with flowered sheets. It's my karma — she complained as she walked up the stairs to the hotel. But her body wanted to be subdued. She no longer cared about the creaky bed where anonymous men and women had loved or hated each other forever in that dump chosen by Leonardo. Uninhibited, anxious, she resigned herself before the animal taken by the fury of possessing another animal by the smell, by untamed attraction. It was part of her new life to accept the man of her destiny as she knew him.

Weeks went by after the night of the second meeting. Leo tried to recall what color the walls of the motel were and learn about her life and her past. Lisa was always elusive, enigmatic, refusing to decipher her secrets:

"I don't know what color they were. I only remember the color of happiness on your face when you put me in that state of madness and complicity."

"I think the walls were green," insisted Leonardo, smiling. Tell me about your life, love."

"Blue, green, red, gray, any color, what matters now is that never have a man so curious made me so happy."

From that day on, when the astrological charts fit for the second time, Leonardo could call her at any time, clear any doubts he had about his solar revolution or trace the white birthmark on her shoulder. Lisa didn't have a fixed schedule any more. She would drive her loyal clients crazy by canceling previous appointments. The phone would ring. It was him, now at any time, day or night. And when the phone didn't ring, the silence tortured her and she despaired. She wanted to hear his voice, always. She could no longer live without his presence in her room and on the flowered sheets where they made love. She would forget about everything, without measuring the consequences and thinking about the "hidden forces".

Chapter 10

AFTER A THREE-AND-A-HALF-HOUR DRIVE, curator Ferdinand Rochemont de Sailly and Father Antoine Duvert entered Porte d'Italie.

Because he had certain privileges granted to members of the General Association of Curators of Public Collections, wealthy Ferdinand Rochemont de Sailly, curator of the Château d'Angers Museum, requested, in advance and without any red tape, a room to deal with a subject of great relevance. His good taste and vanity made him choose the Musée d'Orsay. He would never miss the precious opportunity to worship the famous paintings that had fascinated him since his teenage years. Besides, the windows of the room on the third floor overlooked the Jardin des Tuileries, Pont Royal, and the *bateau-mouches*[5] franticly moving through the Seine River. It was his favorite room. There was no better choice for this important meeting in Paris.

They had lunch at the museum's restaurant. For desert, Father Antoine didn't resist gluttony and stuffed his face with *crème brulée*. After visiting the painting *The Romans in Their Decadence*, by Thomas Couture, curator Ferdinand de Sailly went to meet Aurélien Kléber, his friend's nephew, who arrived on time, by subway, and was waiting for them in front of the bronze statue of a rhino.

The researcher and archery champion felt very honored by the invitation. He didn't know the details of the request

---

5 *Bateaux Mouches* are open excursion boats that provide visitors to Paris, France, with a view of the city from along the river Seine. Trademark of *Compagnie dès Bateaux Mouches*, the main operator for this kind of boat (TN)

for help. As promised over the phone, they would be explained in person that busy afternoon at the old train station turned into a portentous museum opposite the Louvre.

"Essentially, that's it," concluded the curator after exposing for thirty minutes the importance of his mission in that silent room far from the buzz of the visitors. "Thus, we believe you could be of great help to us in Rio de Janeiro."

"I'm sure the rescue will be successful," Father Antoine added with a knowing smile on the corner of his lips.

"If you don't mind, I'd like to know a few details about the discovery. I don't know if I'm fully capacitated to recover this valuable piece of French heritage. I think I..."

"Go on and ask what you want to know, Mr. Aurélien Kléber," the curator interrupted, determined to resolve any doubts.

"How reliable is this information?"

"You know that it is impossible to be sure. Everything leads us to believe that the information is reliable, as the informant saw the image."

"That's all?" questioned the researcher with watchful black eyes, a protruding nose, and a goatee, who looked like a medieval archer holding a bow in a position of attack.

"Of course not," replied Ferdinand. "We've researched the original sketches by Nicolas Bataille and the 1473 manuscripts, archived at the Hôtel de Croisilles to ensure that the scene seen by our informant matches the description of the supposedly original tableau 76. I'll give you the research dossier. Trust me, there are almost no more doubts about the authenticity of the painting."

"Seventy-five!" corrected the priest, raising his index finger in protest.

"But why the hell this tableau 75 ended up in Brazil?" asked Aurélien, making his hosts laugh.

"If we could answer your question, it would probably be here with us already," said Ferdinand ironically, closing his tiny eyes and pressing his moist lips. "It's still a mystery to all of us. No one can explain how this happened. We need someone to go there and find out why and when the tapestry crossed the Atlantic Ocean and ended up in Brazil."

"Can I ask you why did you think of me?"

"Because of your profile and the determining circumstances," replied the historian Ferdinand in a systematic way. "First, because you have experience in this kind of case and know fully well what the recovery of the tableau represents for Angers. Second, because we cannot get the police involved before we are sure of what we've found. Third, because you've been to Rio de Janeiro and have some contacts there. Your uncle says they can help us."

"It's true, I've lived for a few months in Rio. I know the city a bit and speak a fairly acceptable Portuguese-French. I just don't know if my friends would be willing to collaborate."

"Tell him, Aurélien, about the Brazilian prosecutor who came to visit you in Paris," interrupted Father Antoine walking away from the window, not without first glancing for the last time toward the floating restaurant parked at Quai d'Orsay right in front of the museum.

"Rio's Public Prosecutor and his wife stayed at my house for a week. We're good friends."

"This is very good to know. Did he come to Paris for work?"

"Yes and no. He was vacationing in France, but insisted on meeting some of my former colleagues from the *Gendarmerie*, who are now serving at a DAT unit of the Ministry of Justice here in Paris."

"Hmm… It could be a good start to help us confirm the information," summed up the curator, glad to know about the existence of the Brazilian prosecutor, but not interested in deciphering the mentioned acronym of the mentioned French police agency.

"My friend Aurélien, please understand, I'm not here to help a family member," Father Antoine pondered solemnly, straightening up in his chair. "Something very important is in danger. There is a Christian justification that compels us to recover the missing tableau and not allow it to fall into unscrupulous hands."

"How so, Uncle?" asked Aurélien, gently stroking his goatee with his fingertips.

"Nobody knows the true meaning of the book of Revelation," replied Father Antoine, recalling his dark thoughts and concerns when leaving the lecture at the Palace of Arts, during the 21st Journalism Festival. "It's a book subject to interpretation, that has a complex symbolic and prophetic language, containing heavenly visions that go beyond the comprehension of the human imagination. The disappearance of a tableau of this magnitude, that symbolizes the final victory of good over evil, unfortunately allows for a lot of superstitions and speculations."

"Your assessment of the value of the tableau is quite right," said the curator. "It's crucial to recover the picture of the devil and return it to the castle and to religious faith. It's not the purely physical concept of filling a void on the wall or the monetary value of the work itself. It's the message of salvation and of the beginning of the millennium that is essentially at stake."

"The tableau is biblically very important, Aurélien," continued the priest, excited by the preaching. "Its absence can represent hopelessness. Many disillusioned people imagine that the world will soon be destroyed by the forces of evil."

"Soon?" asked the researcher, raising his eyebrows at the apocalyptic omen of the end of the world.

"That's where the great religious issue and the great challenge of recovering the valuable tableau that is now in Brazil lie."

Father Antoine got up from the chair, rubbed his hands

on his rosy cheeks, crossed the room, and took his time explaining the verse: "*Things that must happen soon*" (1:1; 22:6). He explained, frantically, that this time limit was put at the beginning and the end of the Apocalypse to make the interpretation of the intermediate chapters easier. He emphasized, agitated, that the expression "soon" is used in other parts of the New Testament to show that God was not talking about events that will happen in the distant future. He quoted verses from the Fifth Seal, in which persecuted Christians, especially those who sacrificed their lives in the service of the Lord, were crying out for justice. "And were their deaths in vain?" was what Antoine asked and at the same time answered, gesturing a lot with his chubby hands and excited fingers. He explained that they had died trusting that God was fair and that He had assured them that He would punish the evildoers, but that persecution would come before He exercised his vengeance. Tableau 75 of the tapestry has everything to do with this, with the defeat of Satan, before being thrown into the lake of fire.

"Bravo! That's it! We want to hear the seventh trumpet of victory," exclaimed the curator, congratulating the priest for his emotional speech in defense of the recovery of the tableau.

"Let's not forget that before salvation the trumpets of catastrophe were heard", emphasized the priest, getting into a new biblical trance. "The sounds of a world where men were corrupted and hit by the fire of damnation and by the locusts that piled up in the cities. Where plague and violence progressed with no limits until death, threats grew, and urban wars multiplied in the neighborhoods like tumors. It was the victory of the Red Horse's big sword sowing bloody wars to destroy peace on earth and rush the end of the world."

"This historical lesson pulsates in the embossed threads of the tapestry scenes," remarked the curator proudly, excited by the sweeping figurative interpretation of the exposure.

And the priest went on with the same enthusiasm and rhetorical tone.

"A world of catastrophes, in which servitude has intensified, the weak were oppressed, the poor were disowned, the children were manipulated, and the old were abandoned. Everything is magnificently represented by the scenes of the forests disappearing, the waterways putrefying, diseases proliferating, the values of existence being thrown to the ground and the youngsters getting desperate and killing themselves. You can imagine nations destroyed by criminals with demonic weapons."

It was at this moment that Father Antoine, much calmer, said, changing his tone to a confessional one:

"I had a very interesting experience with a group of teenagers the other day. When the visit to the gallery was over, I asked the group who really symbolized evil today. Everyone said that it was still the devil but, to my surprise, a nine-year-old boy told me without hesitation that it was money."

"Correct. Money seen as the source of man's misfortune," the curator chimed in. "It's the distant and the imaginary of the cruelty of the Roman Empire, as suggested in the tapestry, that is present in today's globalized and capitalist world. It's the violent need for power and supremacy of men who think that whoever has money has everything in life."

"The boy got it right," Father Antoine confirmed. "Money is the greatest lie in the universe, at the service of Satan and his worshipers. The devil is free of his thousand years of condemnation and on the loose in the world that raises money to the skies like a god."

In a biblical relapse, Uncle Antoine explained what the thousand-year kingdom of chapter twenty of the Apocalypse represented: "Then I saw an angel come down from Heaven; he held the key to the abyss and a big chain. He held the dragon, the old serpent, which is the devil,

Satan, and secured him for a thousand years; he threw him in the abyss, closed it, and sealed it so he could not deceive the nations until the thousand years were over." He had quoted the passage to make a point that the Satan from the tapestry cannot be on the loose. He had to be brought back to the castle. And no amount of money in the world was more important than that!

"That's where the danger lies," warned the curator, adjusting the uneven bowtie knot. "The devil worshipers try to convince humanity that the absolute value of anything is not life, but the money that corrupts everything!"

"They sell their souls to the devil. Everything is allowed," confirmed Father Antoine, raising his index finger again.

"These worshipers can kill for money. They oppose directly and unmistakably the word of God."

"Are you saying that the representation of the free devil has everything to do with the current violence and greed?" asked Aurélien, astounded, getting closer to where his uncle was seated.

"Absolutely," confirmed Antoine. "These worshipers say that Satan cannot be held by a physical chain or locked up in a physical abyss. They spread the word that only money can save humanity."

"I'll go even further. We're living in an era where we only have liars," added Ferdinand, desolated.

"True," Father Antoine continued. "There are those who bet that the things predicted on the verses will happen and take advantage of that to get rich with radio revenues and tithes. Others say that Jesus is a false prophet and cling to antichrists, preaching that Christianity is a pernicious delusion from which society needs to be cured, like drugs and lust. Trust me, Aurélien, we're on the verge of the Apocalypse!"

They all bowed their heads then and kept silent, meditating about the current monetary and violent times so well portrayed in the tapestry scenes at Chateau d'Angers. Father Antoine took the sudden pause in the meeting room to pressure his nephew into saying he was qualified and approved the adventurous trip to Brazil.

"Any means are valid to recover the missing tableau. Your mission will give hope to the faithful in the victory of God and his army. It will demonstrate that Satan cannot defeat Jesus. Nor can he defeat those who remain faithful to the Lord."

"Can you tell me when the tableau was last seen in Rio?" asked Aurélien, finally showing signs that he was going to accept the mission.

"Somewhere called *Roziná*. I don't know if it's pronounced correctly. That's where our French friend from the NGO saw the tableau."

"Can you be more specific?" asked the nephew, looking at his uncle.

"I've heard it's a low-income community on a hill," answered the priest. "Don't worry about that, Ferdinand will give you the directions to where the NGO is located in the…"

"Rocinha!" Aurélien jumped the gun, remembering the blue sky cut by hang gliders that came from Pedra da Gávea.

"*Roziná!*" repeated the curator, having a hard time pronouncing the difficult word. "These pronunciations kill us. Do you know the place?"

"From what I know about Rocinha, it's not just the pronunciation that kills," replied Aurélien with a sarcastic smile, without the Angevins being able to grasp the meaning of his words for a poor urban area on top of a "hill" on the South side of the city.

*

A few days later, curator Ferdinand Rochemont de Sailly had a meeting in a large room in Bercy, where representatives of the Ministries of Culture and Communication, Justice, Interior, and Finance were present. During the long session, the curator answered several questions about the validity and cost of the mission, and made grandiloquent pleas to convince participants of the need to authorize Aurélien Kléber's trip to Rio, calling it "the last hope of recovering one of the most significant gems of French cultural heritage and the treasure of universal religiosity".

Aurélien sat on a bench in the long corridor in front of the meeting room, reading a book about Brazil. He was surprised he wasn't present at the session, but understood their rites were "secrets of State". In the end, when the doors of the room were opened, he entered solemnly, with firm, military steps, as was appropriate. He was greeted by the authorities present, in a hurry to return to their duties. They only said "Good luck". Father Antoine also attended the meeting. Not a single authority asked about *Roziná*, apparently considering it to be easily accessible and thinking that the researcher would have no difficulty to find it with the precise directions that would be given to him and the ease he would have due to his previous experiences and local friendships.

Curator Ferdinand emphasized that Aurélien would be allowed to travel immediately, in the strictest confidence, and the instructions were not to ask the local authorities for help or be involved in acts of violence. He also gave details of his compensation. He would receive the plane tickets, plus a transportation fee, in addition to daily rates for the ten days scheduled for the mission. If he returned with the tapestry, he would receive a bonus, its value not clearly specified.

When he was saying goodbye to his nephew before leaving for Angers, Father Antoine emphasized the religious content of the mission:

"I've already told you that God used the image of spiritual visions to reveal His message through John, on the island of Patmos, in the Aegean Sea. The message is still alive in the Apocalypse tapestry. Visitors don't notice that there are some scenes missing. But what frustrates them the most it the absence of the scene of the *Caged devil for a thousand years*. They'll only understand and value the unmistakable meaning of the global message of faith, justice, power, and God's absolute victory if we bring back to Angers the tapestry's missing scene. We're counting on you, Aurélien. Use all your skills to recover the tableau."

Chapter 11

THAT MORNING, WHEN LEONARDO LEFT HOME, his promise to the boss that "the traffic would be a money-making factory" exploded like a grenade on his head. He had been able to fulfill it in less time than promised. The drug traffic expansion had taken huge financial proportions. The small tables in the office at Downtown Shopping Mall in Barra could no longer account for so much money coming in and out at the same time in the ledger. It became urgent to computerize the financial structure with competent people so he would be able to manage the portentous profits of the drugs and weapons business. He could no longer bear such responsibility by himself in the new rented offices.

"Are you still looking for an excellent guy for the financial area?" asked the Spaniard denizen, owner of a chain of restaurants and night clubs, leader of drug sales in the entertainment business in Rio.

"Do you know someone?"

"I do. This guy is amazing. He has worked in every administration and loves money. He has helped me a lot in the past."

"Who wouldn't like it, right?" said Big Head ironically. "I need some tips to get ready for the new guys that are coming."

"If these economists were any good, the country wouldn't be buried in so much shit. They don't know anything! I have his phone number, do you want it?" asked the Spaniard, dabbing his sweaty face with a handkerchief.

"Give it to me," said Leonardo, walking toward the bar's counter.

"I'm gonna tell him that you're going to call," said the Spaniard, pulling the fat phone book with the numbers of his clientele from his pocket.

While he waited, Leonardo asked for a glass of water to take an aspirin. Lately, his headache had grown much worse.

*

That night in the comfortable apartment in Barra the stage was set to expose the cheating, proven with the help of a hired private investigator. Ana had endured the pain in silence and had not mentioned the humiliation she had suffered to anyone. Now that her son was with his friends at Maracanã and the cell phones seemed to have calmed down, it was time to face the storm to rescue her husband from the trouble he had gotten into, risking their marriage. She had listened in tears everything that the detective had found out, and agreed to think about the practical advice he'd given her:

"Ma'm, you better lay low and stay at home watching your soap opera. Wait for this to go away. It will go away."

Before deciding for the confrontation, her melancholy gaze was amused with the family photos in a voiceless dialogue. They were all in black and white. The story of her life was there, condensed in such an abundance of photos that the white of the walls was diminished in the terraced room, in the corridors, and in the bedrooms. The woman got sadder when her gaze wandered over the images of days gone by. They were snapshots of her mother and father in Brasília, at a ceremony — her father wearing a tie, very elegant, without the cane he used now. These pictures of the couple brought back good memories. They showed a bit of her father's past, an influential politician with the means to get a good job for others. But Leo had never accepted this kind of help. There were pictures of her and of her wedding at the church and the lavish party; and also pictures of Lucca, since he was a baby until he was an adult, and her favorite, showing her hugging her son by the pool.

A picture on Leo's desk brought tears to her eyes. It was a photo taken at the maternity hospital, with her holding little Lucca and Leo by her side, happy as a clam. It was when he told her that he had opened an accounting office at Saens Peña Square and gave her a gold bracelet with diamonds. Leo said it had belonged to his late mother. The valuable piece of jewelry was bought at an auction. At that time, he used to have lunch at home, and always had a funny anecdote about his annoying clients. But after he moved his office to Downtown Shopping Mall in Barra and the trips to Brasília began, he stopped going home to lunch and talking about his work. He became the shadow man who answered the nightly voices on the cell phones, making family life unbearable. Of this man, there were no pictures on the white walls.

As a mother, she was happy to see that the pictures of Leo with their son, always fun, happy, and joyful, portrayed the good relationship of a loving and present father, irreproachable, worthy of the silver frames in the room. As a wife, with so many smiling pictures on the wall, she was furious and shocked that Leonardo had done this stupid thing. To make matters worse, she had to bear the insult of not having sexual relationships with her husband for over a month. Had it not been for the private investigator, she would have never found out that her husband's sudden impotence was connected to the existence of this "other woman".

So, furious as she was, she didn't want to listen to the advice she had received. On the contrary, she decided that the time had come to put an end to her husband's infidelity. She decided to confront him. Of course, at first Leonardo would deny and fight, but he would finally reconcile with her. He would resume being the "sad and needy guy" he had been during his father's wake. And if — by some misfortune — she wasn't successful, then she vowed to scream like crazy, playing the role of the irrational woman. Too bad she didn't consult the stars. Then she would know that Pluto was shaking the foundations of her seventh house, which ruled her marriage, and that screaming doesn't always avoid the worst from happening.

That night in the couple's bedroom, feeling very emotional, Ana demanded explanations from her cheating husband. At first, she was very disappointed because he didn't engage in the discussion. She was perplexed and disarmed by the indigestible monologue, with Leo just listening, his head down, not showing any reaction. She was starting to panic when, all of a sudden, he answered the accusation in a classic way:

"There's nobody else. It was never my thing. You know that."

Against her husband's hypocrisy, she pleaded to merciful Jesus and, as she was devout to St. Anthony, she asked both to help her save her marriage. In her mind, life only made sense if she kept her family together as they were in the photos. She thought that, after her yelling, she would see the Leo she knew again, the one he was when they were dating and at his father's wake. A deeply regretful husband who would hug her and kiss her, like in the soap operas she watched in the afternoons. However, instead of trying to get around the situation, acting in a pacifying way, resenting the lack of sex, she lost control and began to attack him.

"That's a lie! I know everything. And don't be cynic, I hate that. I don't know how you got the astrologer's number. I didn't give it to you, because I'm sure I threw away the piece of paper with her phone number that Aninha gave me. I could never imagine that she was your lover."

Leonardo was silent. He remembered he had taken the piece of paper with Lisa's phone number from the trash can and, without his wife knowing, wrote it down and then entered it on his phone.

"What have I done to deserve that? Answer me! Did I have to go through this? Cheating on me with a slut who just wants your money?" she shouted, standing up and making a scandal like she had never done before.

Leonardo began to stand up from the bed, but gave up. Ana was too furious to get out of the room. It could worsen the quarrel, which still didn't have a clear outcome. He was patient and self-controlled.

"I stayed all these years by your side, protecting you, supporting you, and now here comes this woman wanting to take you away from me! You are nothing but an ungrateful, wretched thug. You should be dead!"

"Fuck! What are you talking about, 'thug'? Don't forget that it was this accountant that gave you this good life all these years," Leonardo reacted when the word "thug" was proffered, giving rise to a possible connection with the drug traffic and the discovery of the alias "Big Head". He raised his finger to Ana's face. Then, he pointed to her chest and sank his finger into the cavity of her shoulder, pushing her slightly back.

"What are you doing? Do you want to hit me? Don't touch me, I'll call the police," yelled Ana, walking toward the door.

"I'm not violent to anybody, I'd never hit you. You're being preposterous and childish! Stop!"

"You pushed me! Assault is a crime. Aren't you ashamed?"

"Crime? Look who's talking! Miss Holier Than Thou! From what I know, the slaughter of Catholics during the six-hundred years of Inquisition was a crime," said Leonardo in a loud voice. He made a face, as he himself was surprised with his bizarre defense, questioning the sins of the Catholic Church.

"What does the history of the Church have to do with the story of my husband having a lover?" protested the woman, angrily baffled and confused by the shift in the conversation.

"It has ruined my childhood with threats of going to hell. There are no excuses for the crimes of the Roman Catholic Church. You, Catholics, have to keep your mouths shut, because there have never been so many crimes, so many people killed, tortured, burnt alive in hot oil cauldrons at the public squares than at the time of the Inquisition. Shame were the centuries of heinous crimes committed by the Church. Thousands of Christians have died praying and thousands of books were burned publicly in the name of God, now there you are, acting like a moralist, talking about crimes. Since when Catholics feel ashamed? Tell me!"

A gloomy silence fell over the white sheets of the double bed when the religious temporality and its cruelties, kept in secret by the Vatican, were evoked.

"How do you know that?" asked the woman, as if she wanted to change the subject to a possible pardon.

"From my father. He suggested some books from the library that I needed to read and I read a lot of good stuff. I could have read more, but I didn't have time," said Leonardo, with a certain pride. His face took the sad, needy look from when she'd met him.

Ana didn't hold back and ended up revealing that she'd had the help of a professional to decipher the mystery of the cell phones.

"The detective told me that your lover's life would make for an adventure book. She's been married three times and buried two husbands. She lived abroad for quite some time. She must have fucked everyone she met and now she's having an affair with my husband. Jesus, do I deserve this?" asked Ana, tearful.

"Enough! I don't want to know about other people's lives. What I want now is to fix my life with you. That's all that matters," replied Leonardo, trying to put an end to the discussion and propitiate a negotiation. "I've already had a great loss in my life and I don't want to have another one. Let's talk, honey."

"But I don't have anything to talk about anymore. It's all over. I want you out of my life," said the woman, still full of hatred, ignoring the detective's advice once again.

"Calm down, my love. I know I've made a mistake. I regret what I did. Really. I've never wanted to hurt you. I love you."

"Then tell me one thing, just one little thing," bargained the woman, resuming the familiar dialogue after calming down with the delayed declaration of love and the hopes of saving her marriage.

"What?" asked Leonardo, already foreseeing the twist.

"Promise me you won't see that slut anymore. Do you promise?"

"I swear, honey. I swear!" answered Leonardo, holding his cell phone, which vibrated because someone was desperately calling, with his hand in his pocket.

"There's more. Do you promise not to use the phones at dinner? This is killing me! Do you promise?" Ana insisted.

"Give me a break. I can't, all of a sudden, leave my clients hanging."

"No, no. I don't want to hear about it," protested the woman, waving her index finger from side to side. "If this doesn't stop now, I swear that I'll throw you out of here and tell my father and Lucca. They'll know everything that is going on. Can't you understand that what you've done has devastated me?"

"Are you threatening me? Are you threatening the man that supports you, who has given you a wonderful son and who wants to live with you in peace? Is that it?"

"The only reason why I don't go to Itaipava right now is because the old man would have a heart attack!" she blurted out, crying more and more, sitting on the big bed, looking at the joyful family photos on the white walls. A past she wanted back.

"Would you do that?" asked Leonardo, fearful.

"Do you doubt it?" Ana replied, in tears.

But, as if by the miracle of tears, despair was stilled by the memory of her father, holding hands with her mother on the porch of the farmhouse, sitting on the swing with the plaid blanket covering their knees and feet. She hadn't seen her parents in months, since that week she'd left Leo alone in Rio.

"I promise I won't go anymore. Don't you believe me, honey?"

"I'll be watching you. You're a dead man if I find out that you're still with her. I won't give you more than a week to resume being the Leonardo I knew."

"All right. I'm gonna make you happy, you'll see. I promise!"

There was silence in the room. Ana didn't tell her husband anything about the "terrible revelations" that the investigator was yet to tell her, but which he would only disclose if it was at a safe place. She immediately thought of her father's place in Itaipava, where, besides being absolutely safe, if she needed to, she would call her father to also hear all the terrible things he had found out about Leo.

"I love you, sweetheart. Trust me," said Leonardo.

"Do you want me to believe that?"

"It's the truth. I've never stopped loving you.

"I also don't want to lose you for anything in this world," confessed Ana, looking at the picture of them both hugging each other.

"I promise you that things will change. Trust me, honey."

Then came the convulsive weeping, many tears, and finally the passionate kisses on the edge of the bed. Leonardo's whispering and theatrically emotional voice echoed through the room as if reciting a peace prayer, incredibly enabling to the recommencing of sex in the Barra apartment, as it used to be.

"Forgive me, sweetie, forgive me, sweetie… Forgive me, my love…"

"My love, love of my life," replied Ana.

And so, everything seemed to go back to the time they were dating, when Skull and Lisa weren't a part of Leo's life.

After the Christian forgiveness, they made love as they hadn't done in a long time. The woman felt, like the first time, that penetrating blade with which she had lost her virginity. She felt again like the happy woman who had married Leonardo in a veil and wreath, under the blessings of the Catholic Church. In the vows of love, the woman had forgotten that the devil is quite patient and disguises himself as a good Big Head in the nostalgia of the past to create the misfortunes of the future.

*

It was after midnight when the cell phone rang in the office. He had promised Ana not to answer it. It rang once, rang twice, rang three times. Leonardo couldn't restrain himself. He jumped out of bed and went to the office. He answered it immediately when he identified who was calling him at that hour and with such insistence.

He broke the peace pact he had made that night with his wife, who had warned him she would go visit her parents soon.

"What's up, Major?"

"Fuck, there's a snitch going through everything here. He has some nerve! He's looking through everything."

"So?" asked Big Head, assessing the gravity of the fact.

"Now he's digging deep to know who do I get my orders from. What do you want me to do? Do I beat him up or do I kill him?"

The Leonardo that Ana didn't know enters the scene. He whispers something incomprehensible on his leather-covered cell phone. Big Head's most private cell phone, from where the orders came in case of emergency, so things would happen. Then he deletes the number he'd called and goes seamlessly back to the bedroom.

In turn, Ana, with her eyes closed, breathed softly. She pretended to be asleep, after deciding to go to Itaipava without telling anyone. She would only tell her parents when she was already on the road. She wanted to surprise them.

Chapter 12

THE TV STATIONS PROMOTED ROUND TABLES to discuss the war between gangs. Without objective propositions, the participants incited the outrage against the spree of homicides and stray bullets. The population remained silent, fearful, and omissive as always. "I don't know anything" — Leonardo would say. He didn't feel guilty about the illegal drug retail market and the corruption in every level. He liked to repeat the thoughts of his friend Skull: "If a major criminal goes away, someone worse, like me, comes." And he would conclude, laughing: "The other guy, Satan himself, comes," and laughed.

For Leonardo, history repeated itself. In all those years of fratricidal wars in the slums, in which people survived amidst that situation of deaths, prisons, stray bullets, the Beast of the Earth with its seven heads roamed free. The power of money still made the huge engine of illicit business work.

Authorized by Pimpão, Leonardo paid a visit to the famous professor Carlos Alberto Guimarães on a Thursday night. The big shot of finances had worked in every administration before the military returned to the barracks and after civilians were appointed as Presidents of the Republic. He was a recognized monetary authority, with great experience in public finances and familiarity with the dinosaur that was the government administration. And, since no one is immaculate, he was willing to provide consulting services to bypass the scrutiny of the Fed and the tax authorities.

The meeting with the professor, as the economist liked to be called, was scheduled for the same day. Leonardo didn't use the name of the owner of the restaurant to introduce himself, but that of his late father. In the financial world, his father's name was still a prestigious reference, respected by awkward silences. On that late afternoon, with mild weather and a beautiful sunset, the runway of Santos Dumont Airport could be seen from the office windows. The planes took off and landed without disturbing that historical meeting between two old friends with a lot of things in common who had met to exchange secrets and organize plans for the future. After drinking their whiskeys, the uncertainties started to be defused as the professor's voice and his jowl explained how the financial market worked and what the prospects for the coming year were.

"The first problem is to know what to do with the money. It becomes a hot potato burning on your hands. To do nothing with the money, invest it in savings or fixed-income securities, which have low returns and only cover inflation, or invest in high-return investments, which have high risks. The second problem is how to make the money have a higher return, multiply it like Jesus did with the bread. All of this preventing the government from biting off a big chunk of your profit. Do you know what I mean? The choice is entirely up to you, Mr. Leonardo."

"What do you suggest, professor?" asked the accountant.

"That's where the big question lies. Who will handle the money? If it's the bankers, you need to know that they'll profit a lot if they administer it well and will pass on the losses if they administer it poorly. When you administer the money yourself, you assume the risks, but on the other hand, your profits are yours and yours only, you don't have to share it with anyone. The choice is always yours, Mr. Leonardo."

"What do you suggest, professor?" Leo asked again, watching the first lights shine on the other side of Guanabara Bay and the bridge light up crossing the translucent shadows of the ocean.

"Well, the current international crisis is exacerbated by the belligerence of the Bush administration. The global economy's circuits are connected and there is currently a mood of financial euphoria. There is a bubble growing in the air, but nobody knows how and when it will burst. The investors' appetite for risk has never been so big. They began to make a lot of money, even though there were several international crises, but Russia was not erased from the map, and the unsustainable growth of the Asian Tigers didn't ruin foreign investors. On the contrary: the risks are getting higher, and so are the profits."

"Just a minute, please," asked Leonardo, turning his cell phones off. "There. This way we won't be interrupted.

"As I was saying," resumed the consultant, adjusting his glasses with thick lenses, "investors were not intimidated by their losses and inflated the prices of raw materials, making the prices of soy, sugar, copper, and iron ore soar."

"And what will happen in Brazil?" asked Leonardo, not blinking, mesmerized by the pendulum of the money dangling in front of him, faster and faster.

"Good question," replied the professor, pinching and pulling his jowl, pleased with his listener's interest in cutting the introduction short. "As our economy has no solid foundations, the elections had a great influence on the speculative rise of the dollar. I can assure you that, as soon as the electoral process ends, the new administration will signal policies that will lower the dollar value and reverse the downward trend of the Stock Exchange. That's what will inevitably happen."

"Is this the time to act? It this what you suggest, professor?"

"Exactly. Economy is like life itself, full of highs and lows. It's time to bet all our chips and anticipate the facts, before the new administration manages to shield the economy, pay off the external debt with the IMF and increase international reserves. These are the current uncertainties that create the ideal conditions for excellent profit alternatives in the future."

Leonardo heard everything in a state of grace, not moving on the comfortable black leather chair. He listened to the professor giving his master class in another high-backed chair, continually using graphs, indicators, statistics, and printed materials. He admired the ability of the fat and smart juggler to squander knowledge like someone who knows everything about billionaire businesses to wealthy investors, without ever questioning the origin or the smell of the money.

As soon as he drank his first whiskey, the professor realized that Leonardo was a smart, calculating representative, very ambitious, who had a lot of ballast. He could smell money from miles away, as if it was the smell of a good espresso. He liked to compare the financial market to coffee, which becomes a drink when the water boils. When the water reaches its maximum boiling point, it extracts the maximum flavor and aroma from the coffee. Now, when market instability reaches its peak, it is time to make the most of the opportunities. The wisdom lies in knowing what the maximum level of warmth is in order not to spill the water or miss the tasting point.

It was a late afternoon of a lot of information, of many sketched dreams. The smiling consultant, nervously stroking his right ear, gave his final message to reassure his client.

"Everything is done in the strictest confidence, operability, and efficiency. Any questions, Mr. Leonardo?"

"For the moment, no," replied the Minister of Finance.

"Next year, Brazil will face the biggest international credibility crisis ever. With the dollar's ups and downs and stock market speculation, many will make loads of money and many will be ruined. The time to act is now," prophesized the consultant. "Are you going to let the paying train of the future pass you by? Are you, Mr. Leonardo? Will you think about it?"

"I don't have much to think about. I'll talk to my people and call to schedule a meeting and discuss the values. I'll bring a spreadsheet next time."

"Can I schedule an investment portfolio?" asked the professor, frantically massaging the fingertips of his right hand with his thumb, like Scrooge McDuck, anguished with the itch of greed. The jowl got even more bloated with the anticipation of Leonardo's positive response.

"Yes, you can schedule a portfolio that's not conservative. Does it matter if the sums are in cash?"

"No problem. You'll like our laundry. Do you want to own pizzerias and nightclubs?" the professor asked.

"I've never thought about it. Seems like a good idea," Leonardo answered with a laugh, picturing himself eating a mozzarella pizza or dancing with money in his pockets.

"Think about it, Mr. Leonardo. We'll take care of everything."

Leonardo recognized that the professor had been successful in the world economy panel, in which the money from foreign investors is invested anywhere on the planet that promises good returns. He just didn't realize how little the teacher had been didactic and had omitted the information that, with online computerization, the money that comes easily and quickly in the accounts abroad, also comes out with the same ease and speed with which it came in, not always bringing pleasant surprises for the holder of these secret accounts, called off-shore.

The professor predicted the civic euphoria of democratic life in 2003 if the false prophets with their seven trumpets of chaos won the elections and took their places at the banquet of power. The time to make things right had come, it was time to jump on the back of the four horses of the Apocalypse, that here are corruption, impunity, sex, and war, and ride the hectic, frantic gallop, to make a lot of money. The time had come, now that he had the "Relic", for the revenge countdown, because his father's death had taught him that, in this violent world, no one is innocent, no one is exempt from blame and forgiveness in the Last Judgment.

After saying goodbye to the professor, Leonardo went to take care of the Relic, as he fondly called the famous, nameless tableau, which was being looked for in France, and which he had taken after he finished all the "arrangements" with the *babalorisha,* thanks to the help of the Major. With the change in command at Dona Marta Hill and the demands of the new boss, he hadn't had time yet to put the tableau of the devil on the wall.

It all started with the tip from a fifteen-year-old moron at the Dois Irmãos Institution, which belonged to two Frenchmen. The boy stole from the NGO's owners to buy drugs. He told an informant that, approximately six months before, the owners, together with a *babalorisha* from Bahia, were negotiating with the "French people there" to buy a valuable rug for "a million". He gave him all the details of the negotiation.

Since it wasn't something connected to the drug sales, Leonardo didn't need Pimpão's permission to tell Major Runner to kidnap the man from Bahia before he visited the NGO. After the *babalorisha* spilled the beans about the value of the tableau and the government's interest in having it back, he disappeared in the "microwave" (a cave in the slum where bodies are burned and become unrecognizable). With this service from his buddy the Major, Leonardo took full possession of the million bucks rug. It wasn't difficult to replace the deceased *babalorisha* in the negotiations with the owners of the NGO and the French government, which would send an emissary to prove the authenticity of the work and pay the high price of the ransom. But the moron, totally high, freaked out and told them that the NGO's owners already had the money, brought from France, at the headquarters, ready to buy the tableau. The result of this slip-up was that the Major, by Leonardo's request, went there to check it out, tortured the poor guys, and set the shack on fire, out of spite.

On the morning after the consultation with the professor, Leonardo was enjoying the terrifying image of the seven-headed Satan, as he named the tableau, which was finally hung on the wall of the office at Downtown Shopping Mall. An inspiring apocalyptic image for someone who worked in crime, because the devil preached that everything can be done in the land of venal men. The important thing was to wait for the traffic to raise more and more money to feed big business and offshore accounts.

Who can resist corruption and bribery today, Leonardo asked himself, *with all this impunity?*

With more and more money raised and well administered thanks to the professor's competence, Leonardo would have the opportunity to get rich, as it had happened to Joseph Fouché, the French plenipotentiary who obtained special powers to spy and steal the wealth of the kings of France. He would have the money he needed so badly to settle things with his life and establish a partnership with the Beast of the Relic. And even more: with the money stolen from Pimpão, he would renovate his father's manor in Botafogo to go and live there permanently. It was everything he had ever dreamed of and just a matter of time, by his calculations.

Chapter 13

BEFORE THE HUGE 775 LANDED at Antonio Carlos Jobim Airport, the plane flew over the Wonderful City. It wasn't Aurélien's first trip to Brazil. He saw, from afar, the Maracanã stadium, the Christ Redeemer, and the beaches he had never forgotten. He was sure there wasn't a more beautiful city in the world, admired from the small window of the aircraft. It was like a divine blessing for those who spent their day in boring toil verifying dusty documents and manuscripts worn out by the patina of the years.

"*Roziná*, have you ever heard about it?" echoed de curator's authoritarian voice.

Aurélien had taken an intensive Portuguese course. He hadn't brought any radiant dreams in his luggage. Passionate about Rio, he felt comfortable in the city "without knowing why", leaving Paris and his current girlfriend behind, who would take root in his apartment every Friday night with a hanger full of clothes, grocery bags, and — even worse — rolls of toilet paper. From the moment she set foot at the building's foyer, she would complain about the flights of stairs, the dirty subway stations, her family. And she also took the liberty of leaving croissant crumbs and empty glasses with lipstick stains all over the one-room studio, a very common thing in Paris. He didn't know how he put up with it!

Just to think that the Parisian routine was temporarily on hold made him smile broadly in the cabin. During the flight, with his eyes half-closed and time to think, he convinced himself that the girlfriend he'd left behind was a messy, annoying person with fat arms. What he most wanted now was to forget Paris' grey skies and enjoy the sunny beaches and the way *cariocas*[6] waddled when they walked, with the money of his daily fees filling his pockets.

As soon as he got settled in Botafogo, with the help of his friend, the prosecutor, Aurélien called the Frenchman who owned the NGO, confirming that he would go immediately to Rocinha. But, since it was already late, the other man said he'd rather see him early the next morning. He described the meeting place in a casual way: "Anyone who lives here knows where Dois Irmãos' headquarters is". The only thing that intrigued him was the insistence that he brought the money "cash". What money? — Aurélien wondered. Neither the curator nor his uncle had mentioned anything about any sum of money.

"I'm going to Rocinha tomorrow," he told his friend.

"What for? Can you tell me?" asked the prosecutor.

"The municipality of Paris saw on the internet the work of a French institution that helps abandoned children and they were very impressed," lied Aurélien. "And now they're interested in the model to create something similar. I'm going to pay them a visit and write a technical report. Everything will be done in the utmost secrecy."

"I see. Do you have any idea of where are you getting into?

Aurélien preferred to hide his mission and omit that he had read the story on *Libération*, which gave him a bad first impression about the *favela*, where the beautiful scenery was associated with the rawest urban violence of a big city.

"By the surprised look on your face, I see that I'm in trouble."

"You're going to the biggest and most famous *favela* in Brazil, which lives up to its reputation. Rocinha is ruled by a gang of drug dealers. They enforce their cohabitation laws

6   Those who are born in Rio de Janeiro (*TN*)

on citizens who lead quiet, honest, hard-working lives. Go easy, my friend. Go easy so you won't disappear."

"*Merde, alors!*" he exclaimed in French. "I thought it was going to be an easy task. I'm going to charge a high-risk fee."

Aurélien remembered curator Ferdinand's emphatic warning to stay away from the police. Due to an excess of caution and the intuition he had, being a *gendarme*, he felt it was premature to expose his mission to his friend, the prosecutor, without first knowing the extent of the dangers involved. There had been violent incendiary demonstrations on the outskirts of the city of Paris as part of the daily life of human rebellion and dissatisfaction. Rocinha should not be different. He believed that it was the media that turned the violence of that *favela* into sensationalism.

"What do you suggest?" asked the visitor.

"It's better to get in one of these tourist transport jeeps that will take you, totally protected, inside the *favela*. Which institution are you going to visit?"

"Dois Irmãos."

"Good choice. The French guys who run the institute are well known. They're honest people. They have never been involved with the drug dealers or the militia. For the love of God, please don't take your passport with you this time. Do me this favor."

"I won't repeat the same mistake," said Aurélien, recognizing he had been careless with his passport; its disappearance drove his friend and the French Consulate crazy, and he had to postpone his return to Paris. Which didn't seem so bad at the end of his short vacation.

It had not been easy for Júlia to change her habits, get adapted to the urban hectic pace, away from the calm of the mountains, and create a new routine, getting up early, taking the bus, eating hurriedly out, studying at *Aliance Française*, doing her exams for college, and getting out there to look for a job.

Although she didn't agree with what the mirror showed, Júlia was a sexy, slender woman, with smart blue eyes, and long, well-groomed black hair. Even with glasses, she drew attention. But she had a complex about her super skinny arms. She was never conformed with it nor told her mother, who would never understand why her daughter was ashamed of her normal arms.

She met Letícia Boker in Mauá. She was also studying to get into college. The girl had gone to the inn to spend the weekend with a friend. Letícia was from the South. Her parents lived in Porto Alegre and paid for her SAT classes, the rent, and gave her a good allowance. Back in Rio, Letícia would send all her classes' material and tips to Júlia via express delivery mail and e-mail. The two of them got into Communication school. Even before that, she had already invited Júlia to come and live in her apartment in Leme. Since the beginning, Júlia's mother hadn't liked the girl's bossy behavior. But she didn't interfere with her daughter's decision. She only subtly suggested that the housing arrangements should be "temporary", until she found a better place.

At first, the friendship with her college classmate was great. They laughed together and shared the room, kitchen, and bathroomm and how much they missed their parents. They had fun together on their nights out, at beer halls, in the middle of the anonymous racket of talkative, happy people. Until the "incident" happened. Due to it, Júlia only woke up the next day at lunch time. She was forced to call the newsroom and tell them she'd woken up with the flu, with her head and her body aching, besides being very thirsty. She drank half a gallon of water in minutes. That day, her friend only arrived home well after dinner.

"I thought you liked it," said Letícia, sarcastically.

"You thought wrong, very wrong. I don't believe you," objected Júlia, raising her skinny arms in the air, her fists clenched with rage.

"OK… alright," interrupted the girl, trying to calm her down.

"What did you put in my beer?" asked Júlia, who couldn't come to terms with the betrayal. "Tell me!" still with her arms raised.

"If you want to know, I'd do it all over again. It was worth spicing up your drink to have you all naked, all mine."

"I considered you like a sister. It never crossed my mind."

"I did everything I could, but you just wouldn't get there. Do you want to know why?"

"Now, shut up! Enough!" Júlia yelled, furious.

"You're going to listen! Because your insanity is your fucking work. You only think about it twenty-four hours a day! You want nothing to do with sex. For you, writing is enough. I've never seen such a poor, stupid thing!"

They continued arguing and offending each other until late at night. After they both stopped talking, tired, Júlia went to sleep on the living room couch. She recognized she'd drank too much, letting her friend take off her clothes and pantyhose. High as a kite, naked, she was at the mercy of her friend, who took advantage of her and "did everything". But despite being drugged and seduced, it wasn't because of her obsession with work that she did not indulge in sensory orgasms. For Júlia, the "unknown territory" of the female soul, so well studied by Freud and Guy de Maupassant, only surrenders to an "act of love".

It happened, period — reasoned Júlia when she woke up the next morning. As much as no one ever forgets sexual harassment, she admitted there had been mitigating circumstances, such as them being vulnerable, away from their families, in need of affection in a unique, desperate moment of loneliness. Compromising, she decided to forget the incident. So, with their spirits appeased after a sleepless night, Júlia and Letícia talked over breakfast in the kitchen, like civilized and modern people.

Her friend cried a lot. Júlia was moved. She believed in the friendship and in the fact that Letícia was sorry. However, as time passed, the infatuated gazes of the southern girl suggested that further "intimacies" would soon happen.

It was at this time that Amélia Azevedo, the lady who had spent a long weekend at Blue Angel Inn to relax the year before, came into the picture. A chance encounter at the supermarket made Júlia move to another house and gave a new existential breath in her life of many surprises in the big city, but unfortunately without a great love, although she hoped to find it, if only to dismiss that malicious insinuation that she, like the hero Tintin, "didn't want anything to do with sex".

*

Through the auspicious hands of chance, she ended up going to live with Mrs. Amélia, affectionately called auntie, who was the director of a famous research institute. It was a stroke of luck, not only because of her aunt's contacts with the press, but mainly because of the bond of affection that was created between the two in the relationship of surrogate mother and daughter.

Interestingly enough, whenever she saw reporter Júlia in a new dress or a different hair style, Aunt Amélia got emotional.

"You know, Júlia? You look more and more like my daughter every day. The skirt looks cute on you, girl. Every day I pray thanking God that you're here with me."

"I pray for you, too. Look, this is the medal of Saint Thérèse of the Child Jesus that my mother gave me to protect me," said Júlia, pulling up the small medal that hang from her neck since the day she came from the mountains to live in Rio.

Aunt Amélia, a lady the same age as Júlia's mother, with gray hair, had been abandoned by her husband in the seventh year of marriage. She'd lost her only daughter on a night of urban violence, when she was returning with her boyfriend from a party at Ilha do Governador. On Linha Vermelha, they ran into a shootout between drug dealers and the police. The girl was hit in the heart by a stray bullet. The mother kept her daughter's room just as she had left it. And Júlia only occupied it at the lady's insistence. Júlia's joyful presence rekindled the longing she felt for her daughter.

Sheltered in this new home, Júlia finished college and started as an intern in a magazine, then in a small newspaper, and finally was admitted to a newspaper of great circulation. Aunt Amélia helped her a lot with the several jobs.

"I wish someday your parents could come see our house."

"Don't even think about it! Not even a miracle would take my father away from Mauá."

Her father paid for college, the French classes, and the modest, almost symbolic rent. Her mother, on the other hand, secretly sent her an allowance — which was always welcome — enough for her expenses, with a bit of extra money for knick-knacks and the gym. When she was not on duty at the newspaper and could have an entire weekend, she went up the mountain on Friday in the late afternoon bus and was greeted with a party as if she was an illustrious resident returning to the city.

She would tell her mother only the stories she wanted to hear, those who wouldn't make her worry. Her father listened in silence to the two of them babbling until they were not sleepy anymore, and suddenly, with no ceremony, he'd fall headlong on the chair and snored loudly, unabashedly, in the Mantiqueira Mountains.

"Where's the 'love' of my life?" Júlia would ask, leaning on her bedroom window overlooking the neighbors' windows, without Aunt Amélia and her far away mother knowing about her sorrows. Fortunately, the bad moments at her first home were water under the bridge. She liked the feeling of relief, before closing her little blue eyes on her pillow and recalling some of Tintin's adventures — the main inspiration for her coming to Rio and gradually becoming a journalist known for her impeccable writing in form and extraordinarily vigorous in content.

However, in the privacy of her solitude, Júlia nurtured the desire to truly participate in at least one adventurous comics story, and — if that eventually happened — she hoped she would experience it in an *inoubliable* (unforgettable) way and in style.

*

Júlia admitted that, in one regard, the southern girl had not exaggerated: her "madness" in dedicating her body and soul to her profession. She had deepened her research on the relation between comic book art and journalistic writing. She accessed the first Brazilian interview about comics made by reporter Patrícia Villalba. She became interested in the comics about major cases investigations, such as the political kidnapping of Aldo Moro in the 1970s; corruption in Russia with the series of new tsars; and the suspense narrative of the 9/11 attacks. She researched the obscure behind-the-scenes conflicts on a global scale, told by the news with a distant approach, but well registered as articles in comics, such as the American invasion and the torture in Abu Ghraib prisons in Iraq. She saw it was possible to use these graphic works in her job and be a Tintin, even without being the protagonist of the facts.

To Júlia, the important thing now was to live her daily life with her skinny arms and the new bangs that covered her forehead, which did not prevent her neither from dreaming with a future full of surprises nor from hearing her boss' request during the work meeting.

"Júlia, I've assigned you to Rocinha. The readers want a

story about the relationship between the locals and the drug dealers. The degree of violence, fear, and social protection they practice, ok?"

"Are there new facts I'm not aware of? Any tips?"

"The police are setting up a mega operation in Rocinha. I wasn't able to find out when. They told me it will be at the beginning of the month. I'll give you an entire page on Sunday. Deal?"

"Deal," replied Júlia, knowing that the search for news requires persistence, patience, and dedication. "Leave it up to me."

"Dig deep, but be careful. I don't want a female Tim Lopes. Understood?"

"Relax, I can take care of myself. I'm still alive, aren't I?"

Júlia knew that a story is always a surprise, especially in Rocinha, the largest slum in Brazil.

Chapter 14

WITH HIS EYES FIXED ON THE WHITE CEILING of Lisa's room, Leonardo looked back on his life. How everything had begun. He recalled his initial insistence on taking Lisa to a motel because he thought he was living an extramarital affair and that the place was more appropriate and exciting for secret encounters, without the consequences of an emotional commitment. But it was all just theory. In reality, he had been enthralled by Lisa and didn't need a motel. He just had to visit her in that room where she had the blinds drawn and candle lights, to find her passionate, sensual, waiting for him on the bed with flowered sheets. To feel, in that fleeting carnal moment, that whatever past or men she had, there was nothing better in the world than to take possession of her desires.

He recognized he had gotten involved too fast. But, never in his life — and he was being honest about that — had he had such happy moments, even though he was living on the edge.

Now, in his office at Downtown Shopping Mall, in front of Tableau 75 on the meeting room wall — which had not yet been removed to the Botafogo manor, as it was at the final stages of renovations — Leonardo thought about scheduling an astral consultation for Lucca, after having been warned that "mom has been acting very strangely" lately.

Returning from a Flamengo soccer match, with a mandatory stop at a fans' bar where they used to go, Leonardo brought up the subject of the visit to the astrologer. He ingeniously insinuated that it was time for Lucca to seek a "vocational orientation". He added, coyly, the word "astrological".

As expected, Lucca reacted to the "crazy idea" bombarding him with questions and refusing to go, as it seemed unnecessary to him.

Leonardo explained everything, or almost everything. He insisted that it was time for his son to hear someone reliable about his future. He told him about his fascination with astrology. He mentioned, among other facts, that Lisa had warned him about the negative result of a bid he was interested in winning. And, in fact, he lost it. She convinced him not to feel discouraged, as there would be other opportunities to make a lot of money. And, as she had predicted, he started winning a lot of bids from the federal government. His son believed him and decided to check it out. He promised not to tell his mom about the "idea".

Lucca arrived ten minutes earlier at the ample apartment in Lagoa. Since his father hadn't mentioned anything about Lisa's appearance, only praised her prophetic skills, he had imagined, in his innocence, a fat, stodgy, gaudy woman, with a ruby in the center of her turban, her fingernails painted violet and a raspy voice — the stereotypical horror movie. When the door opened: *Wow!* Lucca thought when he saw the tall, curvaceous, beautiful woman, with a soft voice, very polite, who welcomed him with open arms and his chart ready. His father had already given her his son's personal data.

Lisa read his natal chart, the aspects the planets formed among themselves, the transit and, finally, his solar revolution. Lucca was fascinated by the explanation of the astrological terms and the mysterious cosmic symbols united by the dotted red, green, and blue lines. He learned that in the natal chart the Sun and the Moon represent the father and the mother, respectively.

"I'll talk about your mother first. Please interrupt me if you want to ask about something you didn't understand, Lucca."

"My mom is an open book, totally predictable."

"Let's take a look. Our life is influenced by the positive and negative aspects of the mother. On your chart, the Moon is in your fourth house, showing an extremely protective, emotional mother. The Moon forms a quadrature with Pluto, which shows that she's a very controlling person. Her will always prevails."

"You're totally right," Lucca agreed with the summary. "When I was a kid, everything I liked to eat, she forbade. Everything was bad for my health. I couldn't even have a Coke."

"To her, taking care of you is loving you, Lucca."

"You call it love? Calling me all day long to know where I am is an obsession!" he complained to the astrologer.

He added that he was tired of taking orders: "Eat vegetables and fruits". Laughing, he confessed he had eaten, without his mother knowing, all the pizzas and hamburgers with fries he could, and drank all the forbidden sodas. He complained that she had never shown any interest in his dreams. She had decided, without even consulting him, that he should join the army. He didn't want to.

Lisa listened to everything in silence before trying to counter and soften the criticism about his bossy mother, emphasizing the positive aspects of the chart and her way of being a good mother.

"When you were about eleven-years-old and Neptune formed a quadrature with your Mercury, you flunked in school."

"How did you know?"

Although he didn't understand the explanation of the aspects of the quadrature of "Mercury with Neptune", Lucca accepted the astral interpretation to justify his poor performance in school. But that was history, Lisa explained, because, as the aspect dissolved, he went back to being the usual good student. She made clear that quadratures were just challenges to be overcome and could not be considered insurmountable. It was then that she gave him the important message that he should not stop working toward his goals and dreams, even if he felt alone and abandoned in the near future. He furrowed his brow grudgingly when he heard her say, "Every man needs the conviction of faith to grow spiritually". She was saying the same words his mother said.

Having satisfied his curiosity about his love life, Lucca wanted to know about his father's afflictions, to the point of having come to consult the stars. It's true that he'd always liked the occult and *Candomblé*. Lucca dared to ask how he could help his father get along better with his mother.

Lisa answered with her most polite smile:

"Your father doesn't need your help, only your support. He's an anguished person who's trying to know himself better in this very tense, busy moment. It's good to know that, despite all his activities, he has never stopped worrying about your well-being and your future. That's how he shows his love for you." *Of course she wouldn't talk about my father's problems*, Lucca thought. He deduced that the secret of the chart reading had everything to do with the sacrament of confession. It was then that he confided to Lisa, embarrassed to call her by her name for the first time, as she had insisted:

"I really love my father just the way he is, Lisa. I don't know how he tolerates those phones ringing all day long and my mother complaining about them non-stop. At night, it's like hell at home."

After an hour and a half of consultation, Lucca realized that she knew all his secrets. The "witch" had even guessed that his bowel movements would work poorly if he was nervous during his exams, or as a result of a romantic disillusion. In the end, he intended to protest against her advice to "have faith to grow spiritually", but ended up giving up and bowing his head to hear the words of hope very intently, which Lisa had saved for the end of the consultation on purpose.

"Very soon, Lucca, you'll fulfill your dream of studying abroad," she concluded prophetically. "Have faith."

"Be careful, or I'll believe it," said Leonardo's son, smiling happily.

"You better believe," reinforced Lisa, explaining that Jupiter was well positioned on his natal chart, which favored the fulfillment of dreams if he just had more confidence in himself. She advised him to put his show on the road and develop his full potential, because he had talent.

Lucca's eyes widened, surprised, when she suggested that he would have the support of people who were influential and strange to his project of going to college abroad.

"She really helps us. Thanks, Dad."

Although Lucca enthusiastically thanked his father for his consultation, he later complained that the astrologer "was wrong" in the aspects of the Moon. She didn't anticipate that morning, when his mother traveled alone to Itaipava without anyone knowing.

In a phone call the day before, Ana had confirmed the meeting with the detective at her parents' farm. Leonardo knew because he'd put a tap on his home's landline, on the Major's advice, after being threatened by his wife. Ana didn't like to run. She felt safer if she could go at her own pace. The road was deserted, since it was not a weekend. As soon as she noticed the approach of the unloaded truck coming at high speed behind her, she cautiously gave way for him to pass. Then something strange happened: instead of speeding up, the F-350 suddenly slowed down. She had no alternative other than trying to pass him. She didn't even see ahead the dangerous curve, to the left, on the edge of the precipice. After passing over half the length of the truck, suddenly going faster, her car was hit by violent blows on the side, which caused her to lose control of the steering wheel and leave the damp road with few holes. The car pulled over to the side of the road, slid and plunged. It did somersaults in the air before hitting the rocky floor of the abyss in a tragic "accident", which was reported in the newspapers without prominence.

From the gray sedan, only the smashed, deformed carcass and shattered glass remained. It didn't catch on fire. But Ana's body was trapped and bloody in the middle of the twisted metal. In his deposition, the only witness who saw the vehicle fall said to the deputy that the most likely cause of the accident must have been a hole in that stretch of the dangerous curve. The victim must have tried to avoid it and was unsuccessful — this was what was written in the case file.

Lucca defined the deep feeling of mourning to his friends present at his mother's funeral:

"Dude, I miss her a lot, it sucks."

His father looked devastated. However, he remained calm about what had happened. The old man had gone through another tragedy before. His cell phones went silent. This silence made Lucca remember his mother's demands and her concern for his well-being. As much as he was told that life went on, he felt abandoned and wondered what would change in his routine now, his father being more and more absorbed in his work.

Lucca liked the refreshing sensation of the sea foam, bathing his tired feet after running on the long promenade of Sernambetiba Avenue. On his way to the beach, he saw groups of smiling young people, old people with white hair in their faded shorts, happy athletes, and people drinking cold coconut water or draft beer. And eclectically and ecologically happy with the sun in their life.

He came back by the sea with his sneakers hanging around his neck, his head in turmoil. He was always anguished with the questions to which he had no answers. There was a buzz of whys in which he took part, asking what his mother, so predictable, was doing alone on that deserted road in the middle of the week, without anyone having been warned of her unexpected trip to Itaipava. She only told her parents about her visit when she was about to go, and even then she couldn't guarantee. Why was this last trip sudden?

Nobody knew the answer: neither he, nor his father, nor the serene voice of the astrologer Lisa talking about the Moon's eclipse. Why?

Chapter 15

IT WAS LEONARDO'S LAWYER who told him that the sheriff had closed the case due to a lack of "convincing elements to proceed with the task", and that he had "arranged" the silence of the private investigator.

Lucca expected that they'd examine more than the imaginary fatal hole in the "road accident". He wasn't satisfied with the results of the inquiry. He wanted to drop everything, move from the house where he was living, and go on a trip. But his anger was fleeting. He withdrew from social interaction and started to study English and computer science with intent. It was his way of mourning and finding his way.

After the closing of the case, Big Head's life went back to normal at his new home address, where his feelings and his sexual attraction toward Lisa intensified, proving the harmonious and happy accuracy of the complementary charts. As for Lucca, some time after the "vocational orientation" consultation and the tragic accident, Leonardo considered that his son had faced the suffering for his mother's death serenely.

It was not the first time Lucca moved. When he was little, he moved from Tijuca to Grajaú, and then to Flamengo. But it was different now. He never forgot that night when his father called him to the corner of the big balcony of the Barra apartment and, very moved, revealed he was in love with the astrologer. He confessed, without digressing, that he intended to live with her. At first, Lucca was bewildered. He didn't take the revelation well, nor did he like his father's idea of them living together. But then he realized that there was no other way, knowing how stubborn his father was, and now infatuatedly stubborn.

Without other options, Lucca moved from the Barra apartment, where he still felt his mother's presence correcting the position of the pictures on the white walls and handling the china in the kitchen, to live in Lisa's apartment. In a sensible and mature attitude, he realized that he had to support his father in this phase of loss and hard work, now that the ring tones of Big Head's cell phones were nervous back into action. Gradually, Lucca accepted the reality of the facts and "humanized" his friendship with the astrologer.

From the moment that Lucca learned to deal with Lisa's presence in Leonardo's grief-stricken heart, he started to benefit from the "witch's" magic wand. So much so that a phone call from Leonardo to a high-ranking military officer in his commercial relations, which she had encouraged him to make, was enough for Lucca to be excused from serving the "beloved country".

"I would never let the boy waste time marching and learning to shoot when he has so much to learn."

The waiver was not the only thing that Lisa took care of in favor of "the boy", as she lovingly called Lucca. She also insisted with Leonardo that he should give sonny-boy a state-of-the-art computer. The only thing she was adamant about was the use of drugs. She would not allow that her lover's son, who would soon turn eighteen, be lost to this. So, being very respected at home, she had no difficulty in convincing the "old man" that Lucca could study abroad, since it was his big dream. She wanted to fulfill other life projects with Leonardo that didn't include taking care of an orphan, especially him being the "other woman's" son. So she kept nagging Leonardo, saying that he needed to fulfill his son's biggest dream, suggesting he turn to an American banker to ask for help. The golden opportunity for the request would come during the semiannual meeting, already scheduled to be held in Rio.

Only one thing intrigued Lucca. His father was talking

about the next visit to the "Relic", and he didn't know what it was.

"Dad, I don't know what's that relic of which you talk so much to Lisa," insisted Lucca, looking tenderly at her, seeking support to make his father give a convincing answer.

"Wait until you go to your grandpa's house in Botafogo and you'll know what it is. Lisa hasn't seen it also and she's impatient."

*

Everything came to Leonardo's mind that sunny morning. Gradually, he recapped what happened on that memorable January 13, 2006, when he received the good news from the New York banker in the morning and, at night, not only he celebrated his professional success but also relived in details the first astrological consultation with Lisa, which had changed his life and made him live on the edge.

"Congratulations, Mr. Leonardo, the board authorized the increase of your credit line. The bank has never granted such a large amount to a Brazilian client."

Big Head knew he'd had to make several "adjustments" after the first reading of his chart to be able to be there, next to Lisa, living in her apartment, where the dogs' barking no longer could be heard. By mutual agreement, the pets were given to friends, before he decided to live with her. Several months had passed and the bankers were now in Brazil. Leonardo was going to meet them at the professor's office. He couldn't stay lazily in bed anymore. It was time to go, in a suit and tie, and preside the important meeting with the *gringos*, scheduled after that auspicious morning call.

The professor knew nothing about the narcotraffic's *modus operandi*, since from the beginning he had limited himself to stamping the destination — without questioning the origin — on the stacks of packages that arrived every early evening through the freight elevator and went straight to the safe in the office. Obviously, he didn't know Pimpão, the boss. The chief had never set foot on the "Special Projects Consulting Office", with its well-equipped network of computers, scanners, faxes, and ample meeting room, in which the professor liked to see his clients.

After Skull was arrested and Pimpão took over, giving carte blanche to his Minister of Finance to organize the financial system, two work meetings were scheduled every quarter in Rio. In the first one, the bankers, whose agenda was the financing and investment of the laundered money. Soon after, there was a meeting between the drug lords, whose agenda was the import of raw materials from Colombia and Ecuador, and their commercialization after refining. The first meeting was presided by Leonardo in the professor's office. The second meeting was led by Pimpão in Big Head's office at Downtown Shopping Mall. Each meeting looked after the specific interests of expanding the traffic's lucrative businesses.

Thus far, Leonardo hadn't organized any social gatherings at the manor in Botafogo, still under construction. Leonardo's father's former residence was repurchased from a developer who was convinced by the Major to "back down" from constructing a twelve-story building. There, without keeping it a secret from Lisa and his son, the famous Relic 666 would be put at a prominent place.

At the quarterly meeting with the bankers, orchestrated by Leonardo and coordinated by the financial advisor, obviously without the presence of Pimpão, foreign financiers were able to verify that Big Head had taken the professor's advice to not give credit to catastrophic prognoses about the country's future. And he had only benefited from having believed in the campaign promises that they would ban the moratorium, value the *real*[7] and the stock market. And, above all, for betting on corruption and impunity. In no time the traffic acquired the status and financial power of a large company, and Leonardo's personal fortune only grew vertiginously in the period.

"Any doubts, gentlemen?" asked Leonardo at the head of the table, after two hours of meeting.

The explanations had been completed after the accounting reports were submitted. The participants, even if only to justify their presence in Rio, checked the numbers, analyzed the graphs, exchanged opinions and points of view, and, driven by the greedy instinct to invest and make more money, much more so with the prosperous "front businesses" of the organization, decided to question the "Minister of Finance" about his homework.

"The final profitability numbers are comparable to those of China and India, aren't they?" asked the banker.

"These profits were only possible, gentlemen, because we were able to diversify our activities a lot. We set up important front businesses. Today, we operate a successful chain of pizzerias, nightclubs, bingo arcades. We expanded some commercial stores and the advertising agency," Leonardo summed up, enthusiastically.

"Given the high daily volume of cash flow, we couldn't operate without a large support infrastructure. Everything was set up in record time," assured the professor, didactic, reinforcing the Minister of Finance's explanations.

"The pizzeria chain is a huge success," confirmed the short, chubby man, former owner of five restaurants and today general manager and the biggest "stooge" of the food company, which congregated a vast chain of restaurants, including some beer bars and nightclubs. "We have many 'stooges' working."

7   Brazilian currency (*TN*)

"Our advertising agency has signed millionaire contracts with state-owned companies," said the consultant, thrilled.

"Congratulations, Mr. Leonardo," praised the stern banker from Manhattan who wore glasses with fine golden rims, pleased with the results and thankful for the call-girl, provided to him so he wouldn't feel lonely during his short stay in Rio.

"Oh! We're also operating successfully in the main public bids," said Leonardo, his voice overflowing with confident satisfaction. "It's amazing how you can buy corruption nowadays."

In order not to attract envy and greed, Big Head omitted the intensification of his trips to Brasília, encouraged by Lisa, where he showed more and more intimacy with the crowned heads. He had registered the group's companies at all state-owned companies and became familiar with the auction notices to sell weapons to the Ministry of Defense, cleaning and prompt delivery services to the postal service, books and notebooks for public schools, overpriced ambulances for the health sector. Swearing has become increasingly useful and contagious in whispered conversations, ensuring fraternal identification and mutual trust in defense of the public and social interest of the country among participants in the allotment of public money. He had full access to the most influential public management offices.

"What about the facilitators?" asked the banker form the Principality of Liechtenstein, who liked the company of young men at night.

"A *dollarduct* pumps into the accounts of the most prominent figures in the government and their allies'. This has allowed us to access the state bureaucracy and win the most disputed and profitable bids in advance.

"Are there risks of this leaking to the public opinion?"

"Good question," answered Leonardo. "There's always risk. The risk is decreasing because our contacts in the government and in Congress are even more reliable. The tendency is to increase our profits even more and be generous."

"Mr. Leonardo is absolutely right. Brazilians tolerate transgressions too much. They don't react. The government knows this. They have been the first to defend us because they know that everything is done with the help of the big shots in the ministries and the owners of the parties of the government's allied base. Without it, the machine gets stuck," the professor joked, sliding his hand through his thin gray hair to the edge of his white collar.

Leonardo nodded in agreement and looked again at the clock before proceeding:

"Profits! Profits were only possible, gentlemen, because we were able to protect our interests. You cannot imagine how difficult our fight against tax authorities has been. The government has increased the tax load tremendously and no one protests for fear of being inspected with a fine comb. And the fees to the inspectors and the police are even worse," Leonardo revealed to the bankers, who were convinced to increase their credit lines for the traffic's activities.

"It's hell having to deal with this sons-of-bitches," said the banker from Miami, blowing dense puffs of his cigar, sucked in through the air-conditioning vent.

"Gone are the days when they were satisfied with pennies," said the professor, nervously drumming his fingers on the table.

"Well, you're not the only ones who have this problem. We also suffer the same extortions from the police and the politicians," remarked the American banker from Los Angeles.

"Don't talk to me about politicians. But here they are increasingly greedy and never get punished," complained Leonardo, pursing his lips.

"Since they have parliamentary immunity, no one gets

punished. They are increasingly hungry. They are insatiable. They don't make politicians like they used to anymore," analyzed the consultant, letting out a long sigh.

"I can imagine! But it's the people who vote. They accept that."

"If someone is guilty, so are we. We want everything to stay the way it is. The more corruption, the better for our business," added another banker. "Isn't it true?"

"Do you think in America it's any different? We have party fees. Those who don't contribute, suffer! They kill us from hunger and despair," said the vice-president of a large American bank, laughing and drumming on the table with his ostentatious ruby ring.

"The difference is that, in Brazil, if someone is caught transgressing, they don't go to jail. They are free pending trial, and can lead a normal life. We all know how the Judiciary works here," sentenced the professor.

Leonardo looked at his watch once again and intervened so as not to prolong the parallel conversations that were starting, out of control:

"Gentlemen, please, we are not here to philosophize. I'll schedule the transfers and financing according to the values of the spreadsheets prepared by the professor. Agreed?"

They all remained silent, agreeing.

After the friendly goodbyes, everyone headed for the door of the office. Leonardo pulled the vice president of the American bank by the arm to a corner of the room. With the title of plenipotentiary minister, he was able to request a "little help" so his son could study at an American university. The Manhattan banker, wanting to maintain good relations with a client as important as Big Head, and having in mind the size of the businesses, all legal, answered immediately:

"If his school documents are up to date, I'll help. No problem."

He even offered to personally interview Lucca if he went to New York, and guide him before giving him the crucial letters of recommendation, which would certainly open doors at the universities. It didn't get any better than that.

The financial contribution of foreign capital, without questioning the origin of the money, was important to the traffic. This would allow Pimpão to buy more raw material and sell more cocaine, profiting more and more. Thus, Leonardo, with the help of the "hidden forces", was becoming increasingly rich and powerful, which was all that the death revenge against his father's executioners needed to make the diabolical final reckoning happen.

Leo was in a hurry to get home. It was no longer the financial world that made him nervous, but the anguish of wanting to tell everything to Lisa, tell her how the job request for Lucca went and throwing himself into her arms. It was no longer profits from operations that interested him, but the contours and excavations of her body. He wanted to breathe in the sweet female smell in the folds of the flowered sheets.

He assumed the danger of playing with the fire from Mars or from another planet, passionately clinging to that woman and being thrilled with the happiness of her being part of his dreams in the happy symbolism of the complementary charts. Without realizing it, he found himself alone in the meeting room, dreaming about his destiny. Then he began to smile, happy, grateful, as if listening to a harp of soft, pink sounds, coming from the garden of his father's manor, arriving slowly and leaving its musical trail down the path of his heart.

Chapter 16

THE MORNING AFTER AURÉLIEN'S CALL to the Frenchman from the NGO, the police conducted a mega operation in Rocinha. Around three hundred agents from twelve specialized police stations, two Águia helicopters, and an armored vehicle from Core[8] were mobilized to search the *favela* in order to carry out arrest warrants, recover stolen cars and seize weapons and drugs.

"Each police station has a specific interest in this operation," said the deputy, breathless, before crossing Via Ápia with quick steps, at the very beginning of the occupation. "That's why we've combined all actions into one." His voice was captured by reporter Júlia's micro-recorder, in the middle of a plethora of microphones and many collisions with her colleagues.

"Are you going to arrest the drug dealers?" asked Júlia, following the deputy's quick steps through the narrow alleys of the slum, while, on the other side of the street, there was a tumult.

"Yes," answered the deputy. "We've mobilized many men to intimidate the criminals and avoid that innocent people get hurt. There'll be a lot of arrests and a lot of drugs and weapons seized." – All of a sudden, he interrupted the interview to shout loudly to the officer across the street: "Tie the thug to the utility pole, right there, and we'll pick him up when we leave."

8 Coordenadoria de Recursos Especiais – Coordination of Special Assets (*TN*)

A woman was drinking coffee from a plastic cup. She got startled with the deputy's shout and spilled her coffee with cream. She ended up soiling the kid's clothes and spilling a little on Júlia's sleeve, who complained about her carelessness.

"It's going to be tough, guys!" warned the police officer, breathless, trying to keep up to the agents' progress. "Rocinha got too big. The residents are terrified, with so many drug selling points and guns. There's only one way to reassure the residents, go in full force with increasingly powerful troops."

Ayrton Senna School suspended classes to prevent students from leaving home. However, only when they arrested the Pavãozinho R9 the criminals fired their first rifle shots. There was a gunfight, but no one got hurt. As they progressed through the alleys, the police discovered that the house that had been burned down the previous night was the headquarters of an NGO. Two charred bodies were found.

The forensic team was immediately called.

From the start of the operation at 5 AM until it ended, at 1 PM, twenty-six stolen motorcycles, twenty-two pounds of marijuana, fifty bags of cocaine, and thirty stones of crack were seized, as well as a submachine gun, a pistol, a revolver, and four grenades. In a shack, several radio transmitters and PCs used in a clandestine cable TV center were removed. Three people were detained for operating the center, but they would be released and would be free pending trial, as the policeman holding a machine-gun and watching the shack said.

"So much work for nothing. It sucks! Once again, the information was leaked and it hindered our whole operation. They're going to pay for it," complained the deputy, covering the microphone of Júlia's mini-recorder with his hand, uttering a series of curse words at the failure of the police action.

"What did you expect, exactly?" asked a reporter.

"A cocaine refinery and the dealer's arsenal with weapons recently arrived from Paraguay. The Intelligence department did their job. We were on to them. Unfortunately, everything disappeared. Thank God no resident or police officer got hurt."

Júlia watched the deputy flee the crowd of journalists. She also fled, because she had a lot to investigate, starting with the strange destruction of a single shack during the night. She sought information from the neighbors about the fire and the charred people. She found out that it wasn't a shack, but the headquarters of a well-known NGO belonging to the two dead Frenchmen. This alone would make front page headlines in all the major newspapers in the world.

*

It wasn't the first time that information leaked. Just recently, Leonardo's informants warned him that agents from two police stations would make operations at Ladeira dos Tabajaras. They informed Pimpão, who, through his phones, told his men to "clear the area". Nothing was found and the press released the failed invasion of truculent police officers to a peaceful Copacabana slum, disrupting the lives of easygoing residents. The supremacy of organized crime was celebrated by Major Runner at night, in another slum, dominated by 7.62 rifle shots. And he seized the moment of celebration to do a little service for his friend Big Head. He would never break his word.

On that celebration night with shots cutting through the moonlit sky in Rocinha, Leonardo jumped out of bed several times to answer his phone, since it wouldn't stop ringing. Lisa had never seen Leonardo so agitated. She asked if he needed any help. Tense, he would say no as he left the room. Back from his den, after so many comings and goings, he gave her a loud kiss at 5 am, whispering in her ear:

"Don't worry. Everything is under control. Sleep tight, my love."

Another leak happened on the day of the mega operation, when reporter Júlia and Aurélien were in Rocinha. Having been warned in advance, Leonardo and Pimpão plotted everything to demonstrate that police war operations in densely populated slums were a dangerous mistake with tragic consequences. The press would show pictures of terrified residents and violent police officers, unprepared to deal with the increasingly organized crime. They would report the humiliations of which poor communities, occupied by military force, were victim. And how, afterwards, they were abandoned, despised by the State, received no social investments, being at the mercy of the traffic's welfare, which even paid for funerals.

"Everything is cool, man," Pimpão's general manager assured over the phone from his hiding place at the top of the *favela*, in his tenth call to Leonardo to tell him that the police forces were leaving Rocinha.

"I've heard everything on CBN. It's time to put the NGOs on the street to protest. Pimpão wants them to go now, so the protest will be shown on TV today and will be on the papers tomorrow. Focus, Runner."

It was past noon. The killer Runner went out in a hurry to gather the crowds and "make one hell of an uproar" to demoralize the mega operation. He placed in the alleys the noisy demonstrations of the NGO for the Defense of Human Rights, financed by the drug dealers, who came out shouting and holding up protest signs against the police invasion, thus polarizing the news.

The Major returned from the protest, as the slang says, "brand new", and then made the lines of cocaine, newly refined in the shack lab, which was not found during the operation, located right in front of the clandestine TV center.

As he inhaled the first line, the thug recalled the previous night, when the two *gringos* were tied to chairs and tortured. Having not obtained the information requested by Big Head about the suitcase of money, he had decided, on his own, to set the NGO headquarters on fire. That was when Major Runner, to celebrate, snorted his last line, entered paradise, and smiled happily.

Aurélien woke up early that morning, anxious to see the Frenchmen's NGO at Rocinha. He remembered the fear in the nervous voice of the man on the other end of the phone when he talked about "the tapestry" and "the money" as if he feared some imminent danger.

He decided to take a cab, instead of taking the tourism jeep. The transit was slow in Lagoa towards Barra. He got worried because he was going to be late for his meeting. The traffic jam was consequence of the mega operation and a police blitz in the Zuzu Angel Tunnel. Cars and motorcycles could only go to São Conrado after they were inspected. Residents were frisked at the access to the *favela*. It was absolute chaos.

A policeman stopped him at the entrance. When he said he was a tourist going to visit his French friend at the NGO, the policeman made a face.

"That's not good, man. You're too late," he said.

"Why?" asked Aurélien, surprised.

"There was a fire at the NGO last night and the owners died."

"That's awful! How did it happen?"

"Only forensics will be able to tell. You can go through. Go up to that green house, then turn right."

Aurélien had nostalgically accepted the folkloric version of the name "Rocinha" as a result of the fact that, in the past, there had been a large plantation with cassava, pumpkin, watercress, banana, kale, cabbage, which supplied the residents or was sold by teenagers along the road. More people came to live in Rocinha and it grew until it became a city. A resident explained it to him while they walked uphill:

"Today, we have all the good things that other *favelas* don't have: butchers, drugstores, rental companies, public squares, bus companies and several supermarkets. On the bad side, we only have the drug dealers and the deaths. But the other slums also have it."

At the top, close to the green house, Aurélien contemplated the fantastic view, that work constructed naturally, meshing natural assets, the ocean, the beaches, and the hills, that made Rocinha an idyllic scenery for foreigners, despite the human violence. When he got closer to the burned down NGO, he saw the area isolated by tape and the journalists at work. Nobody had called the fire department. The law of silence ruled.

Up ahead, very close to the tape around the burnt down house, Aurélien saw a young journalist with red-rimmed glasses, holding a tape recorder, listening to the dramatic description of a neighbor:

"I had left a crack in the window open, and I could see the yellow traces of the bullets in the sky. After midnight, they cut off the electricity. Right then, my heart started to race. When this happens, we know it will be bad. We heard a lot of screaming and then we saw a flash. Then the fire started. Poor guys, what a terrible death!"

Forensics had taken samples and covered what was left of the victims with black plastic sheets. Many reporters and photographers had already left the scene. He got closer to the reporter wearing glasses and found that she was more charming up close than when he had first seen her from a distance. Still, Aurélien couldn't hear what an old resident of the *favela* said while being interviewed by Júlia.

"I lived on the streets when I was a kid, but I was honest, I didn't want to steal what didn't belong to me. I asked the rich ladies for food and they gave it to me. I raised myself.

My first job was delivering food to the construction sites. I worked as a bricklayer's mate and as a mason, and then I began to sell ice cream. It was the Frenchman's wife idea. I remember the day she bought me a Styrofoam box and I went through the *favela* selling popsicles. Now I have an established itinerary. Another thing the Frenchman did was teaching me to read."

"Where did they come from and what did they do for the community?" asked Júlia, raising her glasses with her left hand and looking around to make sure her colleagues had gone to interview other residents in other parts of the slum.

"The only thing I know, Miss, is that the Frenchmen did charity work in Bosnia and Mexico, and that they created this NGO here to help rescue young Brazilians from a life of crime and poverty," answered the resident with a sad look.

Júlia suspected that the old man with the white hair had more to say, but was afraid to speak. She was clever and used deception, appealing to the man's vanity.

"Apparently, they liked you very much, wasn't it? Readers will love to know about it. Don't you want to tell us a little bit about it?"

The resident was moved by the memories he had. He was going to stay in silence, but he couldn't resist and spoke in a heartfelt voice:

"I'm very sad, Miss. I am devastated by what happened. I remember their happiness seeing the girls with dolls and the boys with marbles. I had never had that in my childhood. I started to work very young. The Frenchmen said that children needed to play because life is an endless game. That was not what happened to them, was it? They were very nice people, you better believe it. They promised me a key chain with the Eiffel Tower. I wanted it so much! There was no time. They weren't able to give it to me, Miss."

Looking over her shoulder, Júlia noticed for the first time a man with his arms crossed, impassive, with an ugly goatee, watching from a short distance away. He had very pale skin, a telltale sign that he wasn't a native from Rio, which was not a plausible reason to be intruding. She laughed at her childish reasoning. The stranger didn't look like a foreign correspondent or a police officer, let alone a criminal. She suspected he was a curious, nosy foreigner, just like her father.

"Do you think it was arson?" Júlia asked boldly, not worrying about the stranger. It was something she needed to know from the ice cream seller, as he would be able to satisfy her curiosity.

"I believe so. There was a lot of cruelty, Miss."

"Have you told the police or anyone else?"

"God, no! I don't want the police around!"

"Why are you so sure?" insisted the reporter Júlia, feigning naiveté.

"They were tortured to death. It was very mean! The Frenchwoman suspected that a boy was stealing from her. I don't think that that was it, Miss. There were some very strange things happening this past month at the NGO. I don't even like to talk about it."

"Like what, for example?" urged Júlia. "Can you tell me?"

"No, it's nothing. I don't want any trouble," the old man avoided the question, scratching his head nervously.

"You'll be telling only me. I swear, no one will know."

"I rather leave it for another day. I can't do it today. I'm very sad."

"I just wanted to know the truth. I'll only publish it if you let me."

"OK. I'll clear my conscience. The Frenchman was terrified of a rug that a guy from Bahia wanted to sell. I think his wife died without knowing about it.

"A rug?" asked Júlia, astonished. "Are you sure?"

"He said it was very valuable. It was something from Satan. I don't know if I got the story right. Someone was coming from France to buy it. With the money he was going to receive, he was going to travel and remodel the headquarters of Dois Irmãos and the NGO. He said that whoever kept the rug died. I get goose bumps all over when I remember this. I'm scared, Miss."

Suddenly, the old man stopped talking, frightened. Júlia looked back and saw the stranger standing very close to her, snooping. He must have heard the resident's last words. She didn't like the unsettling look of the eavesdropper, but continued her work.

"Did you see the rug?" she asked nervously.

"Hell, no! I didn't and I don't want to see it. I suspect that the Frenchman died because he saw too much. Please, I have to go," mumbled the old man, walking away, disturbed by the presence of the intruder. "Don't tell anyone about what I've told you. They'll think I'm crazy, Miss."

As she was about to leave the crime scene, Júlia felt the stranger's strong hand gently tug on her thin arm:

"Could you give me a few minutes, please?"

Júlia put her glasses back on and fixed her investigative gaze on that serious and provocative face. She was curious about the stranger and especially about his insistent interest in the interview.

"Why?" asked Júlia, annoyed.

"Because I have important information you need to know. I ask you not to publish anything about the rug before you listen to me."

"Isn't this too much to ask?" protested Júlia, reluctant, not hiding her annoyance at the boldness of the request, which she considered to be a joke or a rude pass at her.

"I can explain," said Aurélien. "The rug that disappeared from the NGO on the night of the fire is part of the largest tapestry in the world."

"Really?" asked Júlia with a hint of irony.

"Believe me! The rug is part of the biggest comic strip in the world, the Apocalypse saga. The French government is committed on recovering this missing piece from the Chateau d'Angers.

Júlia backed off. She believed the stranger. He must not have been lying when he spoke of the castle and identified himself as a French researcher on an unofficial mission. This was good. She agreed to his proposition to exclude the "rug" from the story she would write about the fire, but only until she heard the full Apocalypse story and the "important information" to which she would have access. They understood each other better in French. They smiled and set up a date for dinner that night.

The story of the NGO's fire simmered in Júlia's head. Her journalistic sense soon detected that the "rug" of inestimable historical value was a hot subject. There was no reason to doubt the "researcher" to discover the true cause of the barbaric executions of the two Frenchmen in Rocinha. She agreed to hold the news. She knew that there was a sensational scoop, with information from reliable sources capable of making fabulous headlines in all the newspapers on the planet. Indeed, the night promised many revelations and surprises.

Júlia didn't find in Rocinha only an unprecedented story by Tintin. Fate wanted her to find the story of her life.

Chapter 17

LEONARDO HAD PLANNED SOMETHING exalted so that Lisa would never forget the day of her first visit to the manor where he'd lived with his late father. He picked her up in a rented white limo and went for a ride along the southern shore, sipping a cold rosé Perrier Jouet, in crystal flutes. A limousine like the ones that ride around Manhattan at dusk with their tinted windows. But, if anyone could see it, they wouldn't understand why Lisa was curled up in the back seat, away from Leo's hands and passionate kisses. From experience, she knew that if she let things happen, the game of seduction would lead her to lush scenes and she would arrive naked at the "ceremony".

They entered a quiet street in Botafogo and finally arrived at the place so present in Leo's past. Since she had curiously waited for the visit, everything was a surprise to Lisa, even the neighborhood of luxurious buildings that Leonardo didn't like, especially a newly built twelve-story next to the manor. He had heard that it had underground parking, and that the noisy cars exiting through the ramp could be heard inside the manor. A few streets away was the Dona Marta Hill, lit up at night like a Christmas tree.

Inside the manor, Lisa, wearing a new dress, was surprised by the splendor erected under vestiges of reminiscences and glories of the good times. Everything was restored to what it was at the time of Leo's father: the paintings, the silverware, the china bought from auctioneers and antique dealers. Not always the same precious items, but almost identical. She saw Leonardo get emotional with the Brazilian rosewood table in the dining room and the Dom

José chairs, where the family used to gather for meals and talk about amenities. The dream of living in the manor was about to come true. He just needed her to agree with the idea.

With all the lights on and the chandelier crystals shining on the ceilings and walls never empty, they walked the manor in slow steps through the long corridors, furnished rooms, bathrooms, pantry, kitchen. They visited, on the top floor, the large empty rooms with high ceilings and sumptuous mirrored bathrooms. Then they went back down the pink marble staircase and finally entered the library and, silently, looked at books of all genres lined up on the shelves.

Seeing the books, Leonardo thought about his son, who might have been present. But he had decided that Lucca would visit the mansion later. That day was dedicated to Lisa, who received a gold and diamond bracelet. He got emotional when he told her that the jewel belonged to his late mother and that she would be glad to see her wearing it. Lisa was very moved by the honor. Since Leonardo didn't want her to cry, he pointed to draw her attention to the bookshelf with the row of books about the Inquisition, his father's great bibliophile pride, and, without her noticing, approached the fireplace.

There, standing by the fireplace with marble columns, Leonardo pulled down a large lever. They heard the sound of a noisy mechanism that made the fireplace disappear. A gloomy corridor appeared and, at the end of it, a narrow spiral granite staircase. After calmly going down the steep steps, they reached the underground of the house. Then they went through an iron gate, similar to those of a graveyard. A spacious room welcomed them, where guests waited for them to begin the ceremony.

Leonardo's green eyes shone in the shadows when his feet stepped on the inverted pentagram at the entrance to the "temple". Lisa saw all the *babalorisha's* followers wearing their *axos*, gathered there, immediately move away from the center of the room and line up, side by side, opening a clearing for the prevalent crossing of the owner of the manor and his companion, who proceeded to the end of the human corridor, where a tall man stood waiting with the pomp and fluid apparel of *eshus*[9]. He wore a long black hooded robe with two flashy red lines in the center. In the back, on the central wall of the room, shone, magnificent, tableau 75 of the Apocalypse.

In this gloomy, dense atmosphere, characteristic of darkness, feeling heavy, disturbing magnetic radiations in the air, a lump in the throat chocked Lisa, even if she was standing beside her beloved, unabated by the morbid sensations emanating from the underground. She gazed around the room filled with floating shadows moving slowly, sinuously in that grim room, lit by long kerosene torches. She looked to the right and saw a throne lit only by two candles, one red and one black, on top of two skulls.

The *babalorisha*, after welcoming them, standing solemnly, began the ceremony, asking for peace, health, and prosperity for everyone present and for all his followers, who silently knelt down at the sound of the *adjá* (a small metallic bell with three mouths), greeting all *orishas*, from Bara to Oxala.

Then, the followers responded with the specific greeting of each *orisha*. The *ogans* called the *erês* so that those present could respond. At this moment, the *babalorisha* walked to the throne where the *eshu* "Tatá Caveira" was incorporated. As if struck by lightning from the sky, his body shaking in a trance, the manifestation took place. He immediately asked for his offerings, which the *ekedes* handed over to him. He drank brandy from a skull-shaped goblet and smoked a cigar. Soon, he started to sing and dance. Then he called the great Leonardo to talk.

9 An Orisha — spirits sent by higher divinities — in the Yoruba religion (*TN*)

"*Laróyè Eshu, Laróyè Eshu,*" greeted Leonardo, clapping his hands. "*Mo ju mojubá, Exu Oba Baba awon Esu! Iba se, o!*"

Eshu Tata Caveira shook in a state of euphoria. Invoking the spirits of nature, he inhaled vigorously his cigar to expel dense clouds of smoke. And then he declared in the most absolute egocentric superlative:

"I am the energy, the primitive force of embodied nature. I am the great magical agent of universal balance, because I am the greatest enforcer of karmic law. I am the *eshu* who never loses the battle. You, who are the owner of this house, have the keys to the portals, crossroads, and paths in your hand, and you have the obligation to think about yourself if you want to quench your thirst for justice. You, who today lock, unlock, and move money, and have overcome the complaints and groans of dark spirits in the hour of suffering."

Then the sound of the drums was heard. The *eshu* shift his gaze from the spotlight that lit the daunting image of the devil on the central wall to Leonardo's face and continued in a loud voice:

"You're not the only one who's thirsty. The fields are dry. Frogs are so thirsty they cry, and the rivers are covered with dead leaves that have fallen from the dying trees. Now you must fulfill the determinations of the Karmic Law. Take revenge on evil by doing the right thing, 'an eye for an eye, a tooth for a tooth'. You won't be breaking the law if justice is not achieved; therefore, you don't need to fear the law of action and reaction turning against you later. The fields will turn green and the frogs will jump happily again in the swamps, and you, great Leonardo, will quench your thirst for vengeance and money. You'll win over darkness."

Lisa, still in a state of shock before the terrifying Relic, which she was seeing for the first time, decided to join Leonardo, when the *eshu*, seeing her approaching the golden throne, ordered:

"Come here, Miss, come here. Someone wants to talk to you."

Eshu Tata Caveira came down from the throne and gave way to Ogum, the oldest son of Odùduà. Leonardo whispered to Lisa the words she should use to greet him, recognizing the power of those who "live at night" and to ask him to "free her from ambushes".

"Ogum Onirê, my father, Ogum Onirê," greeted Lisa.

"I am one of the enforcers of the law. I am the messenger of the *orishas* who fight poison with poison."

Mesmerized, Lisa heard Ogum's voice, shivering:

"I'm here to help you free your "trousers" from the bad thoughts and attitudes of the incarnated spirits. Help this beloved son of God to be free from mean feelings, hatreds, revenge, unbridled sensuality, from vices of every kind, which feed his greedy, loving soul. Only you can help him put an end to the bloodshed, which he is attracted to and makes him believe he is more and more powerful, and to the deaths of innocents and the cries of unhappy mothers who lost, due to the violence, their husbands and children."

As she listened, frightened, confused, Lisa looked over the gray wall behind the throne. She spotted a dozen small plaques, not identifying the meaning of the engraved capital letters and dates, looking like *ex-votos* in churches to celebrate and thank for the miracles. She heard the sound of the drums getting louder, because Ogum gets angry if it's played softly, which is considered offensive to the entity. She heard the god of war continue to preach like it was a commissioned sermon:

"You'll try in every way, by faith and spiritual work, and, above all, by the great love you have for the great boss, to attract him to the path of light. Each step you take in that direction will increase your capacity for discernment, thereby making your light stronger. Only then he'll be able to evolve and be happy."

While Lisa was talking to Ogum, Leo's eyes were drawn to the magnificent image of Satan, dominant in the center of the room. He could only rejoice in its radiant presence, which brought him fortune, power, and love.

Thanks to satanic protection, he had reached the most evolved and prosperous stage of the "Minister of Finance", having incorporated the most modern financial management into the drug traffic. Not at all similar to Skull's times.

Drug and arms trafficking were at its peak, with computerized accounting of the profits. Big Head had everything from the cocaine empire accounted for, including the numbers of people from the barbarity. The fifty-two "*ex-votos*", recently spotted by Lisa, celebrated the ritual of "devout enemies" that Leonardo supposedly believed had driven his father to suicide. Major Runner had not spared anyone from Big Head's "black book". All deaths deserved an "*ex-voto*" with the capital initials of the graves and the corresponding dates of executions. There were also the initials of the innocent who had died to ensure him possession of the Relic. According to the Excel spreadsheet, Leonardo had not spared money to "set the records straight" and achieve his bloody revenge. The death of a businessman who cursed his dead father at the Stock Exchange had cost 38,798.00.

Accounting was so meticulous that it recorded all expenditure on corruption in all areas in which Leonardo was interested in, from the Army to Justice, from the police to journalists, including politicians and phony human rights organizations. Everything was written down with its exact values. All payments to informants and even the salary of a telephone engineer to maintain an efficient anti-bug system were logged. An impressive working capital amount. Few companies could rival the financial transactions of the empire of cocaine and barbarism.

Things tended to "evolve" with Satan at the manor. For the first time, traffic's sales reached fifty million dollars a month, consistent with the shipment of tons and tons of cocaine to the United States and Europe. Together, Pimpão and his uncle Marcola became powerful drug lords. In their shadow, Big Head prospered at meteoric speed. This could only be explained by the fact that Pimpão hated memorizing numbers and doing math, delegating such "chores" to his Minister of Finance, who, in a plenipotentiary way, started to control all the money that came in and out, the cash flow, the financing, and the millionaire investments of the traffic abroad. He also controlled the stooges and the phony accounts, in Brazil and in tax havens. The great Leonardo had the key to the drug operation's safe in his hands. His thoughts dissipated when he heard *Ogum* warn Lisa:

"My daughter, I see loyalty in your eyes and I don't see the hate that leads to betrayal. I came here to give you a message. You have a very dangerous *egum* near you."

Lisa shivered when she heard all she didn't want to hear:

"You have to work on your inner peace, you have to get and seduce this spirit that is obsessing you. To rescue the "fallen spirit" from darkness, who approached you with a soul tainted by vengeance and greed, and wanting to impose evils and spells on you, you'll need to do something. You'll have to send this *egum* away, it needs to be removed so your life can go on peacefully! If you don't, there will be no salvation for you, you'll kill your beloved in the fire and in the fire you will also die, if you don't act with intelligence and cunning."

That said, with the assurance that only with the immolation of animals would she be forever protected, *Ogum* wielded his sword and buried it in the ground. It was as if the earth opened and disappeared before Lisa's eyes, who was completely astonished, since the four-legged *bori* was already ready for the offering. For the sacrifice, they'd also killed four white roosters, each placed at the goat's four legs, a bowl with flour, palm oil, onion, pepper, lemon, and castor seed. Everything was prepared in advance by the *babalorisha's* followers on a black cloth on top of the pentagram near the exit door. The "head strengthening" was done in order to improve the general conditions of "the missus". The participants stood side by side, forming a circle holding hands around Lisa and dancing to the rhythm of the drums, which increased in intensity.

Once the sacrifice was over, Ogum again gave way to the *eshu*, who resumed drinking his brandy and smoking his cigar and abruptly "ascending", without even waiting for the sound of the drums. At this point, Leonardo and Lisa left the room, leaving the *babalorisha's* followers to end the ceremony.

"Come live here, Lisa. I promise you'll be my goddess."

"I thought I already was," Lisa mocked, smiling.

"Please, Lisa, I mean it. Think about it. I can't live without you. Come live here. The only thing I regret is that my father didn't get to meet you."

"I'm too shaken by the entities to give you an answer right now."

"Please, don't deny that light of hope in my life. Say yes."

"I have to consult the stars, my love. This manor has very negative karmic energies. I need some time to get used to the idea."

In order not to displease Leonardo, who was thrilled with the inauguration ceremony of the temple and the consecration of the Relic in the manor's underground, she tried to buy more time. Lisa didn't want to tell him she had already decided not to live in that sanctuary haunted by ghosts and misfortunes. The gold and diamond bracelet, dangling from her wrist, became the seal that reminded her of *Ogum's* words: "If you don't do it, there will be no salvation for you, you'll kill your beloved in the fire and in the fire you will also die". But as much as her face contorted with anguish, for the time being she would not break the promise she had made to herself that she would consult the ephemerides to predict the course of her life. She hadn't done so perhaps for fear that they would confirm Pluto's entry into the twelfth house of her birth chart, which meant the beginning of a cycle of death and rebirth in her life. She was sure the god of darkness was near…

Chapter 18

JÚLIA MADE THE RIGHT CHOICE, predicting that, at the big patio of the restaurant at Lagoa, the researcher would feel more comfortable to whisper the secrets of the diabolical rug. Traffic flowed very slowly at Epitácio Pessoa. When he was about to start talking, Aurélien Kléber saw a white limo passing by. The impenetrable windows didn't let them see who was inside. He pointed the limo to Júlia, who was also surprised with the extravagance, unusual on Rio's busy streets.

Aurélien first showed the pictures of the tapestry at Chateau d'Angers, stressing the importance of recovering the tableau lost from France's heritage and religious faith. Then he replicated the anguished and enigmatic call from the Frenchman from the NGO's headquarters in Rocinha.

"Is this all you have to tell me?" asked Júlia discouraged, after listening carefully to him. "You don't even know if the image brought from Bahia is authentic. There's no tangible evidence."

"True. But I know that everything is a matter of time and persistence to find the treasure map. Don't you believe that?"

"No art expert has seen the rug and no one knows where it is. How will you do it?" asked Júlia, pessimistic.

"Don't you think the answers will depend only on us?"

Júlia didn't answer. She was pensive. She ran her tongue over her lips to moisten them, without taking her eyes off the "little Frenchman's" face, as Aunt Amelia would define him if she met him. She had been amazed by that unusual face. At the top was an insolent tuft, protruding from the middle of his forehead, and on his angular chin, an unexpected goatee. He also had piercing eyes, with lashes that wouldn't stay still. A strange, but nice composition. Júlia weighed the pros and cons and came to the conclusion that she had nothing to lose with the offer to work together. After all, it was something completely professional that moved them in the shadows of the Apocalypse, attracted by the fascination and mysteries of the great cause and the religious crusade.

They agreed to divide the search tasks. Aurélien would research the tapestry's coming to Brazil and its authenticity, and she would look for leads to the whereabouts of tableau 75. Just to be safe, no news would be published, until they had some proof.

Aurélien was happy with the professional meeting, since Júlia seemed to be trustworthy. She had the wit of a stubborn reporter. He noticed in the aquamarine of her eyes a certain anxiety that was not at all journalistic. But he didn't want to dwell on mere psychological speculations. He was anxious to report the latest events to the curator and receive instructions on his destination after the unsuccessful meeting at *Roziná*.

A few days later, he was summoned by the French consul and appointed as the attorney for the families of the Frenchmen from the NGO. He was charged with repatriating the victims' bodies to France and listing their belongings. It was the crafty way of prolonging his stay, thus giving him time to overcome the unexpected aspects of the mission. With the appointment, he was able to come clean to the prosecutor, who, if necessary, would make the connection with the police without exposing himself, and in a way he would have a partner. He remembered the white-haired old man from the slum and the demand for the miniature Eiffel Tower that the dead Frenchmen owed him.

He returned to Rocinha, and, under the pretext of listing the few undamaged goods of the NGO, he went after the ice cream man in his "established itinerary". It wasn't difficult to find him, or to make him talk. Aurélien only had to give him his own keyring with a miniature Eiffel Tower, feigning he had found the promised souvenir in the debris, for the old man, moved, to become chatty and cooperative, as well as cheerful.

"Do you remember if the Frenchman kept the rug or if he gave it back to the person who brought it?" asked Aurélien, after hearing everything.

"I'm not sure if the guy from Bahia took it back. I believe so."

"Think hard," insisted Aurélien. "This is very important."

"I'm sorry, mister, my memory is not good. It fails me sometimes."

"Who else saw the rug?" asked Aurélien.

"I know Tinhão saw it. The Frenchman asked him to examine the rug. The guy said it was worth a lot of money."

"Do you know where I can find him?" asked Aurélien, anxious and also surprised with the nickname, which seemed like a swearword to him.

"He was a teacher at the NGO. He's a nice guy, you're going to like him."

In Rocinha, he learned that the Frenchmen had been savagely beaten and tortured by the thugs with a saber, before being burned to death, and police suspicions fell on the minor who was raised by the French couple and stole from them to buy drugs. But residents thought there were "powerful people" behind this, involved in the arson.

Having obtained the precious information, Aurélien worried about reaching the address given by the ice cream man. He called to find out when Tinhão taught at the Professional Qualification Workshop. He didn't set a meeting over the phone. He still remembered the tragic telephonic experience when the Frenchman from the NGO had postponed the meeting until the following day and died. Had he received him immediately at Dois Irmãos, he might still be alive. Therefore, he quickly went to meet Tinhão, who welcomed him as an old friend of the Frenchman.

"Are there any doubts about the authenticity?" insisted Aurélien, after they'd introduced themselves and liked each other due to the mutual trust that the situation required.

"None. I had a scholarship for the course at the Textile Training Center in Quebec, Canada. It was immediately clear that it was an ancient, authentic embossed tapestry by the embroidery of woolen threads and bright colors. To make the paints, they used flowering plants. Resedaceae for the nuances of yellow, rubiaceae for the reds and the pastel shade for the blues."

"Was it too damaged?" asked Aurélien, anxious.

"It was a stunning work of art. It only had a tiny little hole on the top corner. Very small. My pinky wouldn't go through. It must be worth a ton of money in the market."

"Do you know who brought the rug to the NGO?"

"A *babalorisha* from Salvador. I met the guy."

"*Babalorisha*? What's that?"

"Forget it, my friend. The guy only came to Rio to show the rug to the Frenchman. He said that, if it was authentic, France would pay millions of euro for it. And he knew it was."

"Do you remember the scene depicted on the carpet?" asked Aurélien, showing no interest in its monetary value and concerned only about its authenticity. Even because, if there was any money involved in addition to his daily fees, the curator and his uncle would have warned him since the beginning of the mission.

"Of course! You can't forget the caged devil and the big padlocks. An impressive image."

"Could you replicate the image? I'll pay for it."

"Don't even think about it!" reacted the artist, embarrassed and offended. "No, the Frenchman was my friend, damn it! Come by tomorrow, I'll give you the sketch."

"Couldn't it be today?" urged Aurélien, wanting to immediately obtain a sure indication that the tableau was in Brazil and that it was authentic.

In the evening, the archery champion policeman called Júlia. They set up a new meeting. Then he told everything to the prosecutor, including about the dinner he'd had with the reporter. The prosecutor wanted to see the image and learn more about Júlia. He showed the artist's drawing, but omitted the physical description of his partner, her moist lips, her round breasts and the nimble figure of the young reporter. He only said she was a "cool" journalist and praised her professional competence a lot. The prosecutor heard everything and summed up the story of the discovery and the reporter:

"Yeah, yeah… a cool journalist with blue eyes. Be careful, my friend."

Aurélien understood the message: he should not let the news of the tableau leak to the press, even if he had to shut the reporter's sexy mouth with a good French tape or, if he didn't have any, with his own full lips to keep the diabolical secret.

The headlines of the evening TV news and newspapers the next morning talked about the murder of the NGO's Frenchmen in Rocinha and the community's tumultuous protests against the police invasion. No news report mentioned the missing rug from Chateau d'Angers.

Júlia was happy with the professional meeting because Aurélien seemed trustworthy. He had the obsession of a savvy researcher. Up close, she noticed that he had the sad eyes of an unloved man. Well, she couldn't waste any time on psychological speculations. She had to investigate in the police stations to find information on who could have the rug they were looking for.

She had heard Aurélien's explanation that the lost tableau represented a caged diabolical figure. There was great curiosity about it, because no one had ever seen the authentic image of Satan in a cage. She was perplexed: she held a thirteen kton TNT bomb in her hand, but she didn't have the detonator to blow the news up on the first page. Who had stolen the piece? She thought that, if she got that answer, she would get the scoop of the year for publishing the cause of the NGO's arson.

Júlia spoke quickly to Aurélien over the phone, and he told her that he had good news, without saying what it was. She was worried she had not yet uncovered any new facts.

She was leaving the police station when she crossed with a released suspect and his lawyer in the hallway. His face wasn't totally unfamiliar. When she casually touched the cuff of her shirt, she remembered what had happened in Rocinha. She was interviewing the deputy when he ordered that the muscular black man be arrested and handcuffed to a pole. The drug dealer kept cursing the police. She had the scene of the screams in her memory.

"Who's that guy that's being released?" asked Júlia to a detective she knew before the man disappeared from view.

"That thug over there?" the police officer wanted to be sure.

"Yes! He has a tattoo on his forehead and another one on his right arm."

"He was at the clandestine TV station in Rocinha. It's all on the records. Go, before the record falls in the graveyard of lost souls," said the officer, laughing and winking.

Júlia had seen small numbers tattooed on the thug's forehead. She was sure one of the numbers was six. She didn't see the other numbers. She also saw a medium tattoo on his right hand. She wouldn't be able to describe what she saw at a glance, but she would recognize the strange image if she saw it again.

When looking in another room of the police station for the clerk, who was an old friend also from Mauá, the throbbing on Júlia's temple indicated that her intuition was on the right track. When he saw her from afar, he immediately grinned widely. The gold necklaces rattled a lot while they embraced affectionately and kissed each other on the cheek.

"Have you seen that guy from the clandestine TV station in Rocinha?"

"It's on the record. Do you want to see it?" asked the officer.

"No. I want to know if you saw the tattoos."

"Yes, I did. The drug dealer had a number 666 on his forehead. Three tiny sixes," replied her friend, showing the size with his fingertips. "-But what caught my attention was the one on his arm. It's unforgettable."

"What was so different about it?"

"It was a monster with seven heads. They say it brings bad luck."

Back in the newsroom, the "important things" revealed and uncovered were enough to make her head spin. She was impressed by what Aurélien told her about the reading of the Holy Scriptures by his uncle, Father Antoine, a scholar of the Bible and the Apocalypse. It was written that a leader would rule the world for seven years. He would make a revolution in the economy and influence men. All his followers would be marked with the number 666. The justification for the number 666 was simple: 6 is the number of man, because he was created on the sixth day by God; 3 is the number of God, because He is a trinity (Father, Son, and the Holy Spirit, the Holy Trinity). Therefore, the number 666 is the man (the 6 repeated three times) who declares himself a god (represented by the number 6). In the book of Revelation, this man is called the Antichrist, and so the number would have a connection with the mark of the Beast, personifying the seven-headed dragon that brought down fire from heaven on Earth. She also recalled the other story told by the researcher.

"They say that the Louvre pyramid, which gives access to the museum, was going to be built with exactly 666 glass panes. At the personal request of François Mitterrand,

President of the Republic, to the Chinese-American archi-
tect Ieoh Ming Pei, the pyramid now had six hundred and
three rhombuses and seventy half- rhombuses, in a total of
six hundred and seventy-three panes. This version has never
been officially denied."

According to the archer, the sign or mark of the Beast
has always been subject to interpretation, taking into account the supremacy of evil. Because of his uncle's influence, Aurélien believed that the number 666 was the sign of
the devil engraved on the right hand and on the forehead of
Satan's worshipers. The expression "is the number of man",
known by everyone, including illiterate people who recognize and accept Satanic numbers with ease and adoration.

In the evening, Júlia called Aurélien and told him everything that had happened at the police station. Then she told
Aunt Amelia how the dinner with the researcher went and
their latest discoveries. Very frightened by the journalistic
report, the aunt wanted to know if she wasn't afraid and if
she wanted to know a little more about the "little French
guy". Júlia reassured her and hid his physical details, telling
her the researcher was just a "nice guy". In her maternal way,
the aunt summed up the story of the suspicious rug and the
first meeting with Aurélien:

"There's something wrong, darling. Be careful with this
devil on the loose out there!"

Chapter 19

TIME ONLY CONFIRMED THE ASTROLOGICAL predictions, coincidentally after the Relic appeared in Big Head's life. He started to live on the edge, increasingly rich and powerful with a cut in the profits of the drug trade, the fraudulent public tenders, and the front companies that he organized with the help of professor Carlos Alberto Guimarães. The only thing he had not yet managed to do was convince Lisa to live in the mansion, and the first disagreements arose between the couple, even after he gave her his mother's bracelet, and she took part in the *gira* and heard Ogum's advice. However, since he had adopted Lisa's favorite motto, "everything has its time", he was confident. He knew that if he took her to visit New York on their honeymoon and Lucca to study in America, she would change her mind.

The fact is that the Candomblé *giras* were a success. But the owner of the *terreiro*[10] chose to keep the devil worship ceremony with the Relic restricted to practitioners, with rare exceptions. The public and the authorities didn't know about the rituals within four walls. This stirred up the curiosity of the Satanist community, interconnected by secret channels of communication, to the point that Leonardo one day received a call from Grand Master Pierre, the leader of the powerful French secret religious cult, based on the outskirts of Avignon. They talked over the phone and exchanged e-mails several times, until he became interested in talking to an emissary.

Thus, Leonardo couldn't travel to New York. Unavoidable

10 How temples are generally called in Candomblé (TN)

commitments, such as meeting the unknown French "religionist" coming from the south of France, kept him in Rio.

After the formal greetings, Leonardo and the emissary went to the basement. They stepped on the inverted pentagram surrounded by the two rows of large diameter columns supporting the two floors of the manor. The host watched as the visitor's piercing eyes roamed the smooth walls of the room until they focused on the bottom, where the dominant figure of the devil occupying the central wall was exalted. Leonardo saw the grim figure of the eerily thin religious man, dressed all in black, and stroking his pointed gray beard, take two steps forward, tilt his head saluting reverently the prominent image, and standing there for a few minutes with his mouth open, as if waiting to receive a wafer.

"The image of the Beast is magnificent. It was worth the trip."

The visitor also saw a golden throne at the center of one of the side walls, surrounded by two series of small white marble slabs, as if they were mortuaries.

Leonardo asked the French visitor how he knew he was in possession of the Relic. The intermediary replied that there were no secrets for the Devil's Order. With a malicious grin, he insinuated that black magic entities were gossipmongers and that the news spread quickly through the internet. The conversation about Satanism and the Inquisition with the stranger reminded him of his father, who'd told him what inquisitors in the Middle Ages did to distinguish between Catholics and heretics in the courts: "Kill them all. God will take care of His own."

"The vision of the Beast is stunning," confirmed Leonardo smiling, knowing the origin of the biblical piece and its value. Before dying, under torture, the *babalorisha* from Bahia had given all the indications of interest to the French government, even admitting that someone was coming to Rio to buy the tableau.

"Is it asking too much, Mr. Leonardo, if I want to examine the tableau up close?" asked the visitor, staring into the eyes of the Beast.

"Of course not. You can examine it as long as you want."

A deep emotion, as if from a secret communication, took hold of the Satanist, in ecstasy at the contemplation of each detail of the image.

"You can't imagine how the hatred accumulated in these centuries is appeased by this illuminating vision for the Devil's Order. Trust me, it's been an integral part of our history since the foundation of the order by Abbé Chevalier in 1314, after the death of Grand Master Jacques de Molay and the Knights Templar. They were chased all over France by agents of King Philip IV, with the support of Pope Clement VI. They were tortured and sentenced to the bonfire, accused of heresy. Our order was founded under the symbol of the Templar curse. It was the first religious organization of satanic creed in the world."

"My father also died wronged. I know how it feels."

"The Catholic Church accused the Templars of worshiping the devil, spitting on the cross, and practicing homosexuality. The devil became the scapegoat for the condemnation and burning of all Templars. The Grand Master burned to death, defying the Pope and the king before God and shouting that the devil's curse would catch everyone in its revenge."

The intermediary stroked his long beard and talked about the Satanic Bible and the "infernal accusation", which were part of the cult. He emphasized that Satan had always been the best friend the Church had ever had because, without him, its existence would not have been possible for all these years. For the cult, it's the obligation of every Satanist to "make the new man achieve material success as his reason for living". He made a slight digression about the ritual performed by a satanic master, which consists in spilling the blood of a child put in a silver chalice on the body of a naked woman. And his last words made clear that the order had more and more followers, willing to make any sacrifice to ennoble it.

"We'll use all means to prevent the scene of the Beast, which is in Brazil, from returning to the tapestry of the Apocalypse, in Chateau d'Angers. We'll use whatever is at our disposal."

"What do you mean?" asked Leonardo, curious about the threat.

"Do you know the biblical passage about the caged devil?"

"No… No…" stuttered Leonardo, embarrassed he didn't know it.

"Allow me then to recite it: 'And I saw an angel coming down from heaven, who had the key to the abyss and a great chain in his hand. He caught the dragon, the ancient serpent, which is the devil and Satan, and tied it up for a thousand years. And he threw it into the abyss, and there he closed and sealed it, so that it no longer deceives the nations, until the thousand years are over'. Do you understand why Catholic pilgrims will glorify the scene of the devil if it returns to the Apocalypse? They will reject it to the abyss of evil. That's the main reason for us, ministers of true Satanism, to rise up against the prison for a thousand years in Chateau d'Angers. We want to set if free and live in communion with the devil. Do you understand now why we will use all means at our disposal to prevent it from being incarcerated? Its incarceration represents a threat to our cult. We fear a loss of power and money."

Suddenly, in the underground where they were, there was the sound of a car braking in the garage of the building next door, followed by a slight tremor behind the golden throne adorned with two skulls.

"Don't be scared. I had to sacrifice the side wall to open space for the throne. It touches the underground wall of the building next door. Sometimes we hear a screech, that's all."

"Mr. Leonardo, Grand Master Pierre asked me to offer you to buy the tapestry. Now that you know its importance and its meaning to the Order, say your price."

"You know it's not just a matter of price."

"Don't be fooled, Mr. Leonardo, the French government has the money available, but I doubt they'll pay. They still don't know that you have the tableau. They are looking for it. Thus far, only we Satanists know about the Relic, and the Order is willing to pay a fair price. Be careful, they are very serious about their business. Please, make your offer before it's too late."

"It's not the price that prevents me from selling it. The Relic brought me a lot of money and luck, much more than I could ever imagine. The ritual reunions on Thursday are held here. The tableau is now part of the *gira* and of my father's manor. I don't know if I want to sell it."

"I can't imagine you refusing a considerable sum."

"You have to see beyond people. It's faith that drives men. Money comes later," said Leonardo, with the petulance of someone who did not intend to dispose so easily of the Relic.

"We agree. The Order will never allow the image of the devil to return to Angers, even if we have to blow the castle up to do so. And we will, if it goes back. We, in Avignon, believe that the tapestry belongs to us since the day it was woven in Paris, in 1378. But, if it stays in Brazil, it will be in good hands. We respect your faith, Mr. Leonardo."

"ok. Tell Grand Master Pierre that you've moved me and, if I decide to sell the tableau, it will be to the Order."

"You won't regret it. If your father were alive, I'm sure he would approve of your wise decision," justified the intermediary, ceremoniously saying goodbye to the host and pretending to be grateful for the final arrangement. "See you soon!"

The Satanist was able to disguise the mission he'd been commissioned to do in Brazil. He should certify the authenticity of the tableau and hire good local professionals to break in the manor and steal the valuable Relic, without spending a dime on the purchase. Everything had to be done before the French government paid the ransom.

After meeting the "religious" man, Leonardo, in turn, went back to the manor's underground, without the resonance of the braking noises and the sound of the *adjá* close to the first columns of the temple, and thought about his Plan B. He had to find a way to receive millions from the French government without having to hand the tapestry over, and sell it to the Order with no remorse for the noble cause, but, of course, only if he decided to pass it on, which seemed unlikely, due to his increasing attachment to the loose devil.

What Leonardo liked most about the conversation with the Satanist was to discover Grand Master Molay's last words before he died at the stake: "Don't worry, soon the curse of the devil will take care of those who condemned us". He explained that, months later, Pope Clement VI died and King Philip IV was murdered. Therefore, wherever the devil's tableau "lived", at the manor or in Avignon, Satan would be free to assist his followers in the victory of revenge.

*

Meanwhile, at General Tibúrcio Square, in Urca, Júlia met Aurélien again. It was a neighborhood in the south part of town where there was almost no crime and, therefore, it was very valued for being one of the few in the city that had no slums. A pleasant and peaceful place to talk, under the cable cars of the Sugarloaf Mountain, turned into messengers that took exciting news back and forth from above. They talked, exchanged ideas, getting to know each other better and, with a little help from heaven, they would unravel the enigmas.

Both Aurélien and Júlia had seen, on the previous day, on TV, the scenes of the police invasion in Rocinha, the protest demonstrations, and the moving reports about the brutal murder of the Frenchmen on Good Friday, exaggerated by the appalled voices of the residents on the slopes and alleys of the largest *favela* in Latin America. Violent deaths still reverberated in the local and international press, while authorities again commented on the Armed Forces' ever-delayed intervention to combat organized crime.

"You told me the tableau was given to a priest in Salvador," said Júlia, as if she doubted the information.

"Not me, father Antoine's students said it. They got confused and translated 'pai de santo'[11] as holy priest."

"Wow! A *pai de santo* is the owner of the temple in *Candomblé*. It has nothing to do with Catholicism," explained Júlia, laughing at the mistake. "It might be a good lead to start."

Under the swing of the cable cars, sitting on a bench in the square, Júlia told him about the discovery of the tattoo with three numbers six and the one of the strange monster she'd glimpsed on the forehead and arm of a thug at the police station where she'd been the day before their dinner at Lagoa. Could she identify them if she saw them again? Aurélien showed her the sketch made by the NGO teacher, Tinhão. She was fascinated by the image of the devil. She looked at the sketch from all angles and couldn't contain herself:

"Oh, my God! What a coincidence! The seven-headed monster of the tattoo is very similar to the sketch of the devil."

"What do you suspect, Júlia?" asked officer Aurélien.

"It doesn't hurt to go to the police stations and find out in which *favela* the thugs with the 666 tattoo work. I think

11 In Portuguese, a *babalorisha* is called "pai de santo" (saint's father) (TN)

the two evidences, *pai de santo* and tattooed criminals, may be connected. Do you know what I feel now?" asked Júlia, taking off her prescription glasses to clean them.

"Tell me," insisted Aurélien, betting on the reporter's instinct.

"Remember the hide-the-thimble game? A child hides an object and the other children try to find it. And every time they get near the place where the object was hidden, the kid who hid it says: 'It's hot!' and when they are far, they say 'It's cold!'. I think things are boiling. We're very close to the entrance of hell." Then she asked: "Do you have your laptop with you?"

"It's always with me, after we fell in love," he replied, laughing and showing her the laptop inside his backpack.

"So let's make a list of names of temples and addresses of tattoo artists in town and go out in the field. Are you in?"

Right there on the bench in the square, under a tree, between the statue of Chopin and the sea, the two of them began to make a list of Candomblé temples and tattoo artists. As they sat close together, Aurélien could breathe in the fragrance of her mountain flowers perfume. It was as if Júlia exuded her delicious, enveloping feminine smell, which, for a moment, made him nostalgic. He recalled the time when his regiment climbed the Mont Blanc flank and he smelled the edelweiss. It was just like Júlia's skin.

"I'll go to the police stations to research."

"I can go with you, if you want," offered Aurélien. "Someone has to protect you. Satan has the habit of being dangerous."

"All right," replied Júlia with a mischievous smile, clutching Saint Thérèse's medal.

There was something different in the air on that sunny morning. It wasn't the cable cars that, like soap bubbles, used to carry dreams and bring hope. It was the promises from above. The Sugarloaf Mountain, formerly called Pain de Sucre by the French invaders, witnesses love rising on the horizon of the wild sea of Praia Vermelha, or simply whispers to Iemanjá that the devil was about to be caged for a thousand years.

*

Curator Ferdinand could celebrate the good news of the week. He had received an e-mail from police officer Aurélien with Tinhão's neat sketch. For the first time, the General Association of Curators of Public Collections had a reliable lead to recover the missing scene from the Apocalypse. In addition, at the same time, he had managed to trace on the world map — with the help of Father Antoine's geeks — the long pilgrimage of tableau 75 through the Old Continent until it arrived at the welcoming Baía de Todos os Santos, in the state of Bahia.

"Not even Jason was so adventurous in the rescue of the Golden Fleece," said the curator to Antoine, toasting the discovery with a Saumur, to the aromas of *petits fruits rouges*.

Together, dumbfounded, they looked at the drawing they had received. And, with dreamy eyes, they imagined themselves retracing the path the tapestry had supposedly made, reconstituted by Antoine's geeks, from the Loire Valley, in France, to the Krakow Voivodeship, in Poland, believing that the tableau left the hands of Monsignor Angebault to those of the jew Ladislau Zalsupin around 1845. It was found that, within the Zalsupin family, there were disagreements about the tableau never shown in public, due to the suspicion that it had been borrowed, without ever having been returned, or worse, that it had been stolen. Fearing the scandal and the police, and because it's the figure of the Seven-Headed Beast, the patriarchs kept it in the attic of their houses for decades as a cursed treasure. Suspecting that the tableau could carry a curse because of the increasing number of deaths in the family, and fearing their extermination, especially since the Nazis had invaded Poland, the patriarch of the last generation of Zalsupins decided, during Christmas in 1939, to donate the tableau to the castle. Coincidentally, at the time the French city housed the headquarters of the Polish government, which had been moved from Poland to settle at Pignerolles Castle, in Angers.

Augusto, the only bachelor of the grand-grand-grand-grandchildren, left Krakow with the cursed tableau. When he arrived at the Loire Valley, he faced the following situation: the Polish government, in exile in Angers, had already left the city, since it had become the regional center of the Gestapo in June 1940. Fearing being deported or dying in a concentration camp, he crossed the Pyrenees and fled to Portugal.

The Polish grand-grand-grand-grandson remained until the end of the war in Lisbon with the rug hidden under his bed. He went to live in Salvador when he fell in love with a beautiful black girl from Bahia, stewardess of a Constellation plane from Panair do Brasil. As director of an insurance company, he prospered and became known in Bahia as a lover of vodka and samba. In *cordel* literature, a wood engraving was discovered that shows the man from Krakow with the supposed "rug" wrapped under his foot and a glass of Wiborowa in his hand. They also found the insurer's last letter to his sister in Warsaw — the only survivor from Auschwitz. In it, he said he'd left the rug in a Candomblé temple. A "local holy priest" had convinced him to do so, or he would die by the curse of the devil on the loose since the death of the Templars. After sending this letter, Augusto died of a massive heart attack on the stairs of the Church of Bonfim.

In later transcripts and records, Father Antoine's "kids" mistakenly translated "*pai de santo*" as "holy priest". This did not nullify the evidence that the French owner of the NGO provided to curator Ferdinand de Sailly when transcribing his conversation with the *orisha* from Bahia in Rocinha. The *babalorisha* would have told him that, on a night when he consulted the sixteen whelks, the interest of French entities to acquire the rug at a good price was revealed. He then scheduled his trip to Rio to visit the foreign owners of the Dois Irmãos Institution. It was this unprecedented clue that would hasten the curator's interest in quickly sending someone to assess the tableau's authenticity.

Then the curator lost the thread. The *orisha* from Bahia was kidnapped when he was leaving the institution in Rocinha and would confess to Leonardo, under torture, that very few people had seen the rug in Bahia, since he hung it over the bed in his room as a "Relic". Thus was born the venerable name of tableau 75 in Brazil. And, in the wake of the facts, while Aurélien arrived in Rio, Leonardo was informed by the drugged boy who worked at the NGO that its owners had money from France. The result was the fire at the NGO.

Most of the records, apparently preposterous, were obtained through bibliographic citations, internet search engines, and messages from the dead Frenchmen. Ferdinand reread the document search without taking his eyes off the rough reproduction. He digressed about the longevity of the "Heaven's curse" in the light of well-known obituaries, with emphasis on the dead fellow-countrymen of the NGO. Would the researcher be in danger? — Ferdinand worried in the quiet office room inside the castle, overlooking the drawbridge. Grumbling, he had told Father Antoine his fears about the direction of Aurélien's mission, after the fire in Rocinha and the receipt of the celebrated colored sketch.

Chapter 20

AURÉLIEN AND JÚLIA VISITED the specialized police stations. At Narcotics, they were informed that the thugs tattooed with the seven-headed dragon belonged to Pimpão's gang, who took over Dona Marta Hill after Skull's arrest. The thugs are identified by aliases that hide their real names and become their "christening name" in the world of crime and in police records. Crazy Tião, Captain Hook, Jackal, Ace, *Furica*, are some of the best known nicknames.

At Narcotics, they heard that Big Head had been killed in the war between rival groups, and now the general manager for Pimpão's gang was Major Runner. Júlia verified in the paper's files Runner's fame as a bloodthirsty killer. In fact, he'd been arrested many times and, in all cases, he's been released for lack of evidence or witnesses.

As for the tattoo artists, the task was more complex, due to the immense amount of little studios spread throughout the city. They could never have thought there was such a huge demand. In a commercial building downtown, three studios catered to clients of every age and social status. Júlia researched the tattoo artists and their artistic specialties. They all showed their catalogs with several psychedelic types of Satan. None of them admitted they had made the demonic design shown by the couple, but they were willing to produce an identical one "in a jiffy" if they were interested. They said that, looking at the handicraft characteristics, it was a "rookie's work" and had probably been made in a shack in one of the hundreds of *favelas* in Rio.

There were numerous telephone calls and several visits to the Candomblé temples before Júlia and Aurélien concentrated their research in a place in Botafogo. After insisting a lot, they learned that the meetings were held on Thursdays.

The attendant asked her:

"Who has referred the temple?"

Júlia said it had been a friend. She used every argument to convince the woman to allow her and a foreign friend to attend the service that night. The woman did not authorize it and warned her that it would be useless for them to go to Botafogo, because she would not allow them to go in. It was Aurélien's turn to insist, with a heavily accented Portuguese, that she be condescending. When she heard Aurélien's voice, the attendant consulted with her boss and, magically, they were allowed to attend as "visitors" for a fee. She warned them that photos would not be allowed.

At the time of the service, they arrived at the gates of the house, guarded by security guards. Even with the lights out, the manor impressed them with its palatial appearance. A security guard checked if their names were on the visitors' list. Then, Júlia and Aurélien were taken to a small house at the back of the manor, next to a large garage. The ticket window was there. After paying for the consultation and, strangely, having had their IDs photocopied, they were ushered to a steep stairway. They went down the steps and came across an iron door, which, when opened, gave access to the manor's underground.

The security cameras had recorded the images of Júlia and Aurélien entering. Leonardo was immediately informed about the presence of the awaited intruders. Having been warned earlier by the Satanist, he suspected that the foreigner was the envoy of the French government, snooping around and making sure of the authenticity of the Relic. The guy should know where the money for the tableau was, and how the payment would be made. The security guards received precise instructions on how to act, without disturbing the meeting. Aurélien would have to be surrendered and Júlia deliberately entertained by the consultation.

As soon as the visitors entered the underground room where the *gira* took place to the enthralling sound of the drums and *ogans* summoning the deities, they saw the women with their round and colorful skirts already organized in circles, and the men in chemises and turbans clapping hands and humming evocation chants, waiting for the entities to "descend". The flickering light of the torches embellished the room and provided a supernatural connection between the temple and the darkness.

After the emotion of being there, it was not long before they saw the Relic from afar at the back of the central wall. They held their breath when they discovered tableau 75 in perfect conditions, causing a great visual impact on the unwary. They were fascinated by the image, but had to restrain themselves from showing excessive surprise, just the normal wonder of people who had never been to a Candomblé temple. In the room, they learned that each *orisha* represents one of the four elements of nature and, when summoned, they use the mediums as vessels. Thus, they understood why, after the songs and dance steps specific to each entity, they were presented with offerings, such as cigarillos, red roses, *cachaça*. The leader of the drummers started the beats to greet the arrival of the Pombagira, queen of the seven crossroads. *In red and black… Dressed in the night… That the mystery brings… She's a beautiful girl… Hey, spinning, spinning, spinning there…*

It didn't take long for the Pombagira, circling the golden throne, to point to Júlia, calling her for a consultation. She hesitated before taking a step. Due to the originality of the religious ceremony, she was nervous as a bride walking down the aisle.

"Come here, Missus. Come and discover about your life and love."

Júlia was surprised to have been the first and afraid that her love secrets would be revealed in public, when she heard her name being called, as it was, out loud. However, when he saw Júlia heading toward the throne, Aurélien left where he was, in a place reserved for consultants and visitors, and discreetly walked behind the followers. Without raising suspicions, he approached the central wall of the room to see the valuable tapestry up close and photograph it with his cell phone camera. He was very close to the ideal angle when the Pombagira, with her hands on her waist and in a voice only audible to Júlia, began to predict:

"Missus, you know that almost all the *orishas* stayed in this world for a very short time, went through heroic or divine events, were enchanted, and then returned to the *orum*, leaving here on Earth many teachings that shorten the connection between the material and the spiritual. Here, in this house, we uphold and use this connection for all the people who come to us. You, Missus, who came here, have light illuminating your heart. Love is blooming strongly inside you, like the flower that blossoms in the garden of life. It's coming like the moonlight. He has good ancestry. He will purify your soul and your body. You will reach the depths of the feeling of love and the pleasures of hot sex."

Júlia had never imagined that the Pombagira, incorporated in her horse[12], smoking a pipe and speaking in a very low tone of voice, could, in her clairvoyance, give advice to those in love or those in need of love. At that moment, Júlia wanted to hide in a dark corner, behind the column to her left, feeling embarrassed or panicked. She didn't know what to believe. Be it by being immersed in the darkness listening to mind-boggling voices or floating in paradise listening to divine chants. Her heart was beating faster. Her veins were also throbbing, full of curiosity. Not knowing where she had gotten so much courage, she managed to stutter her request:

"Please, can you tell me more?"

---

12 The name given to the mediums in Candomblé (*T.N.*)

"You will suffer with him, not out of disappointment or disillusion. You'll need a lot of perseverance and compassion to appease the pain of your beloved sufferer. He will come from a passionate trail. You'll soon find passion, and you will reciprocate it with love songs, protecting your beloved from the evils of the world."

While Júlia listened to the words of Pombagira, Aurélien photographed the tableau without being noticed. Then he put his slim cell phone into his long sock and walked back toward Júlia. Suddenly, his steps were interrupted and he was taken in another direction. He didn't even have time to think. Everything changed tremendously into something unreal and dangerous. As if by magic, security guards immobilized and gagged him, dragging him out of the underground. Everything was very professional. Nobody noticed the sudden departure of the "French correspondent" in the intense buzz that resonated in the temple. In the small house at the back of the manor, Aurélien was tied to a clunky chair.

The man tattooed with the circle of the devil on his right arm hung up his cell phone and his yelling voice was heard.

"The boss is coming."

He had received instructions from the boss to wait for his arrival. Soon after, Leonardo arrived, nervous, and a black man called Windstorm, who was specialized in open-hand slaps used in Guantánamo, the American naval base on the island of Cuba, started the interrogation. First, they mistreated the mother of the French "fag", tied without a hood. Then, Aurélien was punched many times on his body and face, which reminded him, without longing, of the dirty war training of the time of Saint-Cyr. If was the same feeling of terror.

"Tell me where the money to buy the tableau is!"

"I know nothing about it... I don't know..." stuttered Aurélien with difficulty, his mouth and lips bleeding as he answered to the big boss standing before him, yelling angrily:

"Liar! Where are the euro you brought, you faggot?"

Aurélien was clobbered more. He was kicked. He then decided to answer the first thing that came to mind in order to survive.

"The money is at the consulate."

"What the fuck is this? Is it at the consul's house?"

"No, no. it's at the consulate. I know how to bring it here," said Aurélien in a voice that was increasingly difficult to hear. "I promise…"

Because he spoke too softly or because they had not heard the information or didn't believe what he was saying, the fact is that Windstorm, enraged, at Leonardo's behest, slapped him so hard that made the chair sway and almost knocked him to the floor.

Dizzy, Aurélien started to recite a Buddhist mantra, asking the Daimoku universe for protection. He chanted Nam-Myoho-Renge-Kyo, as he did every morning, and his body began to shake in a frightening convulsion. And, without any notice, suddenly he was completely still. It had been years since he'd had a catalepsy attack. The last one had been under the stress of military maneuvers at Saint-Astier.

The sensation was dire. Total paralysis came over him. At first, he heard a chorus of voices almost like mantra sounds around him. He felt like he was floating or leaving his own body. He could see the people but wasn't able to make any movement.

But Aurélien kept the perfect use of his mental faculties, his intelligence, and perception. Vegetatively, he was alive. However, he had all the symptoms of an apparent state of death: his heart couldn't be heard, he didn't breathe, he didn't move anymore, and he was insensitive to pain. It was rigor mortis in the strictest medical terms. Thanks to his previous experience with the disease, he gradually calmed down in the still state of consciousness, listening to the voices and seeing what was happening around his false death.

Aurélien clearly heard the "soldier" say:

"My bad, the guy is gone, boss."

Since his chair was very close to Leonardo, he heard everything he said to his gang. He heard him rage in a series of words that sounded like cursing. Suddenly, he heard a cell phone ring and Leonardo's nervous voice answered and laughed, saying that he would not "need to blow the castle up" anymore. He heard Big Head pronounce the word "*Agê*" and repeat that he "was going to sell". He presumed a price negotiation was taking place when he heard the word "euro" several times. He heard the name "Pierre" at least twice, preceded by "Grand Master". When Leonardo hung up his cell phone, he saw that the expression on the boss's face had changed. Gone was the apprehension, replaced by a relieved smile. On the other end of the phone call, without Aurélien being able to hear him or even guess who it was, was the Satanist from Avignon, insisting on buying the tableau, and Leonardo asking a fair price to get rid of the Relic.

After a confusion of voices, there was a pause and the boss's order came:

"Take him to Aterro do Flamengo. Stab him twice with a pocket knife, like street robbers do. Only twice."

And in a short time, a black van pulled up to the garage door, near the small house. Aurélien was thrown into the trunk, without a hood or a gag. The van crossed the gates and disappeared into the city streets, carrying the false tourist, falsely killed by false street robbers.

Júlia had never imagined that she would feel so stunned by the revelations whispered by Pombagira, even though there was no illegitimate desire, unreachable aspiration, or objectionable fantasy that deserved to be reproached. She had never thought that she would be perplexed to see Pombagira's feet hit the ground, evoking mother earth, and for her to penetrate people's souls, unveiling a hidden, personal world, which the *gira* only praises with messages of happiness and hope. Something entirely different from the materialistic world that existed outside the manor. All she could do was hear the prophetic voice of Pombagira, aimed at her anguish:

"Dismiss hatred for joy, fear for courage to arise. Increase your faith, so that you can give hope. Make your charity always grow to be able to donate peace. Multiply the fraternity so that you can give love. And when you leave here, be interconnected with the light where the stars shine, even though they are far from each other. Dark clouds are coming, Missus, but it's in this sky that you'll find the bright star that came from far, far away, from another planet, and arrived here, landed on solid ground to bring light to your blue eyes and your heart. Soon you'll know what it's like to feel true love that will make you very happy."

And the Pombagira said no more. She turned her face away and pointed her finger to the next consultant, who hurried to get closer.

When she returned to her place, Júlia didn't find Aurélien. A security guard came, very politely, to tell her that he had been called urgently by the French consulate and that she shouldn't wait for him. Júlia thought the message was weird and was very worried about his disappearance.

She was politely led to the exit door. As she crossed the high fence and the manor's imposing iron gates, she immediately called his cell phone. But it was out of the coverage area. She got even more worried.

Already on the street, she called the French consul. In that Gallic mood, the man said it had been days since he'd last heard from Aurélien. He complained about the inopportune night call and the fact that the researcher had not presented the documents of the listing of the dead Frenchmen possessions, as he had promised to do urgently. He ended the call by hinting that she should solve her sentimental quarrels out of the consulate.

Júlia then called the prosecutor, who also didn't know where the archer could be. He was surprised that Aurélien wasn't in her company, since they had gone to the temple together. She began to experience visual discomfort and a slight headache, signs of tiredness and that she had recently abused reading without her glasses. It was no longer Pombagira's hopeful words that swirled in her aching head, but the cry of her inner voice: *Where is Aurélien Kléber? What should she do now?*, Júlia asked herself in the silence of the night that had silenced the voices of the city, without drowning out her cry of despair for the "little Frenchman".

Chapter 21

EVERYTHING CONTRIBUTED FOR LISA to have a sleepless night punctuated by nightmares after her visit to Leonardo's father's manor. She was very upset, as she told him when they arrived at her apartment in Lagoa. It was not just the luxuriant tour, the valuable bracelet given to her in the library, or the fact that she participated in the *gira* and heard the *eshu*'s disturbing prophecies; she was very shaken by the emanations that came from the underground of the devil's temple. She was rattled by dark thoughts and doubts about what would happen after that unforgettable day.

She thought the Relic was splendid in its symbolism and terrifying force. But she feared the curse, if the prediction of Grand Master Molay, who died at the stake, was right. She recognized that the demonic presence in the manor had brought Leonardo wealth and power in the culmination of his vindictive ambitions. However, she believed that the famous scene carried an inexorable damnation for straying from the mother tapestry at Angers. Which made sense, even though she was unaware that the influential Zalsupin family, who made a fortune in Krakow, had been wiped out by the Nazis, and all those who'd had temporary possession of "rug 75" had died mysteriously. Intuitively, she guessed that only when the devil was trapped in the shackles of the Apocalypse tapestry would the evil effects of the Relic cease.

In truth, Lisa feared the worst the next day of the visit, as if she had predicted an apocalyptic warning, after seeing what she'd seen and hearing what she'd heard in the depths of the manor. She feared the "obsessors of *ex-votos*", which she suspected were connected to the avenged deaths. She feared the truth on the only black marble plaque, without initials but with the fateful day of the accident in Itaipava. In addition to that, on the night of the visit to the manor, she had a terrible nightmare with a ghost with a blind eye, chasing Leonardo and brandishing the scythe of death at him. She was afraid of the final confrontation between the warrior of the bad dream and the man with whom she had fallen in love and made her happy in the flowered sheets and in her day-to-day life.

Lisa had decided not to live in Botafogo. Leonardo insistently tried to convince her otherwise, in a troubled period when he was very involved in the complex financial negotiations of the biggest cocaine shipment of all times and had agreed to receive a French Satanist obsessed with seeing the Relic. Leo had to stay in Rio. After all, the person who accompanied Lucca to New York to help him enroll in an American university was Lisa, who was happy as a clam to travel abroad.

As much as Lisa called regularly, it was Leo's son who kept him informed about what was going on. It was Lucca who told him of Lisa's dedication the week they were in Manhattan together and of the banker's effective collaboration, whom he described as a "character", a widower with a huge ruby ring on his middle finger. It was the banker who told the bank's HR staff to help him and follow-up the enrollment process at the universities the bank sponsored. He had already contacted them before Lisa and Lucca arrived in New York. As far as Lucca knew, Lisa was by herself to buy the latest in makeup and beauty products just one morning and one afternoon.

"Poor thing, Dad," Lucca felt sorry for her. He told his father about the conference calls and the joyful celebration the three of them had had at the Four Seasons. "It was awesome, Dad!" concluded the boy, thrilled, on his way to the campus of a renowned university that had accepted him as a "visiting student" until the process of registration was finalized. At the farewell dinner, Lisa was dressed in a new, low-cut dress, a detail Lucca forgot to mention to his father, as well as the question she asked the banker during dessert: what year, day, time, and place he was born.

As soon as Lisa returned from the trip, Leonardo told her that, during her absence, he had met the "religious Frenchman" and had been impressed with the cult. In turn, the astrologer told him that Lucca was very happy on the university campus in Boston. It was then, after a night of a lot of sex, that he signed some forms in English, brought from the trip. She said they were a requirement from the Immigration Service to regularize his son's stay in the United States. Leonardo didn't even think about asking the professor to examine the paperwork, printed in small, medicine-leaflet-like letters. He trusted his wife blindly. It was a family matter. It concerned only him, her, and Lucca, and no one else.

*

"*Au secours ... Julie ...*" said Aurélien, after having made a great effort with his arm and hand to turn the fully charged cell phone on.

Júlia heard the distant, whispered voice, as if it came from a tomb, but with an unmistakable French accent:

"*Julie...*'

She immediately recognized Aurélien Kléber 's voice.

"Oh, God! Where are you?" asked Júlia nervously on the phone, and heard an even weaker whisper:

"Aterro..."

"Where in Aterro?" asked Júlia, her voice getting more apprehensive and distressed when she found out where he was calling from.

"In front… *Pain Sucre*… Statue…" and his voice completely disappeared on the phone, which proved not to be damaged.

*

Júlia soon arrived at the deserted place and found Aurélien's body, thrown behind the lookout low wall, in the shadow of the statue of Dom Henrique, erected on the site, and, as he had correctly indicated, in front of the Sugarloaf. She couldn't help covering her mouth with her five fingers, in a gesture of astonishment and horror at his deplorable physical condition, with his head swollen and his clothes soaked in blood.

She called the prosecutor on her cell phone, and he recommended a trusted clinic that provided services for the Federal Program for Assistance to Victims and Witnesses Under Threat. When they arrived, Aurélien's friend had already arranged for emergency care.

In the silent waiting room, the prosecutor and Júlia talked a lot about the latest events. She reported in detail the visit to the temple and the disappearance of the researcher during the *gira*. They would not report the incident of the "tourist victimized by street robbers" at the police station, nor publish any news in the newspaper without first knowing Aurélien's physical condition; they would wait to decide together what to do. Finally, the doctor came to reassure them, saying that the surgical procedure had been very successful.

"He's fine. He was very lucky to have narcolepsy; it's saved him from worse. He must have suffered a violent stress that triggered the paralysis. The left side of the face was badly injured."

After the effects of the anesthesia had passed, the doctor allowed them to enter the room and gave them the final clinical information:

"Fortunately, the two stab wounds were not deep. Only the hemorrhage in the posterior retinal artery is severe."

"What were the consequences, doctor? Can you explain

it, please?" asked Júlia, not being an expert on the subject and concerned about the extent of the injuries.

"Unfortunately, he has lost the sight on his left eye."

When she heard that he had not recovered his left sight, small tears slid behind Júlia's glasses. As much as she wiped her face with the palm of her hand and pretended to smile, as soon as she entered the room Aurélien realized that the crying woman had already been informed of his irreversible eye injury.

"Tintin, Tintin, it wasn't this time that they caught me. For a thousand thunders, don't cry," mumbled Aurélien with some difficulty, but very relaxed, perhaps because he felt revived for the second time. He fixed his gaze on Júlia and found that without her red-rimmed glasses, the journalist's watery blue eyes were even more beautiful than usual.

"God, what did they do to my Captain Haddock? You look like an eggplant," replied Júlia, keeping her friend's playful mood when she saw his face completely purple due to the bruises, except for the white patch made of adhesive tape protecting his left eye. She also saw the stitches on the corner of his mouth. There were gauzes around his chest, covering the two stab wounds. She was impressed by how well he took the "clobbering", as her mother used to say.

"Just you wait. I'll be good as new tomorrow. Ready for the Crusade against the heretics," said Aurélien softly, struggling to speak, although the jokes seemed to alleviate the headache and scare.

"Since you want to speak, talk slowly and tell us everything that's happened," pressed the prosecutor, standing with his arms crossed.

Authorized by the doctors to speak, even though his jaw and neck still hurt, he told them slowly, without laughing, how he'd saved the cell phone with the photos, how he was beaten up, and summed up the mysterious phone call received by the big boss when he was tied up and paralyzed on the chair. Aurélien pointed to his phone and asked to see if the photos had survived the catastrophe. Júlia opened the lid and confirmed that they were perfect. There was no longer any doubt that the Relic existed and the Seven-Headed Beast had its days numbered until it would be definitively locked up in the majestic Chateau d'Angers.

They discussed extensively what to do. The promoter's suggestion to stage "the disappearance of the tourist stabbed by street robbers" prevailed. Hiding the "corpse" was the best solution to gain time and think of a way to recover the damn tableau "the hard way". The prosecutor, based on current experiences, confirmed that the thugs would do anything to kill Aurélien and that they had a vast network of informants in public hospitals and hotels to locate him. It would also be impossible for him to return home, which was probably being watched by now. They all worried about where to hide the resurrected man.

The main thing was to make the thugs believe that the Frenchman was gone. Make them think that he'd fallen into the ocean and was dragged to the bottom of the Guanabara Bay, in the arms of Iemanjá. They would keep quiet. He would not inform the police, nor would Júlia inform the newspaper, to leave the thugs inactive and perplexed by Aurélien's simulated stabbing and death. Thus, they would have enough time to provide a counteroffensive to rescue the valuable French historical heritage. That's when Júlia snapped her fingers and, in a childish way, screamed:

"I got it! I know a place. Leave it up to me, it's all gonna work out."

"Where?" both men asked almost simultaneously.

"My parent's house in Mauá. Nobody will find our eggplant hidden there. He will be completely out of the thug's radar and will be able to recover as long as he likes on the mountains. Tell me, is there anything that would be better for him?"

"Great idea," the prosecutor congratulated her. "It's decided."

"Mauá?" asked Aurélien, still unhappy that his thick eyebrows and bizarre goatee had been shaved.

Now Júlia only had to convince Mrs. Maria Tereza, her beloved mother, to host the "little Frenchman".

"After all, wasn't she the one who 'melted' the Walloon King's heart in the past and, just before, had given the decisive "push" to find her king? So? Her European nobleman didn't need to be so hurt, though — regretted Júlia to herself.

*

No police report. No news. No trace.

Leonardo took the third aspirin of the day. He didn't like the grim silence. He could deal with cell phones, screams, numbers, but the void unsettled him. The mystery of the dead man's silence disturbed his cold mathematical reasoning.

"Are you sure you left the dead son of a bitch at Aterro?"

Major Runner and all the tough guys confirmed that the job had been "easy", that "the guy was dead as a doornail", and that he hadn't even felt the two stabs they gave him.

That void with no dead body or trace was unbearable to Big Head. He sent his henchmen to check the Coroner's Office. See if there was a police report at police stations about the ordinary fact of a tourist being mugged by street robbers, preferably with the Frenchman's physical description He put his network of informants and "undercover men" in public hospitals to work, who were paid to tell him who were the people shot or dying who entered the emergency room and were in danger of falling into the hands of corrupt police officers. He read and reread all the newspapers, both of small and large circulation. The fact that there was not a single line about the disappearance was weird. Through the newspaper's newsroom, they learned that the reporter who requested the *gira* had traveled to Brasília to cover a case of misappropriation of funds, coincidentally in the health care area, where he sold overpriced ambulances.

Leonardo had a good idea and handed over the photocopy of the Frenchman's passport, obtained when he visited the manor, to the law firm to check the missing person's record from the Ministry of Justice, responsible for controlling foreigners' entry in the country. Thanks to the bribes he handed out, he was soon informed that the "dead man" had never been a journalist, much less from a famous magazine like *Paris Match*. But he could be a cultural attaché with the French government or simply a tourist with a known address on vacation in Brazil. It was not the first time that the intruder came to Rio for a tour. Or, in the worst case, he could be an agent of the *Gendarmerie* — a French corporation equivalent to BOPE[13] — on a secret mission. To be on the safe side, Leo ordered his men to look through the dead man's apartment, hoping to find some elucidative document. As a precaution, he ordered the entrance to the building to be guarded day and night.

Leonardo thought quickly. If he was a bureaucrat or a tourist, the deceased would be harmless, but if he was an agent on a secret mission, the ghost would become a dangerous element. He hated to know that the Frenchman's disappearance could cause retaliation. To protect himself from possible external forces, he reinforced the surveillance and electronic security network of motion detectors in the Devil's Castle. *Even dead, that shitty Frenchman is giving us trouble,* muttered Leonardo to himself, omitting from Lisa the incident with the "dead as a doornail" — as the group led by Major Runner had referred to him — man in Aterro.

13 Batalhão de Operações Policiais Especiais/Special Police Operations Batallion: the police tactical unit of the Military Police of Rio de Janeiro State (*PMERJ*) in Brazil (*T.N.*)

*

For old Baldo, nothing better could have happened in all those well-lived years in Mauá than the arrival of the brave Aurélien Kléber. He arrived at the inn at night, in a medium-sized, rented black vehicle, so as not to attract the attention of the neighbors. He had bravely faced the shaky ride on the bumpy road, which gave no respite to his aching body. And even making faces because of neck and lower back pain, his congeniality won everyone over. Júlia's mother, at first, wanted to be ceremonious in her demonstrations of affection. But she soon surrendered to the evidence of the facts and her daughter's happiness on the happy face of only smiles and eyes for the Frenchman from Paris. She let the flames of the kitchen's wood stove, from where tasty delicacies would come out for the very special guest at the inn, burn.

The two foreigners, after dinner near the lit fireplace, exchanged stories about Brussels and a few more about Strasbourg, laughed at the European past, and nostalgically reminded themselves that life is full of matches and mismatches. On her mother's chaise, Júlia smiled, listening to everything, like the child who'd read Tintin's adventures for the first time.

Aurélien told Baldo that he considered losing his left vision a personal tragedy. The worst thing was that, after the nurses removed the patch, no one realized that he could see with just one eye. In appearance, his eyeballs were identical. It could have taken forever to absorb this irreparable loss, had it not been, however, for something transcendental that had happened, making his recovery surpass the most optimistic ophthalmic diagnosis in the world. He praised the incredible healing power of love. That was when he told Baldo, moved, about his passion for Júlia, since the first day he saw her interviewing the old man at Rocinha. It couldn't be different when you felt your heart beat faster.

Aurélien confessed that he had used all his cunning at the clinic. He took advantage of the fact that they were alone in the room and that Júlia approached him to see the wounds on his face up close to seduce her and declare himself. That's what he told Júlia's father. Nothing more than that. He didn't tell him that she was very close to the eye patch and his violet face with shaved eyebrows and goatee. His right eye saw the gleam of the reporter's blue eyes, her mouth and her sexy face. He took advantage of that magical moment so that his unique look, full of desires and promises, penetrated Júlia's empty heart. He saw her calmly close her restless eyes, hold her breath, and slowly let "the depths of the feeling of love and the pleasures of hot sex" take over her thoughts, as Pombagira had predicted would happen. Of course, he omitted from Júlia's father the details of how their first kiss was, very soft, on the lips, and the others, more lingering kisses. When he later recovered from his mouth injuries and couldn't stop the garden of love from blossoming, certainly not the size of the Mantiqueira Mountains or Mont Blanc, but of his inner world at peace with himself, they had no way to deny it: they were in love, by the force of destiny, and united by the adventure of living.

At the famous inn, it's easy to understand why, with so much care from the owners, so many delicacies served at the table, and so much love received from a passionate woman, Aurélien recovered so quickly from his injuries and resigned himself to the permanent loss of his left eye. Holding hands with Júlia, he visited the Cachoeiras da Saudade Park, with three miles of trails going through more than twelve waterfalls, and saw the famous Silver Waterfall, where they kissed a lot and where plans of complicity sprang up listening to the birds chirping on the green trees.

For the first time, Júlia asked for a short leave from the newspaper to do some medical check-ups and take a few days of vacation to which she was entitled. She had never imagined the long nights of love in Mauá, let alone at the Blue Angel Inn.

"Love is a very beautiful mystery when differences unite people," repeated Júlia in the kitchen to her happy mother, wearing an apron peppered with béarnaise sauce. Maria Tereza had saved the best room for the two lovers and began to speak the French from recipes again. Thus, in the peacefulness of the orchards, the waterfalls of crystal clear waters surrounded by forest and araucaria woods, Júlia wrote her love story. And the Gallic king, listening in silence to the whispers of the wind and the rippling waves of Rio Preto, found the well-deserved mountain rest and the sweetness of love. He saw for the first time the hummingbirds that suck nectar from the flowers to survive the challenges of daily life and the bright sun of a tropical country.

Now Aurélien knew perfectly well why he liked being in Brazil so much, without, however, forgetting the violence of Rio, a city that decides who should survive or die.

Chapter 22

AURÉLIEN HAD TOLD THE CURATOR at Quai d'Orsay, and repeated to Júlia when they met in Urca: he rarely went out without his laptop. Fortunately, however, as an exception to the rule, he had left his portable computer at the prosecutor's house before going to the religious ceremony. Thus, he was able to use the electronic carrier pigeon, transmitting from Mauá the small report that the curator read at the chateau.

The researcher summed up the episode of the discovery of tableau 75, without detailing the violence he had suffered in the manor. Aurélien focused on the two cell phone photos of the missing tapestry image that no one had ever seen in French museography. Since he didn't want to confuse curator Ferdinand, he didn't use the word *Candomblé* in his message. He told him of his concern about what the big boss had said to an unknown person, who must have been important, judging by the strange dialogue. He reproduced the names heard from the mouth of the one who had ordered him to be abducted and beaten, and repeated "Grand Master Pierre", "Angers", "chateau", "euro". He didn't say anything about the loss of his left eye, because the mental acceptance of his misfortune bothered him much more than the pain in his optic nerve, nor did he tell about his miraculous physical recovery in Mauá.

Owing an answer to Aurélien in Brazil, who had asked for urgent instructions, curator Ferdinand de Sally and Father Antoine Duvert had a meeting with the high authorities of the Ministry of Culture and Interior, with the presence of the commander of the Directorate-General for External Security, the famous DGSE. At the meeting behind closed doors in Paris, and under pressure from the General Curators' Association, special agents were authorized to come to Rio immediately with the mission of bringing tableau 75 back to Angers, which, for all legal purposes, had been stolen from the French NGO. Quai d'Orsay diplomatically called Itamaraty, which in turn informed the Ministry of Justice in Brazil. It was the way they found to keep them informed, avoiding future problems in case there were any mishaps in the recovery of a stolen jewel of the French historical heritage. They anticipated, on Brazilian soil, the secular outcome of the terrible fight of good against evil, glorified in the superb scenes of the Apocalypse tapestry.

While waiting for the curator's response, Aurélien managed to communicate with his mother. She broke the news bluntly: "He's going to leave us soon". Sighing, his mother told him that his father was very ill. He had acute lymphoid leukemia, the symptoms of which he hid until he could no longer conceal them. Desperate, she tried to put him in a hospital in Strasbourg. Sobbing, she confessed that Colonel François would rather spend his last few days at home. After an awkward silence, Aurélien justified the reasons for not being able to leave Brazil. He promised to visit them as soon as he arrived in Paris and to introduce his Brazilian bride.

When he hung up the phone, the mosaic of shattered memories was quickly reconstructed, piece by piece. From the Alsatian shadows, the pathetic image of his father's goodbye at the train station emerged. He hadn't had the courage to confess in the farewell that he was moving permanently. A military man of high rank and position couldn't reveal his incurable disease to his closest friends, and took upon himself the duty of silence, so as to not upset his family. He missed his parents, and went to take a look at the photos in the laptop. All of a sudden, the bedroom in the inn was taken by the mild summer in Trouville, with his parents on vacation, happy in their traveling lives.

*

Even with the blistering heat of that late afternoon, Lisa didn't bypass the warm bath with scented salts. She liked to wait for Leonardo with velvety and fragrant skin. When she got out of the bath, she took time to take care of her peach skin with imported products bought at exorbitant prices. It was her only big consumerist luxury. Around the bathtub, she collected eye-catching pots with striking labels and golden sayings with rejuvenating promises. In those moments, she used to linger in front of the mirror and still feel young from head to toe. She had no reason to doubt it, since she looked younger than she was and had less wrinkles than the years could have etched. She liked to be noticed, even if it was just for Leonardo to wrap his arms around her from behind, kiss the back of her neck and whisper in her ears: "You look hot, baby".

"Is the dream over?" Lisa asked to herself, curious, as she got out of the bathroom. Whose dream? Leonardo's dream that she lived in the manor in Botafogo, or hers, to stay in Lagoa? To answer it, she broke a promise she had made to herself that she wouldn't read her natal chart anymore. She felt a shiver of fear when she consulted the ephemerides and saw Uranus dangerously prowling the complementary maps, forming concerning aspects with her personal planets, and creating instability in her marriage. She wasn't surprised to see someone entering her love life. She tried to find out more from the stars regarding this new love, but she got no clue. Anything could happen with the sky flashing under Uranus' rule — Lisa thought, sitting at the head of the big table in the room, used to oracles and dreams, which take some time to become reality. She was taken by the memories of her trip to New York.

*

After the meeting behind closed doors in Paris, the director of the Directorate-General for External Security (DGSE) received the report 0655-72 from the Interior Minister's office. It contained a brief history of the measures underway to recover the disappeared tableau 75 in Brazil, highlighting the violent way in which information had been obtained in Rio de Janeiro, in a torture session led by criminals. It was even suspected that they were the murderers of the French owners of the humanitarian aid NGO in Rocinha. The statement was clear and said that the value of the information could not yet be judged, although it acknowledged that the simple reference to Grand Master Pierre, correlated with the city of Angers, should be investigated.

The director-general and his trained men from the Action Division, used to the most unpredictable coincidences, considered that the information really deserved credit and did not seem so surprising, since the first name mentioned was that of a head of a powerful religious sect, and so, in fact, there could really be a threat to the city of Angers and, more precisely, to something that was inside the castle. Everything was possible in matters of religious violence, because attacks and destruction of mosques and churches had recently occurred. Besides, Satanists were dangerous.

Since the call received at the manor in Botafogo had been made from a cell phone, the research focused on intercepting the France-Brazil communications network via mobile telephony. Frenchelon's "big ears" tracking system in the Périgord was used, and the Domme's secret military base took action. It was one of the largest listening centers in the world, with its immense parabolic towers, spying on international communications, captured by satellite, day and night.

The DGSE director promptly sent a memo to the head of the Anti-Terrorism Department (DAT). The man, an experienced colonel, had no doubt in classifying the call from Grand Master Pierre Flaubert as a threat to the impregnable castle and the city of Angers. Without wasting time, he called curator Ferdinand de Sailly, who, immediately upon hearing the department's identification, was annoyed and snorted grumpily when they asked for a copy of the castle's floor plan, the security system, and a list of its employees.

The head of the DAT hadn't anticipated anything to the curator about something suspicious in Angers. He told him it was just a routine operation. He also didn't reveal his conviction: anything could be expected from the dreaded Devil's Order sect, if they were involved, considering the history of violent actions attributed to them, without having been able to prove the authorial participation of Grand Master Pierre Flaubert and his group of fanatics.

Deep inside, the colonel liked the terrorist news. This extraterritorial case was the golden opportunity he needed to demonstrate the real value of his department and justify the secret funds they received. The successful dismantling of the Basque cells no longer excited French public opinion or the Minister of the Interior. The threat to France's honor had come at a good time, demanding a major mobilization of the national security force, as it jeopardized the preservation of a great historical and cultural heritage of humanity situated in Angers. The Colonel breathed contentedly at the news.

Chapter 23

FINALLY, "J DAY", AS THE FRENCH call the day when a combat operation should begin, arrived for Júlia and Aurélien.

At the inn, before traveling, Júlia saw on the internet the news that "the dangerous criminal Skull and two of his partners had escaped at dawn from the federal prison through a 230 feet long tunnel". Nothing out of the ordinary. Every month prisoners escaped from penitentiaries, usually on holidays.

When she arrived in Rio, Júlia had a meeting with the newspaper's editor-in-chief, who was enthusiastic about discovering the tapestry, without her revealing where she had found it. He promised her the front page, betting all his chips on the international repercussion of the news.

Aurélien, in turn, met with the French consul and the two French agents of the feared National *Gendarmerie* Intervention Group (GIGN, in French), who had come from Paris. They had mapped the place, without entering the temple, and already had a plan of action, without having to resort to the local police, as the Ministry of the Interior had forbidden the involvement of Brazilian police in the rescue of the tapestry. They were glad because they had discovered a weakness in the enemy's manor, making the secret paramilitary operation entirely feasible.

The consul confidentially complained to Aurélien about the delay in delivering the list of the NGO's assets, which had been entrusted to him, as he urgently needed to dispatch it to France, because the "higher authorities" needed the document to collect the receipts. Aurélien tried to find out what these "receipts" were, but the consul evaded the question and insisted on receiving the list.

"It has to be the French bureaucracy," huffed Aurélien, annoyed with the demand.

*

In the past few months, Leonardo had been receiving death threats on his cell phone from Skull, in the federal prison: "I'll get you, you shit. You've always been just a messenger". The former boss wouldn't give up on reclaiming his cocaine empire, much more prosperous now than before.

It was Pimpão who first informed him of Skull's escape. To calm down his uncontrollable nervousness, Leonardo fired orders over the three cell phones and talked to Major Runner several times. They both knew they would suffer a violent retaliation, since the former boss had never forgiven the betrayal of his two right-hand men. At dawn, Skull was in Rio de Janeiro and, with the support of Comando Vermelho, wasted no time. He immediately took over Dona Marta Hill. Soon, his thick voice echoed in the shadows of the slum: "I want you to break them, Zé. Fill the ditch with these idiots". The residents were reliving the horror movie. The radio and TV stations reported non-stop the shootings and killings in the war for the control of the *favela*. The police decided to watch the confrontation from afar, without interfering. They would then face the group that won or simply cross their arms.

At the end of one week of war, the Major complained:

"They attacked us badly, Big Head."

"Did you give them all the weapons Pimpão bought? Didn't it work?" asked Leonardo desperately.

"Fuck! Pimpão fled to São Paulo and, when the boys saw they were going to lose, they joined them. The sons-of-a-bitch have already taken the main accesses to the *favela* and, in Rocinha, the guys joined the ADA. Fuck, I'm alone!"

"Get out while you can, Runner."

"The sons of bitches are saying that Skull will leave the *favela* alone to kill you at the manor. Be careful, man!"

"Let him come! We'll set a trap for him here. You need to come."

Leonardo believed that, in the manor, he would win the battle. He imagined the infrared light cameras controlling everything and locating the enemy in the shadows, and the security guards would exterminate him, without him having set foot inside the manor. There was no need to kill the former big boss, just wound him and bring him by the neck to have Major sever his head with a saber blow in the underground.

"A ceremony!" exclaimed Leonardo, imagining the scene of the former big boss' head as an offering to the Relic's devil.

But Leonardo, though he knew that drug addicts will do anything to satisfy their addiction, they would steal, kill, betray, everything to get their hands on an eight ball, had misjudged the fascination that bribery exerts on human beings. He had no idea that Skull had a man inside the manor who gave him information about the *gira* in the "temple" and about his personal life, including how to reach the Professor. Furthermore, fear left Big Head blind, to the point that he didn't realize that the invasions were only successful on the *favelas* because they were carefully planned well in advance, in Skull's fashion, who'd learned since he was a child that no one becomes king if the "honey" (blood) and the drugs don't flow freely in the slums.

Big Head had not anticipated the surprises that his former boss had prepared for him with vengeful diligence. He only became aware of it when, suddenly, the lights of the manor went out. The images on the screens that controlled all the cameras disappeared simultaneously, and the house, inside and out, was in total darkness. Thus, security guards were unable to fire even a shot to prevent the invaders from entering the manor.

In effect, the infiltrated element carried out the sabotage with chronometric precision. He deactivated the circuit breakers of the house's power distribution switchboard at the right time, causing the blackout. This allowed Skull, with the help of his general manager, to jump over the gate, enter the manor, and then hide near the main door of the house. Little by little, in the darkness, he beheaded, with a sharp knife, one by one, the security guards who were making the rounds outside the fortress, with his new general manager standing outside to watch the entrance of the mansion.

His partner was already waiting for him where they had agreed to meet to lead him inside the house to the library. And, once there, Skull just had to pull the big lever on the wall for the front of the fireplace to move inwards and the rocky passage that would take them underground appear. They went cautiously down the steps. Everything had been carefully planned at the federal prison.

Leonardo had barely recovered from the sudden lack of energy when he heard the sound of the fireplace mechanism being activated. Without the cameras, without the sensors, and with the secret access door to the underground invaded, it was up to Big Head to, nervously, wait to do the honors to the raucous arrival of his greatest enemy in the catacombs, lit by long torches. He had never thought that this diabolical place would be the one of the final settlement, dominated by hate.

The two house security guards and Major Runner fired their first shots in the manor's underground. They received the answer as soon as the positions of the enemy camps were defined behind the columns. Fortunately, the location of the shooting was restricted to that area of the mansion, without the uncontrollable evil effects of the Relic wanting to destroy the decoration of the house and its valuable art objects, and, above all, the precious collection of rare books, kept intact in the library.

A few bullets bounced off the temple walls. The empty cartridges piled on the floor behind the columns. Gradually, the shots became more intermittent. The bullets made less sound. Suddenly, there was a brief silence and an unmistakable, arrogant voice echoed in the room:

"Your time has come, Judas, to pay for what you've stolen from me," said the figure distorted by the shadows on the floor behind the first column at the entrance to the room, near the pentagram.

"You got out of prison to die here. I'll take care of you," said Big Head, hiding behind another column near the central wall. "I'm gonna bury you in my father's house."

"You're alone and fucked. You're gonna die like a daddy's boy," said Skull, letting out a loud laugh.

"Come on, show your face," said Leonardo, forging ahead, out of his mind, toward his rival and holding the pistol with a shaking hand.

"I'm gonna kill you," said the thug, laughing.

Big Head winked at Runner, who didn't even have time to obey the order to shoot, because when he came out from behind the column, he was shot in the middle of his forehead with a bullet from Skull's Sig-Sauer. Major Runner fell at Leonardo's feet, who nervously pulled the pistol's trigger. The bullet got nowhere near his rival's bearded face, who had been aware for a long time of the ineptitude of the man who was good at giving accounting tips and make small talk, but sucked when it came to handling firearms.

The former big boss laughed when he hit the first shot in Big Head's left ankle, who reacted with two random shots, which were lodged in the ceiling. The host started to cry out in pain. The new king laughed again. He didn't even have to step forward to fire the second straight shot into Leonardo's right ankle. Leonardo fell, kneeling in excruciating pain, and then hitting the floor in front of his rival, who had a sadistic smile on his lips.

Suddenly, there was a blast behind the throne, which soon disintegrated into small, shiny golden pieces on the floor. The two skulls rotated until they stopped facing down, announcing the invasion of the French agents. Thanks to the well-rewarded doorman of the building next door, they learned of the manor owner's disagreement with the condo over the building's thin underground walls. This made the GIGN rescue operation possible, the only anti-terrorist group that prides itself on the precision of its members with weapons, who are trained to incapacitate and injure, not to kill.

They heard cracking near the floor. There were stunning flashes. Toxic smoke from tear gas grenades covered almost the entire underground, making their eyes sting and their throats choke. Everyone who was fighting underground began to cough. Nobody could see. Much less shoot toward the shadows that moved over what was left of the throne. Everyone was caught off guard, coughing a lot. They could no longer stand without holding on to the columns. Skull initially thought they were Big Head's reinforcements to reverse the adverse situation, but then realized that they were extraterrestrials engaged in a private war.

Aurélien and Júlia waited for the gas's paralyzing effect to take action with their protective masks. The two GIGN agents fired a few warning shots, giving them total cover. The couple, bordering the well-known walls, arrived at the central space where the Relic beamed. Within minutes, they took the rug down and rolled it up. No further warning shots were fired, only gas grenades to ensure the four invaders escaped through the hole that had been blown in the wall.

Before everyone in the underground recovered from the scare, and slowly started to see, a squeaky car tire was heard coming from the garage of the building next door. With his eyes still red, but breathing better, Skull headed to the center of the room, where the smoke was dissolving into a thin veil, already harmless. He took a few more steps and saw Big Head, covered in blood, crawling through the floor, still holding a gun. He laughed at his former friend's pathetic figure, trying to flee from death. He approached his agonizing enemy, gritting his teeth:

"The time has come, buddy. Your daddy is already waiting for you in hell."

Leonardo agonized and breathed hard on the foundations of his parents' home, plagued by tragedy. He could no longer move his legs. He thought of the sister he never sought; his wife dead on the cliff; his son, far from his eyes and the curse; and in the crazy passion he felt for Lisa. Everything became more and more distant after Uranus set up a terrible conspiracy to unleash the wrath of the skies and destroy him. It was too late for regrets and dreams. In a last effort with his right arm, holding the pistol in his hand with only one bullet in the needle, he managed to raise the barrel to his temple and shoot, as his father did before losing his manor and his life.

Skull gave one last laugh and complained:

"The messenger died like a pussy."

Before leaving, the new boss of Dona Marta Hill killed the wounded and ordered his partner to throw a torch at the empty central wall. The kerosene spread quickly and the flames began to burn, approaching Leonardo's blood-soaked legs and shoes. Skull was delighted with the sight of the scene before climbing, with a torch in his hand, the steps of the stone staircase that led to the imposing library. Angrily, he looked around and asked:

"What are all this fucking books for?"

He didn't even wait for his partner's answer. With the torch in hand, he put the whole house on fire. The flames took over carpets, books and antique wooden furniture.

To better enjoy his revenge, the new owner of the slum

stayed for a long time on the other side of the street, watching the voracity of the fire consuming the manor. He saw a desperate figure, running away in a taxi at full speed, while the first onlookers huddled on the street before the spectacle of fiery flames and black clouds smoking under the water from the first hoses of the prompt firefighters.

Skull could never imagine that Leonardo's death scene resembled that of tableau 68 of the Apocalypse tapestry. In the catalogued image of this painting that disappeared in the middle of the 20th century, mysteriously stolen, the condemned prostitute stood out, surrounded by four animals that watched her burn in flames *ad aeternum...*

*

While the manor went up in flames, a black van with three armed men entered the garage of a building downtown. The security guards were already used to the arrival of the well-known vehicle at that time of night. The vehicle entrance was cleared, as usual, without any problem.

At the consulting office, everyone was waiting for the bags to arrive. The security guard recognized the three light knocks on the door and opened it. He was shot between the eyes by a gun with a silencer. With no explanation, two thugs came in shooting and killed the three employees. It sounded like popcorn in a pan. The third thug went straight into the meeting room and surrendered the professor, who got livid when he saw the pistol pointed at his head.

"We're here with Fatsy," one of Skull's managers warned on the phone. There was a pause. "All right, boss."

The new owner of Dona Marta Hill arrived at the office without having to identify himself at the door. He entered the meeting room, where the professor was held hostage, seated in the president's chair, at gunpoint. When he signed, the infamous Windstorm slapped the host for the first time.

It was a warning that, in the absence of collaboration, he would be rewarded with other gestures of kindnesses.

"Get into the corpse's private accounts right now, you asshole."

That's how the professor was informed of his boss' death.

"Are you gonna type or do you want more, you faggot?" shouted Windstorm.

The professor immediately opened online Leonardo's account in New York, which was kept confidential. A surprising balance of $ 6.66 appeared on the screen. Someone had withdrawn from Leonardo's private account and left the enigmatic figure. He opened the secret accounts in Liechtenstein and tax havens. They all had been wiped out and were blocked. The professor was indignant with the balance of the American bank and the other withdrawals, and swore that it hadn't been him who had withdrawn the sums from the accounts.

"Who the fuck did it, then?" asked Skull, shouting. "Who knew the passwords?" he asked, now without the triumphant smile he had when he arrived at the luxurious office.

"Only Leonardo and I. No one else."

"Where's the money?" Skull complained, looking furiously at him.

"I swear, I don't know. I don't understand what's going on."

Another slap, weaker, so he wouldn't pass out.

"I swear. Trust me," repeated the consultant, in tears.

The cries of pain, the convulsive crying, and the piss in the pants were quite convincing. The fat man wasn't lying. The king forced him to check the transactions of the day regarding the European secret accounts on the screen. It was proven that the withdrawals from European bank accounts occurred before Leonardo died like barbecue, with the exception of the American account, in which the last transaction happened minutes after the fire. Skull was not happy.

"Who withdrew all the money from the American account, then?"

There were more cries of pain until the professor was able to mumble:

"I swear, I don't know. It must have been the account manager. Someone warned him that the account holder was dead."

"What about the $ 6.66? Did Leonardo give the password to anyone?"

"No, he didn't trust anyone," answered the professor. "Not even his stupid son or the crazy astrologer, who was his partner. They were fighting. She didn't want to live in the manor."

"What the fuck do you suggest?" asked the boss, resuming his bloodthirsty smile and clenching his fists as a sign of nervousness.

"There's nothing I can do right now, but I can help you to get the money back."

The king did not believe in the good faith of the fat man, forgetting the precious time he had lost on the sidewalk in front of the mansion, when he was enjoying the choreography of the firefighters in action, while someone acted and transferred money from the accounts.

He punched the table and beat the professor up. He told Hammer Joe to do his job before he sailed angrily through the garage of the commercial building, taking all the computer hard drives with the cash flow records.

"Nail him!" ordered the Dona Marta Hill Caligula as he left the room. So the professor had his hands and feet nailed to the conference room table. He was like Christ on the cross when he stood up and jammed the head of the table on the window sill, with Guanabara Bay in the background with its dazzling necklace of nightly pearls.

Hammer Joe was inspired, thought Skull, laughing inside the van and nervously scratching the slight protuberance on the surface of his tight pants. He had seen the dramatic scene in his head: blood coming down the sides of the wooden table, dripping onto the posh carpet, and the professor's eyes wide with dread, with the adhesive tape over his greedy mouth.

*

The French consul insisted: "We don't want problems with the Brazilian government."

Júlia resisted accepting the "request" to change the true version of the facts. To ask that of a journalist, an intrepid warrior of the truth, was to ask her to commit suicide. However, for "State reasons", invoked to prevent another "lobster war" between Brazil and France, a convincing fanciful "official version" was forged in which the illegal invasion of the manor to recover tableau 75 was omitted. Some newspapers reported, without much emphasis, the arson committed by thieves in the mansion of the art objects collector, son of the former stock exchange broker. There were praises to the "finance genius". Nothing was said about Big Head nor about his successor in the criminal underworld.

All the headlines on the front pages of the newspapers focused on the Relic. International newspapers reproduced the Reuters Agency photo of the French consul in Rio, displaying the famous tapestry. They all published the "official version" of the facts.

Many pages were written about the tragedy of the "French martyrs", based on the surrealist version of the excavation at the NGO's headquarters. They falsified the truth of the facts with the sensational news that the French died without saying that "they had dug a hole under the bed, where they hid the valuable rug, which was only discovered thanks to the police instinct and the successful excavation carried out on the spot by the researcher Aurélien Kléber".

Thus, in a world where emotions are worth more than true history, the general public believed in the tragic end of the French who were tortured and murdered while protecting the valuable religious secret. Júlia explained on TV5 that she closely followed the laborious "archaeological" work in the *favela*. She didn't say anything about the invasion of the manor. And, at her side, Aurélien swallowed the consul's praise "for the incomparable historic achievement in a democratic country". So, the *gendarme*'s father, if he were alive in Strasbourg, would be proud that the *petit* had found the famous tableau, which had disappeared in 1863.

While the international media covered the news of the sensational recovery, the police in Rio sought to identify who had set fire to the businessman's house and who had murdered the professor in the downtown office. At Dona Marta Hills and Rocinha, they made graffiti on the walls and there were fireworks to announce the return of the great Skull. They were also celebrating the arrival of a shipment of weapons and cocaine of the highest quality, coming from Paraguay to move the organized crime and supply the Wonderful City.

Chapter 24

IN AVIGNON, THROUGH THE INTERNET, the Grand Master was informed of Leonardo's death and the rescue of the tableau. A hired professional, nicknamed "Gorilla", received orders to visit Chateau d'Angers immediately, before the gallery was closed off, with the construction of a prison to cage the seven-headed dragon. It was not so long ago that the gallery had been closed for the installation of the most modern lighting system there was.

Gorilla made a long tour as a tourist fascinated by the fortress. Accompanied by a young woman from the area, whom he'd met at a bar in Place de la République, he took pictures of the future stage of the war operations. He went down the stone stairway that took him to the imposing gallery, where he appreciated the technology of the new lighting system. He pretended to be interested in the scene in tableau 74: the beasts thrown into the lake of fire, which preceded the white space left on the wall. There he assessed the double ceiling and the vertical fastening of the tapestry, without raising suspicion about his curiosity.

On the surface of the castle, he walked with his girlfriend hand in hand through the narrow passage at the top of the towers fourteen to seventeen of the walls. They protected the tapestry, in front of Boulevard Général de Gaulle, which crossed the Quai de Ligny and the A11 highway to Paris. He saw that there was only one entrance to the fortress. He memorized the vulnerable places on the walls that protected the tapestry. Everything he researched on that first visit was duly recorded in his notebook. At the gallery's bookshop, where he bought some brochures, he also acquired a floor plan of the castle, perhaps useless for the average tourist, but very useful for a tourist passionate about fortifications.

Before returning to Paris, he also visited the small town of Saumur, known for its castle, and located less than half an hour's drive from Angers. The place was thoroughly evaluated. It was chosen for the possibility of having a plan B in the offensive operations or if he had to flee.

The visit allowed Gorilla to obtain all the information to put together an action plan. He was going to start taking action to blow up the castle. That was what he confided to Grand Master Pierre.

*

For local newspapers, the main headlines were the war on the hills between rival drug dealers and the fire at the big house in Botafogo. Few lines were dedicated to the professor's crucifixion in the office downtown. For the world, there was nothing more sensational than the news of the discovery of the valuable tableau of the Apocalypse. It made headlines in foreign newspapers and was the main story on the front pages of French newspapers. Nothing that could explain why the recovery of a tapestry scene, not so famous, would have such repercussion. And the press took a fancy for the small town of Angers, which was praised, even with some exaggeration, as the capital of the Loire Valley.

The story of Chateau d'Angers and the tapestry of the Apocalypse was told in prose and verse all over the world. Regent Blanche de Castille could be depicted as boldly resurgent in her beauty and battling in armor on the top of the seventeen laced towers of the battlements. The narratives about the impudicity of the beautiful warrior regent who got naked before the members of the Parliament were enthralling. The legend spanned millennia and even today it still instigates contemporary imagination, similar to what Phryne, whose beauty in ancient Greece was immortalized in the arts and in literature, did in Areopagus. There were also many pages dedicated to exalting the Loire Valley region, place of the pacification of the royal power in France after the battles of Rocheaux-Moines and Bouvines.

The repercussion in the media caused heated debates in the meeting room at the Tourism Office, at number 2 of the suggestive *promenade du Bout du Monde*. The mayor of Angers, the curator, the director of the Center for National Monuments, the board of the Journalists Union, the head of the notary office, were all excited to honor Angers as a top tourist attraction in France, alongside Paris and Mont Saint Michel.

With so many crazy plans spinning in his head, the mayor repeated to himself: "The castles of the Loire Valley will tremble!" excited to transform the first exhibition of tableau 75 in the castle into the most notable cultural event in the area. Having the funds and the discreet support of the Minister of Culture and Communication, in order not to arouse jealousy from other locations, the city was preparing to advertise the great party. They launched the suggestive slogan: "Come to Angers to cage the devil for a thousand years". An advertisement full of charm and religiosity to keep the Angevin city in the media and an excellent excuse to resume the thread of history, from the more than six hundred years of weaving the tapestry of the Apocalypse in Parisian workshops. Furthermore, the mayor knew he would have something very appealing: the good food and the excellent wines from the Loire Valley region.

Aurélien Kléber and Júlia traveled to Paris, he as the person responsible for the air transportation of tableau 75, and she as the guest of honor of the city of Angers. When they arrived at Charles de Gaulle Airport, they were met by the mayor, the curator, Father Antoine, the worthy representatives of the Ministry of Culture and the Interior, as well as

the head of the DAT with his agents and city and castle officials, all smiling and happy with the demon's triumphant
arrival in a crate.

The press wanted to watch the painting being unpacked
at customs, but they were forbidden to enter. All the honors
should be kept for the solemnity in the gallery of the presentation of the chained Beast. Frustrated, the press blamed the
board of trustees for preventing them from witnessing the
arrival on French soil of "one of the most valuable pieces of
historical heritage in France".

From the airport, Aurélien and Júlia left for Strasbourg
by train. They would stay there for a few days and then return to Paris, where they would stay for about ten more
days until they traveled to the opening of the exhibition
of the tableau in Angers, for which the mayor had not yet
set a date.

Also from the airport, an entourage of cars departed for
the castle, with the devil traveling in a van, wrapped in thick
bubble wrap inside a wooden crate, like a coffin. The curator grumbled the entire trip, because he was in a hurry to
meet with the organizers, interdict the gallery to finalize the
preparations for framing the *bienvenu* in the empty space
and send the invitations for the solemnity, to be held, probably, in the following fifteen days.

Aurélien's sudden departure for Strasbourg was due
to his mother's call, the night of the fire at the manor in
Botafogo, telling him, desperate, that his father had passed
away. That was the reason that made them leave Paris temporarily to stay at his grandparents' home in the capital of
Alsace. Aurélien spent most of his time in the company
of his mother. Júlia got along very well with her, who was
still shaken and had not yet recovered from the depression
caused by her husband's death. On the night when the family members were talking in the dining room, the women on
a corner and Aurélien and the men on the other, Júlia seized

an opportunity when she was alone with Dominique in a small room to present her with a gesture of kindness, winning the heart of her fiancé's tearful mother forever.

"You know, I've known you for a long time."

"How?" his mother asked, raising her eyebrows.

"Well, it's very simple," said Júlia in perfect French. "Your son has all your pictures in his laptop. The photo I liked the most was the one you took in Trouville with your husband. Honestly, you haven't changed at all."

"You're so sweet. My son chose well."

In the remaining atmosphere of mourning, the joyful spontaneity and congeniality of the Brazilian girl, happy to show her knowledge of French culture, conquered all the family members, even the most serious ones. Everyone looked after Aurélien's fiancé with affection, as if she were family. She was in awe with the library, with great classics on the shelves. Grandpa Jojo offered her selected readings in great style for the solemn occasion of the visit of the international journalist and the apple of *petit* Aurélien'a eyes. Jojo took great care in the choice of texts, including reading a passage from the *Physiology of Marriage*, in which Balzac recommended men to pay attention to women's pleasure during sexual intercourse. Júlia loved Balzac's advice on the "bed theory" and smiled at the message given to the *petit-fils*, withdrawn in a corner of the room in his sadness for the death of his father.

Even with little time available, the couple visited the cathedral, strolled along the River III, which bathes the plains of Alsace, kissed at *Petite France* and on the beautiful Merchants Bridge. The two of them just didn't get to see the European Parliament inside, only from a distance. On Sunday night, they boarded the train at the TGV station, the same station where Aurélien had said goodbye to his military father in the silence of his hidden pain. It was thus, with sincere emotion, that Aurélien's suffering mother shed many tears at the station when she said goodbye to her son and his fiancé. Deep in her grieving heart, she had been very pleased with the visit of her hero and his young lady.

"Each person has their own silent pain," thought Júlia as she melancholically left Strasbourg and lovingly approached the City of Light. She would finally see it through Aurélien's passionate eyes, on the banks of the poetic quays of the Seine and the alleys of Île Saint-Louis. The sensation was unique, indescribable, while the mysterious adventure train increased its speed along golden tracks to make the dream of stepping on the platform of Gare de Lyon a reality.

*

The "terrible boys", as curator Ferdinand wittily called the young internet users who worked with Father Antoine, found the company Bel France Montgolfière, specialized in promotional and touristic balloon flights. It was the priest who convinced the curator to celebrate the "imprisonment of the devil for a thousand years" in Angevine heights. The curator endorsed the priest's idea and presented the ballooning suggestion to the mayor, as if it were his own idea. The secretary contacted the company's director, responsible for several balloon flights over the majestic castles of the Loire Valley and arranged the interview at city hall to address "a matter of mutual interest".

Days later, the curator and the company's director were seated on the armchairs of the mayor's office. The mayor's table was covered with papers, pens, medicine bottles, and touristic brochures. It was part of his profile as a traditional politician with faithful constituents, won thanks to his congeniality and effective work. He quickly became interested in the proposition for the day of the party, which he called "brilliant", to paint Angers sky with dazzling balloons.

"*Merveilleux! Merveilleux!*" repeated the mayor enthusiastically.

The director explained in detail how the financial plan of the promotional event would work. He had suggested the possibility of having zero cost for the city, if he managed to gather a lot of balloons and advertising shapes from major brands.

"Despite the short time that we have ahead of us, I believe we can get about twelve balloons. Tomorrow, I'll send the brochures to our registered customers and activate the mailing list. I'm sure there'll be a lot of interest in our VIP package, which offers balloon rides in an itinerary that includes accommodation and gastronomic dinners at the exquisite Relais & Châteaux hotel chain. There's always a great demand."

The joyful meeting included many laughs and many stories. Before presenting the ballooning proposition, the director, born in Marseille, insisted on knowing how the tableau had ended up in Brazil, a country for which he had a secret passion for its music and soccer. He mentioned the samba *Orfeu do Carnaval* and several famous Brazilian players. The curator recounted the adventures of the discovery of the tableau. The director's exclamation was of total astonishment:

"It can't be true!"

Then, the businessman raised a controversy by saying that it was false to consider Étienne and Joseph Montgolfier as the inventors of the hot air balloon. According to him, it was a Portuguese Jesuit priest, born in Colonial Brazil, Bartolomeu Lourenço de Gusmão, known as the Flying Priest, who created the balloon, watching a soap bubble rise in the air. But he concluded that he considered the French brothers the pioneers of the first aeronautical voyage.

"*Vive la France!*" concluded the mayor, enthusiastic about the idea of magic balloon flights crossing Angers' skies.

"The balloons will be a floating billboard a hundred feet high. When they fly over Angers, they'll be seen from miles away. There is no better publicity to advertise the big event," said the director, very enthusiastic about the good receptivity of his services.

They planned all the details. The duration of the flight over the seventeen towers would not exceed twelve minutes. They chose the touristic itinerary for the balloons from Saumur. There would be at least three balloons with the catchy slogan of the capture of the devil for a thousand years, inviting people to visit the city and the Chateau d'Angers in the dates and hours of public visitation.

"Visually, you have no idea how spectacular the effect is with all the colorful balloons in the air. You won't regret it. Honestly, there is nothing better to let people know that the devil will now be caged for a thousand years in the castle's basement. Everyone will know just by looking at the Loire Valley's sky."

They all laughed at the exaggerated image the Marseille director had created.

"I just need to know, Mr. Mayor, the exact date and time of the event so I can confirm the day when we can fly."

"What do you mean?" asked the mayor, surprised and pouting. "I thought we had it all figured out."

"Unfortunately, this is how we work. We only know if it will be possible to make flights a few hours before we take off. We have no way of knowing the day before whether the wind and weather conditions will allow the balloons to fly smoothly. There's no other way."

"Shit! This will mess up all the arrangements. I'll have to rethink," complained the authority, huffing like the French.

"Surprise yourself and your guests. No one needs to know about the balloons coming. It's a secret from the sky."

"OK," agreed the mayor, convinced that the colorful view from above would brighten the event, and Angers would teach the world a lesson in how to relive history with art and ingenuity.

"That's how the balloon world works," justified the director in his most convincing speech. "The magic only happens if the wind blows above thirteen miles per hour. God knows!"

In Paris, the attempts to identify the interlocutors in the suspected France-Brazil connection made the week of the Antiterrorist Department busy, after the good news from Brazil. Rio's police department found the cell phone of the owner of the manor, severely damaged, and recovered the serial number, miraculously saved by being protected under the steel belt buckle. Thus, the local phone company identified all the calls received by Leonardo.

Interpol agents in Rio passed the information on to the French police. It was impossible to identify who actually made the call to Brazil, since the cell phone that was used had been cloned. But it was from the interconnections of the numbers dialed by the cloned cell phone that Frenchelon processed the two-minute and nineteen-second transmission received by Leonardo. The highly sophisticated bidirectional voice decoding system confirmed the use of the words: "master Pierre", "Chateau", "Angers", and "millions of euro" in the short call to Brazil. They reached the conclusion that someone, presumably a follower of the Devil's Order, had called the owner of the manor in Botafogo at the time that Aurélien was being tortured. The DAT chief was the one who established the suspicious and dangerous relationship of common interests between Leonardo and a Satanist.

And, once the Rio-Angers connection was established, DAT agents immediately left Paris for Angers to map the area and all the city's road entrances and exits. It was thanks to the dispatch of the agents and the preliminary survey that the head of the DAT learned of the big festivity scheduled to celebrate the arrival of the famous Apocalypse tableau.

As his duty, the colonel contacted his superiors at the Ministry of the Interior to advise against the event. However, deep inside and in the interest of the DAT, he hoped that the ceremony would be maintained. His colleagues at the Ministry found the threats from the terrorist religious sect preposterous, although they admitted that the devil is not to be trifled with. No one knows whether this was said as a joke or seriously, in terms of national security.

After due consultations with the government bureaucracy, the Ministry of Culture and Communication maintained the priority of the event, which praised the "grandeur of the history and museums of France". The Interior Minister's office, in turn, announced that the scheduled solemnity would not be canceled and that everyone counted on the department's efficiency to take the appropriate measures and actions to protect Angers and the castle.

The colonel, head of the DAT, only had to thank the wise decision, which served the interest of honoring and preserving the department's secret budget. The next step was to talk to the Mayor of Angers. Politicians generally hate police apparatus. They consider it an abuse to be disturbed and, even worse, to be spied on. He foresaw a negative reaction and a tense atmosphere, with many indignant huffs from the local authority, when he informed him of a hypothetical terrorist threat.

The Ministry of Culture had asked him to be very cordial, so the mayor would accept the DAT's actions. He banned the use of the military "national security" buzzword.

"Unfortunately, our department will have to carry out a routine operation that requires some preventive actions."

"So what?" asked the mayor, not hiding his grief.

"We must take some measures of absolute priority."

"That's preposterous! It must be a curse from the opposition" the mayor reacted indignantly. "I hope you don't create political problems for me."

"I will personally see to it that Angers has the preventive security that the event requires. There will be no inconvenience. I promise."

"Well, this is just what I needed. Be careful, I'll be watching."

"Do you know when the event will be?"

"Probably in the next fifteen days. The Tourism Secretary has not yet completed his research. You'll receive everything with priority. It will be an unforgettable day, General."

But the demanding colonel wasn't satisfied with the honorary title of general bestowed on him by the mayor, nor with the promise of late delivery of the schedule, let alone the mapping of the city. He immersed himself on the website Heritage Atlas and other geographic maps. However, the more he researched, the more his suspicions grew, making it difficult to make a secure strategic assessment of the supposed threat to the castle and the historic capital of the ancient province of Anjou in the Middle Ages.

There was an unfathomable mystery in the air that challenged his intelligence and the most sophisticated red security codes. Until then everything seemed very vague, very random, unlikely to happen in terms of an attack to the fortress with its seventeen towers, built in the thirteenth century to "protect from the end of the world". It was difficult to foresee and even more to imagine a triumphant car bomb, bringing down a mountain of stone and destroying the gallery.

There was only one way to put an end to so many doubts and uncertainties: to visit the castle in person and reach his own conclusions. He would go like a Frenchman on a secret mission: incognito, dressed as an average tourist, a fan of war weapons and medieval arts. It could not be different. For government security reasons, no one could recognize the face of the DAT chief. Hence the mysterious code name "the Shadow", the dreaded agent of the French anti-terrorist secret service, with great achievements enriching his résumé.

Chapter 25

GRAND MASTER PIERRE HAD ALWAYS emphasized that the tableau should belong to the Devil's Order. Since it was impossible to steal it or buy it in Brazil, Satanists had to hire a professional to prevent the scene of the caged devil from joining the other scenes of the Apocalypse, and they were willing to go to extremes and "blow up the castle", if necessary.

According to Gorilla, the traditional method of using a car bomb to implode the gallery inside the castle was of high risk and ineffective due to the height and thickness of the walls. Even with a car bomb with more than six tons of ANFO, something difficult to load without being noticed, the chance of causing damage to the tapestry would still be small. He considered the possibility of making a maritime raid, an alternative that no terrorist would take into consideration, as it is not usual in the successful attacks, as seen in Madrid and Algiers. Besides, it would require the handling of long-range weapons, difficult to obtain in underground networks or military warehouses in such a short time. The aerial option of the two towers was also discarded, because it was complex and demanded a long preparation. The conclusion of the survey was discouraging and definitive: there would be no chance of destroying the gallery.

The turnaround happened due to one of these demonic coincidences, bringing the creative solution that they haven't been able to find. When they learned that the company responsible for the event was Bel France Montgolfière, it was enough for an informant from the religious cult, who worked in a tourism agency, to inform Grand Master Pierre of the balloon festival scheduled for the painting's exhibition solemnity, to rekindle the explosive flame of the terrorist attack on the castle.

Gorilla's phone call, giving a false identity, to the company's marketing director, glad to help the new customer, was enough for him to obtain the necessary information: balloon shapes, departure point, and estimated flight time. The director stressed that the exact time would be confirmed on the day of the event, due to the weather or, as she ironically implied:

"It's not up to us, but to Him, up there in the sky."

The big balloons had eighty-eight thousand cubic feet, seventy-five and ninety-two feet high. The professional only admitted the balloon solution after rereading the notes and viewing the photographs of the walls of towers fourteen to seventeen, which walled a good part of the gallery and decorated the sidewalks of Boulevard Général de Gaulle. He only had to study the direction of the winds to define the best point for the attack on the castle. Logistically, at first everything worked.

Gorilla returned to the neighboring city of Saumur. He mapped the planned itinerary of Montgolfière's balloons to Angers. He rented two large balloons, one ninety-two feet high and the other seventy-five feet high. All the weights and measures to carry four-hundred-and-forty pounds of explosives of great incendiary and deflagrating power were strictly projected. He knew, however, that the final decision of the flight depended on external factors beyond his control and reach. He had faith in the Satanists' prayers so that the winds on the day of the party were favorable and did not exceed the prohibitive twelve miles per hour.

After laying out the operation and arranging for the balloons and pilots to be hired, Gorilla informed the Grand Master, in a radio message of a few seconds, that the day was scheduled and, from now on, it was good to keep an eye on the weather, and pray, which Grand Master Pierre and his followers set out to do with all their devotion:

"May the dark force, lit by the flames of hell, guide our moon warrior in the final fight against the blasphemers.

Praise the mighty Satan who has placed my life under the shadow of his spear so that I will battle and defeat the supporters of God. I pray in devotion to the beloved Satan, who represents pure wisdom, rather than the hypocritical self-deception of Christianity. The time has come for Him to impose His vengeance, instead of turning the other cheek."

*

The DAT chief was not happy with the dossier prepared by his assistants. He personally went to visit Angers. He took fifteen megapixel photos. On the right bank of the Maine River, he took a walk through the quays, from Tabarly to Monge and through the port of Angers, and on the left bank, through the quays of Ligny and Gambetta, these a short distance from towers one and seventeen. He examined the castle's only entrance through the drawbridge gate between the twin towers. He examined the uniform thickness of the shale and limestone walls that obeyed the Gothic determinants. He visited the seventeen towers surmounted by bevelled battlements and walked through the patrol paths, as well as through the ditches of the fortress, once flooded. He entered the empty rooms and interiors, all without drawing attention.

When he finished, at the top of tower seventeen, the Tower of the Madman, in front of the Basse Chaîne bridge, he concluded that it was impossible for a car bomb attack to be successful, as had happened in other countries. Even if the bolide managed to pierce the roadblock, the explosion would not cause major damage to the castle.

The terrace on the top of the Tower of the Madman offered a beautiful panoramic view of the entire city and the length of the navigable Maine River, formed by the confluence of the Mayenne and Sarthe rivers, to the north of Angers. The main road that bordered the river until reaching the castle was connected to the A-11 highway. Colonel Lucien Jouvet didn't need binoculars or pictures taken with a wide-angle lens to decide what was needed in terms of maximum security. He ruled out the attack through the drawbridge at the main entrance, since it was too far from the gallery. His concerns were concentrated on the thick walls that ran alongside Boulevard Charles de Gaulle and served as the inner wall of the gallery, where the beautiful scenes of the Apocalypse were hung and exposed. All the attention was directed to that side of the castle.

On his return to Paris, reviewing the castle's *plan de masse* (floor plan) and the photos plotted in 35x24, he concluded that, from a fluvial point of view, it would be enough to previously forbid access on the banks near the castle, closing visitation to the docks, and preventing the anchorage or the navigation of any type of vessel up to three miles on both sides of the fortress. Due to his experience in ballistics, he knew it would be impossible for someone to hit such a distant target, unless they had very sophisticated weaponry, which would be difficult to transport and would quickly be intercepted.

From the road point of view, it would be enough to create an effective block at the entrance to Angers and the streets near the castle. The A11 highway would be closed and there would be a partial blocking of Avenue de l'Atlantique and a total blocking of Boulevard Charles de Gaulle, beginning at the Basse-Chaîne and Verdun bridges. All the side streets that allowed access to the castle would be closed. It would all be stealthily operationalized during the night.

The colonel also took into consideration the surprise element, since it's not only in a terrorist attack that it is important and works. The police must also surprise the enemy with preventive public security measures, preferably taken at the last minute. Thus, all planning would be carried out in the morning before the ceremony, without the mayor's prior knowledge, to avoid protests and problems with city hall.

DGSE had the modern radar and wiretapping system installed and had been operating it for days to detect any mobile artillery equipment and track any kind of suspicious communication within the wide range of action across Angers' outskirts.

Something suspicious was picked up by the Territory Surveillance Direction (DST, counterintelligence services) in Domme. A kind of a "warning" from an unidentified radio amateur from Paris to a mobile receiver of the Devil's Order in the South of France. However, DST was unable to reconstruct the entire intercepted dialogue, and the colonel couldn't decipher the meaning of parts of the recording that would elucidate the order's involvement in the story.

"What could the message say?" asked the director of the DAT, rereading the confused words, with emphasis on the "castle", "RDX", "less than twenty" and "pray". He was not impressed by the acronym RDX, for explosive nitroamine. "What the hell is this number reducer?" wondered the Shadow, biting his lips and clenching his fists, before hitting them hard on the desk. After stroking his sore hand, he decided to ask his superiors for the red alert level, the maximum alert, for the outskirts of Angers, and to add to the ongoing actions an effective emergency evacuation plan for the gallery.

Now all he could do was wait. He trusted the interior minister's positive decision to authorize the red alert. There would be no shortage of men, weapons, or funds to avoid the Apocalypse — reasoned the colonel, tormented by the enigmas that surrounded the castle's insurmountable walls.

*

"Ah! Paris! What an extraordinary city!"
It could sound like a commonplace, but that was the first

impression that Júlia had when she exited Gare de Lyon and walked around the city. She only knew it through photographs, films, and her father's stories. At first, everything was flowers, smells, birds, different and wonderful greens, the mysterious elegance that filled the eyes and senses with enchantment. She could find no faults in the landmarks like the Arc de Triomphe, the Eiffel Tower, and the Louvre's pyramid nor in the city's Haussmannian architecture.

She looked in awe at everything she saw around her. She was very curious to discover the fabulous world of her dreams. Paris became a kaleidoscopic city, each day with a new neighborhood, a different corner, a different street. She understood the dreamy pauses of her father, who discreetly abandoned the readings of *Tintin*'s comic books and slid off the illustrated pages' blank margins to wander indolently, in his mind, through the Luxembourg gardens, Place des Vosges, the alleys of the Rodin Museum, or join the Montmartre bohemia or the packed streets of the Latin Quarter. Her photographic memory rediscovered in awe and reminiscence what European urban life offered her.

With an emotion that could not be translated, she discovered the prodigious Paris of enigmas without needing Aurélien's steps to guide her own or her father's experienced eyes who, a long time ago, had left behind the habits and cloudy days of the European continent, all harmoniously historical, millennial, resistant to the patina of time, to rejoice in the love of Maria Tereza and find inner peace in the art of living in a place far from the past, in an ecologically embedded mountain range, telling him sunny wonders with a passionate heart.

However, behind the thin red-rimmed glasses, her loving view of a Paris of dreams and enigmas had found its best critical sense, of someone who left behind longing memories of Brazil and went to live with a Parisian for a few days. Her little aquamarine eyes were gradually noticing an infinite range of contrasts, from the refinement to her strangeness to certain things, from the rarity of the blue sky to the monotony of the gray sky, from the vanguard of the civilized world to the primitivism of ancestral habits or troglodyte houses, still present and scattered all over France.

After being dazzled, came the first disappointments. Júlia was faced with the harsh Parisian housing reality, quite different from the translucent tourist brochures. Starting with the big studio, pronounced with an open "o" of horror. A 301 square feet cubicle rented by Aurélien, who proudly said it was just like his neighbors'. An unquestionable truth in a charming neighborhood that housed a lot of those Lilliputian studios. However, the tragic thing about this one was the infamous bathroom. The shower was in the kitchen and the toilet was far from there, in a corner between walls, where the building's sewage piping was located.

"This is ridiculous!" huffed Júlia, taking on the Gallic protest habit. "Where can I do the laundry?" she asked awkwardly.

"In the kitchen," said a sweet Aurélien, smiling. The Parisian knew it was the only appropriate answer.

It was difficult for an "Indian girl" with a habit of showering twice a day, even in low temperatures, to adapt. In Strasbourg, she had found the lack of a shower odd. There was only a bathtub in the big house — the ultimate symbol of French domestic comfort. She missed Aunt Amélia's place, with the large bathroom and laundry area, things that did not exist in metropolitan French residences, small or large, rich or poor. Perhaps this explains in part why Parisians turn the street into an extension of their living space. It's because they stay in cafes for as long as they want, taking time to read the newspapers or chat, wandering the streets, the big department stores and gardens, or revisiting the magnificent museums. Maybe the French's contagious passion for bistros, restaurants, theaters, and gardens, is the way they found to forget the discomfort of home privacy. She deduced that the typical Parisian has learned, through generations, to lead an active social life outside the home and make it a healthy joy of living.

But, as she'd told in her letters to her mother, "things were rough". People always think nice cold weather, maybe a little snow, but they don't picture a warm Paris. Not even the French. The city is not prepared for summer days out of the season, nor does it matches its tourist profile. With the exception of the big department stores and some places that keep the air conditioning on, the Parisians, for economy or neglect, don't seem to be bothered by the discomfort of the heat and don't even huff if they are sweaty. Thankfully, it was only two days of heat and sunshine, soon replaced by a light rain.

Taking the subway was even worse. In it, Júlia was forced to endure an unbearable odorous mix in overcrowded cars, as well as in certain public spaces or closed environments, despite the population being surrounded by majestic monuments, works of art, beautiful squares and bridges. This was also not consistent with the aggressive, grumpy complaints, out loud, followed by rude grumbles, which she had to hear while she walked all over the city. Old Baudoin Werhofen said she should bark back to the few lovable idiots. It worked like a charm! They quickly backed down and became common and respectful urban citizens.

Well, the daily coexistence with the small olfactory sin and the winds of bad mood were part of the Parisian landscape; she certainly didn't like it, but in no way it prevented her from being in awe when she saw the great scenario of the great times of civilization, where they honor and pay tribute to the triumph in battles, the guillotined royalty is revered, and the imperial pinnacle is monumentalized, without giving up the rigid principles of freedom, equality, and fraternity.

Júlia began to understand, in her daily life with Aurélien and in her interaction with French citizens, that, however tropical and hygienic her reservations were, they were contested, if not compensated, on a large scale, by the advantages of being in a cosmopolitan metropolis: she was moved by the organ concerts in Sainte-Chapelle, the *bateau-mouche* tour on the River Seine, got addicted to the tour by the *bouquinistes* and the habit of whispering in his ear in search of lost time at Les Deux Magots or being rapt by the look of the big boulevards and avenues. It was as if the chimeras that once made her feel like a stranger had suddenly disappeared in the face of so many prodigious things to memorize. And so, Júlia, now in the shoes of a Parisian, was lagging more and more in the lit streets before returning to their cubicle.

She wrote to her father saying that, if she had to choose the deepest emotion caused by the French cultural hegemony, she would have a hard time picking out and personalize one of many, without being really unfair. But she believed that two intimate perceptions, kept alive in her memory, stood out from the others: the maturity of the French people, always restless and ready by the lights of reason to be indignant and united against the slow social changes, and the tenderness in honoring simple, everyday things. She couldn't explain why such things touched her heart the most. She admitted that nothing touched her more than approaching the shop windows to admire the laborious ordering of the cheese, wine, butcher, fishmonger, bakery, fruit and vegetable shops, where the refinement of the presentation befitted the reverential tribute to a state of mind of those who know how to be in harmony with life.

On her last day, Júlia, reclined on Aurélien's relaxed body on the banks of the River Seine, watching the boats travel under the shadow of Notre-Dame, and was thrilled to hear her beloved talk about the remarkable ability of the French people to bring together men and ideas around existential improvements and fighting for them in protests, marches, rallies and changes in laws, almost always successful and important. Fighting for the national values of a legacy bequeathed not only by kings and statesmen, generals, philosophers, writers, poets, but especially by thousands of anonymous people over the centuries of France's history. *Merci* for the lesson of greatness, Júlia said emotionally, avoiding judging the Brazilian people who cower in their pathetic indignation, preferring not to react, not to close ranks against violence, corruption, impunity, delaying the changes in civilizing advances.

In that, her father and Aurélien were absolutely right. Paris was unique and lavish in offering so many attractions to visitors who loved France, or rather, who understood it in its secular dimension, its glories and its conflicts, its castles and its slums, its contradictions and successes in building the wisdom of its people, essentially universalist. There, in the City of Light, one could lead a structured, culturally rich life, informal in dealing with others, in peace with an intimidating police, as it should be to fight and repress the insane violence of our time.

Her stay in France allowed her to follow the complete recovery of the *grand* Aurélien, admire how he still skillfully handled the crossbow. The day before they left for Angers, he took her to visit the us Tir Gouvieux, a shooting club in the city of the same name, 25 miles from Paris. Since the loss of his vision, he had been anxious to check his aim with his championship crossbow, kept under lock and key in the club locker. Júlia saw how he was congratulated by his sports friends for his beautiful shots. It was impressive to see how he managed to hit the bull's eye from dozens of feet away. He left there under applause. He also deserved applause for the nights when the archer of love went out of his way to make her feel happy in the narrow bed of the studio, as recommended in Balzac's book, which Grandpa Jojo had read for both of them. There was no way that Júlia could not be definitively cured of the complex she had for having thin arms and not be thankful every day for breathing the Paris air.

However, in this existential vision, hovering over the local feelings and the chimneys of the gray roofs, was a question that Júlia could not answer: would she live forever in Paris?

Chapter 26

THE CURATOR'S GUESTS STAYED at the Hotel Marguerite d`Anjou, on the eve of the presentation of tableau 75, right across the castle gates.

*

The entrance to the hotel was through the charming restaurant, where the high counter of the bar doubled as a front desk, where you could get your keys and your messages.

*

From the balcony on the third floor there was a frontal view of eleven of the seventeen circular towers on the walls. When he woke up at 6 AM, a military habit that he'd kept, Aurélien was able to follow from the window, in the twilight of dawn, the great military mobilization in the areas surrounding the castle. After trimming the ends of the goatee in the bathroom mirror, he returned to the rear window to see a wide area around the castle closed off and soldiers moving in the narrow alleys between the towers. The parking lot in front of towers seven, eight, and nine had been completely emptied. When the sun came up, the entire length of Boulevard Charles de Gaulle was empty. On the other side of the Basse-Chaîne Bridge, he spotted two AMX-10 RC tanks with their cannons aimed at the sky. He also saw barbed wire with galvanized steel spirals blocking the access to the castle. Two GIGN policemen guarded Ligny's quay. The preparations were those of a security red code.

The former cop's mind and eyes went on high alert. His intuition warned him that something surprising would happen on that slightly windy morning.

After breakfast, a short distance from the hotel, Aurélien and Júlia stepped on the long red carpet that adorned the entire passage of the drawbridge to the entrance of the large garden courtyard towards the chapel. The festive ceremony had just begun. They walked hand in hand towards the courtyard that would take them to the entrance of the gallery, around the walls of the chapel, located in the central part of the castle. There was a buzz in the air, and the solemnity felt like the Academy Awards, with the curator and Aurélien deserving a statuette for the capture of the seven-headed dragon. The mainstream press was present at the historic event, thus ensuring great repercussion and dissemination in the media.

Receptionists in typical medieval costumes led the guests along an alley of lime trees that ended at the *châtelet's* gate. As you crossed it, you entered the courtyard, from where, from the top of the stone guard rails, you could see the rose garden that beautified the access to the Apocalypse gallery. In this cozy, open-air courtyard, a *vin d'honneur* was offered. The most delicious rosé wines produced in the Loire Valley were served by prompt waiters, also in medieval costumes. All those present were gathered together waiting for the ceremony, scheduled for 11:30 AM. The few invitations with a discreet red stripe in the left corner included a post-ceremony lunch, reserved for authorities and special guests.

But the party had a major flaw, criticized by all, although forgiven by the guests when they arrived at the castle courtyard. All caused by the ostensible public security red code, which, less than two miles away, didn't allow access to the fortress. The guests were taken to the drawbridge on chartered buses. No vehicle could go through the access roads or streets near the castle, except for those reasonably comfortable buses that were available.

In addition, all those present at the event, without exception, had to go, grudgingly, through metal detecting devices. The agents only followed the red code procedures, discreetly commanded from afar by the head of the DAT. Something frightening, that had not been seen in official events for a long time, and that contradicted the promise made to the local authority that it would only use a modest military apparatus.

The mayor cursed, the guests protested, the journalists complained. Only the curator didn't find that this negative advertisement was bad. Parodying Sarah Bernhardt — speak ill, but speak of me — he gladly accepted that people spoke ill of excessive and embarrassing police enforcement, but also that they vented the emotions of bedazzlement about the beauty of the Apocalypse tapestry. Even more so now, with the inclusion of the famous tableau, so well protected by the castle's walls.

At a certain moment, when most of the guests were already present, the curator decided to gift them with the glided flight of a great royal owl, trained in the castle. It was a beautiful bird. Its neck rotated almost three hundred degrees, as if to compensate the fixity of its huge golden eyes. It flew over the seventeen towers to land in style with its giant wings on the outstretched arm, wrapped in a leather protector, of the young, blond trainer.

The entertainment act was widely applauded. The mayor gave a wry smile to the audience, thinking that the flight was just a small sample, a *hors d'oeuvre* of what would come next to celebrate Satan's triumphal imprisonment at Chateau d'Angers. Thinking about the election, he counted the attendance at the event. An absolute success: everyone was present, except for Father Antoine, who should, as usual, be late.

"They're coming," the director of Bel France Montgolfière quietly warned the mayor, who went around the courtyard nonstop, greeting the guests, in the middle of an electoral campaign, smiling to everyone. When he had a greater friendship or guaranteed political return, he didn't hesitate to give a discreet kiss on the cheek of the guest, in a typical French intimacy in solemn meetings.

The mayor glanced at the sky and saw nothing.

At that moment of expectation, from tower one, on the left side of the entrance gate, it was visible that there was no sign of vessels passing by or anchored in the waters of the Maine River or a soul on the docks miles away from the fortress. From the top of the two twin towers, right at the entrance to the drawbridge gate, it was possible to see that the only direct access to the castle was one and a half miles away, where a barrier of heavily armed soldiers and armored vehicles, identifying the guests, was built. At the bottom of the moats, once filled with water around the walls, were positioned soldiers with assault rifles. Despite the lack of an underground passage, soldiers manned these moats, giving the frightening appearance of a well-guarded medieval fortress against the proclaimed "forces of evil". Maximum security was the order of the day at Chateau d'Angers.

"They are coming. Look to your left," repeated the director of the balloon company, this time whispering in the mayor's ear, who glanced at the towers of the castle, but saw no balloons.

"*Merci* for the invitation," greeted the mayor of Paris.

"It's an honor for us to have you in Angers," replied the mayor gratefully, with a broad smile.

The curator, very flattered by the presence of the Minister of Culture and Communication, was on cloud nine after receiving a generous compliment:

"It's a great day for our national heritage. All of us, Mr. Curator, are proud of your victory."

"I only did my job, Mr. Minister," replied the curator standing straight, like someone from the military standing at attention.

Suddenly, the acknowledgements and honors were drowned out by the "Ohs!" exclaimed from all corners of the patio. They foreshadowed the slow and fairy-like arrival of the balloons in their various shapes. They were still far from the seventeen towers. The guests could not yet see that the smaller one had specific words about the ceremony, with three of them sporting the famous slogan: "Come to Angers to cage the devil for a thousand years". The bigger balloons showed ads for big companies like Michelin and Coca-Cola.

Director Montgolfière was euphoric at the magnificent visual show his company had put together in the blue sky. The promotional event proved to be a great financial success. The mayor would be very happy to know that the ballooning cost for the municipal administration was zero.

Everyone was smiling and the "Ohs!" continued to pop around the courtyard as the nice chubby tire man and the giant soda bottle approached the castle. The only person who didn't like seeing the sky full of colored dots was the head of DAT, asking himself, over and over, in the depth of his professionalism: "What the fuck is this now?" He was entirely absorbed in his apprehensions, when he heard the comments of the elderly woman by his side, owner of the most famous local bakery:

"How beautiful! Have you ever seen anything so beautiful in Angers? The animal-shaped balloons are wonderful! I just don't understand why the two smaller ones aren't colored."

Anger took the pale face of the Shadow, forced to listen to the observations of the baker's wife. He got tense, biting his lips. His clenched fists showed that he felt the gravity of the aerial surprise in the air. But as soon as he was done with the unforeseen event, he turned away from the crowd that filled the courtyard and fired a series of orders over the radio. He told the platoon chief-sergeant to stay on high alert for an emergency evacuation. At his sign, with his arm raised and making concentric circles with his index finger, policemen with heavy rifles began to appear in each of the seventeen towers, watching vigilantly in vested combat poses. Although such acts always conveyed to the general public a visual impression of protection, in reality they had no counteroffensive power. They were only rehearsed theatrical performances.

"And now, what am I going to do?" wondered the Shadow, perplexed, with the bluetooth microphone crossing his face, aware of the terrible terrorist threat that loomed in the cloudless sky and the impossibility of being able to react in time to defeat the demon with black wings.

*

In Rio de Janeiro, the headlines of the tabloids asked: Suicide or Murder? The tragic death of the accountant, whose body had been found partially charred in the luxurious manor in Botafogo, continued to produce stories. The police promised to engage in a rigorous investigation, although the normal routine for investigations was to fall by the wayside. Interestingly enough, the professor's death had completely vanished from the news. As always, other crimes appeared and occupied the headlines. And urban violence, both in Brazil and around the world, would remain a dangerously contagious disease.

Lucca learned of his father's death from the Rio's chief of police. He tried to call Lisa, but she didn't answer. He made several calls without hearing a voice on the other end. "Poor thing!" he thought sadly. She should be making arrangements for his father's funeral. He pictured her dealing with the bureaucracy of the Coroner's Office to release the body. His father had left no documents or valuable items at her apartment. He had taken everything to the Relic manor. There should be no money left because everything was concentrated in the hands of the professor, who held the key to the safe and controlled the accounting balance. This was the way his father wanted it to be, there was nothing he could do.

He thought that his father's brutal death wouldn't change his life in America. Big mistake, because it had several consequences and disappointments. The first came with the call from the university's administrative director, who informed him that his enrollment had been suspended due to lack of payment, as he had received a notice from the bank that had canceled the charge directly from the account. To stay in college, he would have to pay the expensive semester fee in the next 48 hours. Interestingly enough, his teachers and classmates, once so cordial, suddenly became hostile, as if he were Bin Laden's son, an undesirable immigrant — a case for immediate expatriation.

He desperately tried to reach his father's banker friend. The Texan's kind secretary told him that he was in a meeting. He lost count of how many times he cursed "Fuck you!" after trying in vain to contact Mr. John Dalton at the bank.

The interruption of his dream of studying abroad and becoming abroad was mixed with the pain of losing his father. Had the dream gone down the drain of a corner in Boston? No! No!, he protested to himself. He remembered to use the card from the Swiss bank account that his father had given him the day before his trip to New York, at the professor's office, without telling anyone, including Lisa.

He would withdraw the money deposited in his father's secret account and pay the university, besides other expenses. He pictured himself enjoying the fun pleasure of counting the pile of hundred-dollar bills drawn from the bank with his fingers. He admitted that he'd already dreamed of going out spending the accumulated millions with no limitations, because he thought his father did not enjoy life; he never traveled, except to Brasília. He was never interested in seeing other cities and getting to know other people. He only thought about that damn manor in Botafogo, as if it was the center of the Earth.

For fifteen minutes he felt powerful, like a god. As he still had 48 hours, the university could wait. He could pay them later. He entered a big department store and chose the most expensive designer sneakers and t-shirts. He also decided to buy a blazer. He had a tremendous desire to wear one. He went to the cashier and handed over the bank card, and was disappointed when the payment for his purchases wasn't authorized. He wasn't discouraged. He decided to buy the most sophisticated laptop advertised on INFO. The salesman explained the configuration and benefits of the new release. At the checkout, no matter how many times the employee typed the card number, the operation also wasn't authorized. He then ran to the bank and saw there were "insufficient funds". He was shocked: of the previous eleven digits, which had made him gap at the office when his father showed him the millionaire balance of his secret account, there were currently only three measly digits left: $ 6.66.

He quickly realized:

"Shit! It was that chubby bastard who left me with this ridiculous sum," accused Lucca, still unaware of the professor's bloody death. He thought that the professor had not wasted any time on the electronic robbery on his father's secret account. He cursed, outraged, back at the university campus:

"I will recover what was stolen from me!"

He knew what it meant to have to go after the missing money and win, just like his father did after his grandfather's suicide, this legendary character that he only knew from the stories that his father told in the bars, on the return from the games at Maracanã. Good times that would never come back.

"I can't understand how my father could entrust all his money to a thief like that! That son of a bitch deserves to die!" thought Lucca in the long boarding line to Brazil.

It was a shame that Leonardo's son didn't know that nine-year-old boy, who, after visiting the tapestry of the Apocalypse with his classmates, confidently said to Father Antoine that the greatest beast in the world was money. He was absolutely right, money was the Satan who seduces to cause violence and evil.

Chapter 27

WHAT'S THIS?, THOUGHT AURÉLIEN, surprised to see the balloons moving in the sky and approaching the castle. In the blink of an eye, he associated the scene with the military preparations seen from the balcony of the hotel at dawn. He quickly realized that the security scheme was flawed. Immediately, the image of the destruction of the Twin Towers in New York came to his mind.

This justified the state of panic in which the colonel of the Écoles de Saint-Cyr was in when he saw the seemingly peaceful arrival of the fourteen colored balloons towards the impregnable walls of the fortress. It was possibly at this exact moment that the archer mentally pressed the crossbow's trigger, as the element of surprise to win the war with modern arms.

"Colonel, come with me, please."

"Me?" asked the Shadow, feeling disrespected by the request made by a civilian in that difficult situation. The head of the DAT didn't recognize the former student immediately, perhaps because of the extravagant novelty of his after-school goatee and tanned skin. But the unmistakable tuft in the middle of his forehead and the unexpected gesture of solidarity left no doubt about Cadet Aurélien. Certainly, the *petit's* military father would be very proud of his son's courageous combat initiative.

"Stay right there," said Aurélien to Júlia, who was mesmerized by the arrival of the balloons.

They didn't even have time to fraternize with an *accolade*, the usual effusive hug between members of the military. Aurélien, respectfully holding the Shadow's arm, led him to where the mayor chatted happily with possible voters, laughing and talking.

"Excuse me, do you know who is responsible for the balloons?" asked Aurélien, skipping the formalities and wasting no time.

"It's the one with the polka dot tie over there," answered the mayor, surprised with the rude interruption in front of the guests.

Aurélien and the colonel didn't wait or thanked him for his answer. They marched at a quick pace towards the director of the balloon company to inquire him, without even introducing themselves.

"Are you the one responsible for the balloons?"

"Yes. I'm the commercial director of the company that…"

The man had barely finished speaking and the colonel was already summoning him with an urgent request, in a military tone of growing annoyance:

"We need the full list of people on the balloons. We need it now! And stay here until I say so."

"Sure, sure. Here it is, sir," babbled the director, a little out of words, fumbling to get the list from the pocket of his jacket.

Suddenly, the director exclaimed, very concerned:

"Oh, God! I've just counted the balloons. It's not possible! There are fourteen balloons in the air. Two of them are not from my company."

From the colonel's glare, the director predicted something catastrophic in the sky, especially when he was surrounded by soldiers.

By Aurélien's initiative, who knew the way by heart, the colonel, followed by orderlies and soldiers, hurried up the stone steps that led them to the Museum of Medieval Weapons. The chief of the DAT raised his police badge and hurriedly passed by the guard and the museum's doorman, astonished by the invasion of the truculent visitors.

"Go! Go!" shouted the Shadow, panting.

Despite the running and the confusion, the archer

managed to share, in general terms, his plan of action, be-fore entering the main weapons room:

"I'll choose the crossbows and arrows we'll use. It's the only way to stop this terrorist threat coming from the air. Any questions, Colonel?"

"No. You can count on me, Lieutenant Aurélien."

"I'll need one of your men to help me carry the crossbow, is it possible?"

"Yes. Are you going to tower sixteen?" asked the Shadow nervously as he gave orders to a soldier to assist the archer.

"No. I'll be positioned on tower fifteen. I'll have a better angle to shoot the arrows from there. I have a hunch that they'll attack from tower fourteen. That's where the attack is easier for them. I think it will work, Colonel."

Suddenly, the confusing words of the last message in-tercepted by the counterintelligence services, which the Shadow hadn't been able to decipher, became clear. It was as if he'd awakened from a nightmare. He immediately cursed himself, feeling guilty for not being able to decipher the numerical message about the wind and the explosive nitroamine that the balloons were carrying, which would be detonated, under any circumstances and without the slightest hesitation, if they were suicidal fanatic terrorists. *Unfortunately, I don't have a crystal ball on my desk,* the Colonel thought bitterly, and then burst out with rage:

"The bastards!"

When he said goodbye to Aurélien, the DAT chief handed over an integration and monitoring system device via digital radio and immediately adjusted the bluetooth microphone on his face.

"I'll be on the terrace of tower seventeen. There I'll have the best view of the field of operations and will be able to better coordinate all backup actions. I think it'll work, Lieutenant," said the Colonel, hurrying with military steps to the Tower of the Madman, where assistants and the intelligence officer were waiting for him. When he arrived, they confirmed that the two black balloons were not on Montgolfière's list. Unfortunately, what the colonel feared the most happened half an hour before the gallery opened: the occupants of two of the balloons were terrorists and were probably carrying explosives. He would have to avoid using firearms, except as a last resort.

Aurélien spoke for the first time on the digital radio:

"Colonel, I'll need two helicopters at the rear to ambush these bastards and distract them, while I get positioned and carry the bows."

"I'll send them. We all trust your skills as a champion archer, since you attended our school. You're our biggest hope, Aurélien."

"Don't say that, Colonel. These guys were very lucky to catch winds of less than thirteen miles per hour at this time of year. But we'll give them a really hard time! We'll throw them a great welcome party."

"The surprise of the arrows awaits them," agreed the Shadow for the first time, with a wicked smile on his lips. The colonel, through his assistant, asked the Montgolfière director to give the order for all his balloons to turn around. The first balloon to obey was the one for Sloggi underwear, with a naked woman showing her back. Little by little, they all turned to the South and slowly distanced themselves from the castle. Only the two black balloons kept their trajectories.

Much against his wishes, the Shadow ordered the immediate evacuation of people from the festive courtyard. The military maneuver proved to be an impressive show of speed and efficiency to respond to a public security emergency. Soldiers from all corners and holes in the castle, like orderly ants, without confusion and not bumping into each other, led the frightened guests to comfortable shelters within the fortress. They were underground anti-aircraft bunkers under the chapel, far from the gallery, and in an absolutely safe place. Those shelters dated from World War II, when they served as the arsenal of the Gestapo command in the Loire Valley. Even so, the colonel talked with the air base and requested that two Cougars helicopters remain on the ground on a preventive basis in case they needed to quickly remove injured people from the castle.

In the following few minutes, only the two black balloons remained in the sky, heading towards the courtyard that gave access to the gallery, which was already completely empty. There were also two helicopters in the air. A Tiger flew in circles outside the perimeter of the castle walls to distract and frighten the balloon occupants. This helicopter had an automatic cannon and Trigat missiles. They could not fire them under any circumstances, to avoid causing explosions. Closer to the balloons, a Cougar surrounded towers nine and ten of the castle. Inside, a sniper armed with an FR-F2 rifle awaited the order to fire. While the flying objects were positioned in the airspace, the archer Aurélien settled in tower fifteen, located in the middle of the second half of the gallery. He was being helped by a soldier who was holding another crossbow and clumsily trying to carry it.

As the balloons approached the gallery, the head of DAT coordinated the counterattack through his bluetooth microphone.

When the balloons lost altitude, the colonel asked the helicopter crew members, with long-range binoculars, to find out which of the two men in the smaller balloon basket was operating it. He then gave the order for the helicopter pilot to approach the balloon, so that the sniper could shoot and hit the head of the identified conductor.

"Fire!" ordered the Shadow to the sniper.

The helicopter flew low and approached the balloon threateningly, enough for the sniper to shoot the conductor in the head. Then the balloon basket started to swing and fall, moving away from the larger balloon and dangerously approaching the fortress. Now it was up to the archer to hit him and tear his rip-stop fabric with the arrows, to deflect it and avoid a collision at the top of the walls, where RDX explosions could reach and damage the Apocalypse gallery.

"Fire!" ordered Aurélien to himself. The archer shot the first arrow. It got very close to the smaller balloon. While he aimed another crossbow, heavy gunfire came from the balloon. He had to protect himself from the bullets and wait.

This time, when he fired another shot, the archer aimed the crossbow at a seventy-degree angle and hit the arrow on the envelope of the smaller balloon. It stopped in midair and then plummeted into the water right by the quay of Ligny. There were no explosions because the helicopter had come close and the long-distance sniper had hit the second occupant, preventing him from detonating the bombs and making it easy for soldiers to assault the deflated balloon, part of it stretched out on the highway. The firefighters didn't have to intervene because there were no explosions and the man was not a terrorist, but a mercenary who, panting, had saved his own life.

After the sniper's shots, the occupants of the second balloon hid inside the basket. The helicopter sniper could no longer fire without risking detonating the incendiary bombs made with white phosphorus, a substance similar to napalm. The archer went into action and fired another shot with the crossbow, which scraped past the envelope of the balloon. Its occupants opened fire. By less than an inch, one bullet missed the archer and another didn't go through the helper's shielded visor. But one of the bullets hit the soldier's thigh, and he was still, with his back to the wall. A trickle of blood spread across the floor of tower fifteen.

Aurélien took a deep breath to contain his nervousness and aim with his good eye. He made the most accurate shot of his life. It tore the blimp's heart. The gondola stopped before it lost altitude, going out of its course to the gallery. He saw the balloon conductor still trying a desperate maneuver to get rid of the gas cylinders, which act like the car's tank, in an attempt to redirect the balloon so that it fell on top of tower fifteen. But the gondola fell out of control in the peaceful waters of the Maine River, near the Basse-Chaîne Bridge, miraculously without the explosive nitroamine and white phosphorus exploding. It was confirmed that the occupants of the balloon hadn't detonated the bombs because they were just mercenaries with no suicidal vocation. Scuba soldiers got into the balloon's wicker basket and handcuffed the criminals, less than six hundred feet from the castle walls. The entire military operation lasted eleven minutes, set on the colonel's watch.

When he shot down the second terrorist balloon, Aurélien felt like the rider on the white horse of the Apocalypse, the beast of the earth, whose characteristic weapon was the bow, the terror of the Roman world in the first century. If Father Antoine was with him in the tower, he would have quoted: "And I looked, and, behold, a white horse, and he who sat on it had a bow. A crown was given to him, and he came forth conquering, and to conquer" (cf. 6.2).

"This way, this way, please," the soldiers repeated, throwing the doors of the shelters open so that the guests could breathe the tranquil Angevine air again on that tumultuous morning.

Gradually, the guests began to walk through the large courtyard again without danger. Everyone was talking a lot and extremely curious to know what happened. With the explanations, and still amazed, they crossed the stone portal at the entrance to the gallery to see the famous tableau 75 up close, which should have never been separated from the ensemble of the celebrated work of sacred art. The adventure had ended on a gala afternoon.

Finally the Beast was imprisoned in Chateau d'Angers. From inside the gallery, entirely walled, no one could see the remnants of the deflated balloons on the banks of the Maine River; the mercenaries wounded by the direct shots of the GIGN policemen were captured, and the inactive charges of the explosives were collected. It was the two anti-terrorist agents from GIGN, specialized in capturing living targets, who prevented the balloonists from having one last reaction before landing on the river. Now it was up to the journalists to research the facts related to the terrorist attack and medieval counter-reaction and inform the details to their readers.

Once again, the city of Angers made headlines in newspapers around the world, and got the front page of the French magazines and evening papers. The mayor, the curator, Aurélien and the director of the balloon company could never have imagined so much repercussion in the media. Now the Shadow could think of retiring, after everyone had seen his smiling face when he saw the devil caged for a thousand years, surrounded by walls and secular towers, which resisted the violence in its most diabolical face.

The solemnity had begun gloriously. After smoothing his thinning gray hair with his hand, the curator started his speech:

"My friends, my first words are to exalt this magnificent military fort, desired and built by a warrior, which was once a luxurious monarchic residence dedicated to painting and poetry, a Nazi prison and military depot, and is currently on the rise as a national museum of international reputation. And much, much more. Today it houses one of the most complete and important collections of religious iconography, consecrating the triumph of good over evil."

He was applauded when he mentioned the famous scene of the seven-headed dragon, finally recovered. Near the end of the speech, he presented a more updated and more confident version of his favorite closing quotation, the same he had used to finish the lecture of the 21st edition of the Journalism Festival:

"We could never have imagined that the battle to recover the tableau of the devil caged for a thousand years would show the satanic face of violence in modern times. But the forces of evil have been defeated and the proclamation of the message of hope continues to live more and more in this gallery illuminated by the light of God. Let us together admire the masterful sequence of visions and symbols of the message of salvation announced by the evangelist apostle St. John. Friends of art and beauty, I now invite you to be enthusiastic about the unique tapestry of the Apocalypse, according to St. John, on permanent display at Chateau d'Angers."

Chapter 28

WHEN THE RED CODE WAS ESTABLISHED, the Angers communes were subjected to a strict siege of media interception. Everything was tracked. Any conversation or message, suspicious or not, private or business, was intercepted and recorded in an outrageous violation of individual rights. With the pretext of combating terrorism, the invasion of privacy became the general rule in all countries of the world after the September 11 attacks in New York.

Many suspected and unsuspected things surfaced, without people knowing that they were being spied on. No one could have guessed that in a quiet town in the Loire Valley, and, by accident, without anyone reporting it, as it's usually the case in these heinous cases, a network of pedophilia and child pornography could fall into the radar. It was a terrifying surprise to discover this network based in England, led by a pedophile under the alias of Son of God, and with ramifications in the Netherlands and France.

Everyone assumed that Father Antoine would arrive late as usual at the ceremony. But he ended up being the great absentee and nobody knew the cause of his disappearance. The priest was summoned to give his testimony on the same day and time of the festivities at the castle and, from the moment he was entered the Vice precinct, he was detained and held incommunicado.

*

It all started when the first shocking pictures of naked children were intercepted on the internet. Despite the use of modern computer coding techniques and restricted access, police officers, with the support of the Child Exploitation & Online Protection Center (CEOP) in London, discovered that many of the images came from a church in Angers, where they seized the suspected computers, after locating it.

Undercover agents from the new Technical Service for Judicial Research and Documentation (TSJRD), disguised as pedophiles, found that the children were taken from school in a luxury black van to houses with swimming pools and hot tubs, where they were photographed, filmed and possibly molested. In these houses searched by the police, were produced the main images of abused children. Around a thousand recorded CDs were removed from them.

When the police discovered the network, they tracked the parish bank accounts and discovered a "stooge" account. The priest's lawyers tried to clear the personal files that had been seized, arguing that the inviolability of the house of God had been disrespected. They also claimed that the bank fund was created solely to raise money for the parish. They justified the creation of the fund because of the cut in the municipal grant, and that the money raised was to rebuild the church roof, which was seriously damaged. They argued that there was nothing wrong with that. They only omitted the fundamental fact that the police had discovered: most of the deposits were of very suspicious origin, since the list of donors included the most famous pedophiles in Europe with a record.

"I have nothing to do with this. I swear. Trust me," protested Antoine, gesturing nervously with his hands, more sweaty than usual, and without the usual smiles of contagious joviality on his chubby face.

After hearing Father Antoine's long deposition, along with his lawyers, the chief ordered him to be held until the complete investigation of the facts involving the pedophile network, which the international police had long sought to dismantle, had been completed.

"These criminals need to know that pedophilia is a crime and that they will be reported to justice."

With his head down, the priest heard the chief's threat and replied:

"This is nothing but a slander. This diabolical little internet gang keeps getting me in trouble and getting all the bad things done, just like the devil likes it. I'm innocent."

*

It was past noon, on the other continent, away from Angers. A uniformed doorman was waiting for an important person to arrive on the sidewalk of the imposing building across Central Park. He looked more like a general in the Disney band, with the fringes on his shoulders and golden cords crossing his jacket. He opened the limo door for the smiling woman to get out, sliding her long legs until they reached the sidewalk.

"Mrs. Lisa," said the doorman, showing the perfect teeth in his most cordial smile. "Mr. John Dalton is waiting for you. I'll tell him that you've arrived. Please, follow me."

Nothing out of the ordinary. The Texan had informed her in advance that it was impossible to pick her up early in the morning at J. F. Kennedy Airport because he had a board meeting. He sent his driver to get her.

"It's the penthouse, on the eighth floor," said the doorman.

Mr. John Dalton, who had just arrived from the bank, was waiting for her with a bouquet of small roses, in the shape of a heart, at the elevator door. They hugged each other right there, and then Lisa entered the stunning apartment, stepping on the glossy black and white rectangular marble floor. He took a few steps forward and gave her a long kiss on the mouth. Lisa had barely recovered from the brash kiss and the Texan was harassing her again, uncontrollable in his effusive welcome and the bold groping.

"Whose are these?" asked John playfully, holding Lisa's buttocks shamelessly with his firm hands.

"Now that I'm here, they are certainly yours, John," replied Lisa relaxed, smiling and pretending to be embarrassed.

"Really?" insisted the gray-haired banker and, with no sign of shame, fondled Lisa's breasts like a starving baby.

With no trace of lipstick, Lisa approached the edge of the large window and admired the splendid sunny day shining in Central Park, the large lawn with the large green *pelouse*, the several artificial lakes and the shaded hiking trails.

"Did you make a good trip?" asked John, hugging her from behind.

"Your travel agent was perfect. Thank you very much."

"Is everything alright?"

Lisa paused before answering. She stared at the landscape of that green oasis in the middle of the bustling city and, suddenly, as if diabolically, by special effects, began to see, projected on the New York horizon, the thriller of suspense and seduction of which she'd been the main protagonist. She saw the first scene: she and Lucca entering the bank. The banker was sitting behind the garish mahogany table with the computer screen open. On the table, only the keyboard, a notepad, and a gold pen. She saw his X-ray look on the two strangers in front of him, like they were carry-on luggage at the airport. She noticed his indiscreet look, after she uncrossed her legs, at the slight tan line on her left shoulder when she took off her white linen coat. The effect was stunning, just like that of a rocket from NASA. For a moment, his eyes went from looking like those of a successful senior banker to those of a needy widower, still dreaming of his good 65 years of age, who wanted to live life's adventures, full of twists and turns, like it happens in movies and comics.

The second scene was of the day Lucca was held in the bank's HR department and she was starving. Maybe Mr.

John Dalton had planned everything. He invited her to lunch at an elegant New York restaurant near Fifth Avenue. They talked about her husband's profession and Lisa implied that his success was due, in large part, to the help of "hidden forces". She stressed the accountant Big Head's vertiginous rise after he'd met her. The banker probably knew this in detail, because no one becomes a major banker with impunity, just for looking out for Latinos' interests, without getting their hands dirty. At the end of the lunch, she began to complain and confessed that lately she had been feeling very insecure and unprotected, since Leonardo wanted her to live in a haunted manor and was threatening her. The topic of her fears and the risks she was taking led to financial confidences and, of course, some intimacy.

"Can you imagine life without adventures? What it would be like?" he asked laughing and, taking advantage of her benevolent smile, dared to hold her hand during dessert. She let him do it without showing any reaction, while the iced chocolate syrup melted.

The third scene was inside the limo, both of them already involved in an irresistible attraction. He pushed a tiny button. A dark glass went up, isolating the back of the driver's seat. They kissed. John went further. He opened her blouse and dared to kiss the protruding nipple on her left breast. She let him, but then stopped him from going on. They held hands, until the limo stopped at the bank door, where Lucca was waiting for her. No one had ever kissed her breast in such an exhilarating way. They had just made a love pact and a profitable risk contract.

The fourth scene was the following day, during the morning visit she made by herself to the bank, as he'd requested. In his office on the twenty-seventh floor, he declared himself hopelessly in love. His greatest proof of love was to instruct her on how she could move Leonardo's secret account, of which he was the manager, and how to formalize the bank succession process in investment funds in case he died. He handed her the forms, which she should immediately send to him, after being signed by Big Head, with the date and the values fields empty. Then he arranged for the papers to open her secret bank account.

The fifth scene was the farewell dinner, the night before the college student left for Boston and she returned to Brazil. In Lucca's happy presence, she, in a one-shoulder new dress, with the tan line barely visible, showed no gratitude or remorse.

"Tell me, how did it go?" asked the banker after Lisa's long pause, fascinated by the scenery and the thriller that reminded her of how Mr. John Dalton had crossed her destiny.

She told him more than that. She omitted the event of the Pombagira and the transits of the natal charts in which she had predicted in advance Leonardo's fateful hour, announced by Pluto.

She began by Skull's escape from federal prison. Leonardo had just moved to the manor. She'd refused to go. On the day of the fire, she took a cab to the manor's gate to make sure the reading of the charts was accurate. She stood on the sidewalk awaiting the outcome of the reckoning and saw a black van speed out of the building next door before the flames destroyed the mansion. When she saw two strangers leaving through the gate laughing, she was sure that Leo was dead inside his father's manor.

"And then?" asked the Texan, getting more and more curious.

"I took a cab home and immediately called you, telling you to do what we had talked about."

"You were wonderful, and very efficient. You know that if you had waited another ten minutes, everything would be lost. You did everything right."

The banker was talking about the forms that Lisa had convinced Leonardo to sign in trust, because the American

Immigration required those guarantees for his son to enroll in college. Days after the astrologer's return to Rio, he received the documents signed by Big Head: the bankfax of his personal account with the blank values and her indication as successor of the investment funds. He didn't even have to go through the Customer Call Center, which only clears the transfer of amounts above fifty-thousand dollars when the client confirms the fax sent by phone. As the account manager, not only he confirmed receiving the bankfax, but also transferred personally the sums to Lisa's private account, besides leaving, at Lisa's request, the symbolic $ 6.66 in Leo's account, to infuriate the professor who, apparently for no reason, never really liked her. Ironically, he became aware of the ridiculous balance just before he was crucified.

As for the funds linked to the secret account, since their values could not be withdrawn immediately, as they were investments, they were blocked, preventing the professor's access. They would be cleared upon the presentation of Leonardo's death certificate, which was in Lisa's possession, in her carry-on luggage.

The professor died not knowing that Leonardo, when he learned of Skull's escape, gave orders to the account managers in Europe to immediately transfer all the money to the secret account and the funds administered by his manager in New York, Mr. John Dalton. He had decided to favor him, for his great effort to help his son to study in the United States. He was unable to warn the professor because death had come early in the manor.

"I had to sacrifice the boy. It was too dangerous to keep him in college. I was able to make him return to Brazil immediately. You do understand how these things work, don't you?"

"Lucca tried to talk to me. Since I didn't answer, he must have thought I died with his father. It's good that you think so. His dream is over. We all knew this on the night of the fire. Isn't that right, John? But he has not figured his destiny out yet. You know, there was a time I was very scared when Leo hesitated to sign the documents. If he suspected anything, I would be dead. I would never be here, safe and sound in New York."

"Me, too. Well, the important thing is that everything worked out."

The Texan kissed her passionately and, as he released himself from her arms, told her about the reservations he had made for a cruise through the Caribbean.

"When do we leave?" asked Lisa, ecstatic at the news.

"The day after tomorrow. Did you like the surprise?"

"I've loved it, darling. I'll still have time to buy some makeup and dresses and look pretty for you."

"Your natural self is enough for me, my treasure."

With Leonardo's mother's gold and diamonds bracelet shaking on her wrist and a Libra with an ascendant in Gemini in tow, she would have time to think what to do with so many millions in her personal account and a banker, born at 10 pm, on October 17th, astrologically good in bed and emotionally needy, as had been all the men in her life, always willing to satisfy all her desires and whims.

But John had kept a secret. The total balance of Lisa's secret account was much more than she could have ever dreamed of when she collected the sum of the values in the European accounts and the bank's funds. Overnight, she had become a billionaire. *But, until when?* wondered Mr. John Dalton, with a mischievous smile on his lips.

As for Lisa, she was anxious to get on the Galaxy and set off on the huge ocean liner to the Caribbean. To let, as she always had done, fate happen with the sun in conjunction with Venus at her house seven, on display on her shoulder as a sassy tan line, without forgetting to beg: Ogum Onirê, always protect me...

Chapter 29

"WHY DID YOU SUSPECT THE BALLOONS and act so quickly?" asked Júlia, still curious, on the morning after the ceremony.

"I saw the military apparatus for the party from the hotel window and didn't suspect anything. But when the royal owl flew over the castle, I sensed that something bad could happen. I was on alert."

Seeing him driving at high speed down the highway when they were leaving Angers, Júlia recognized that Aurélien had overcome his visual impairment. The best proof was the accurate arrow shots in the balloons. The only problem he had was that he still wasn't being able to serve himself at the table without spilling water or wine around the glass.

The newspapers of the day highlighted the skill and courage of the champion archer. His photo was on the front page of *Le Parisien*.

"Your fans from Gouvieux are going to love this photo."

"Are you jealous?" asked Aurélien provocatively.

"It's not that. I just don't give, lend, or lease what's mine," she replied, laughing.

"Since when?" continued the archer, behind the wheel.

"Since the day you shot my heart in Rocinha."

Before they arrived in Paris, Aurélien wanted to show Júlia the Renaissance beauty of Château de Villandry, the last of the great châteaux built on the banks of the Loire River, dazzle her with the wonderful gardens and the beds with the most famous vegetables of the region, for sale. They had time to stroll hand in hand through the ornamental garden with its beautiful flowers, full of fragrant roses and unique colors, put together as if it was embroidery and surrounded by birds; the water garden, with its gentle waterfalls and the gardens of love. After walking through the sophisticated vegetable garden, they went up to the terrace, on the second floor. At the stone balustrade of the lookout, with a panoramic view of the splendid landscape, Júlia blurted out:

"Do you know what was the worst situation in this whole story?"

"No," said Aurélien with his eyes on the waterfalls.

"When I had to accept that preposterous version of the discovery of the rug in Rocinha. I never felt so bad in my life."

"I understand. But Júlia, it was not the government's fault, it was the only way out. The thugs had a plan to get the ransom money."

"What are you talking about?" asked Júlia vehemently, objecting to Aurélien's justification in defense of the French government.

"It was only yesterday that I found out the whole plot. I've been suspecting for a long time that we were part of a disgusting scam. Yes, we were used and betrayed in this historic rescue. There was a lot of money involved and I didn't know anything until yesterday afternoon. I thought I was on a serious government mission, without frauds, or on a romantic adventure in search of the Holy Grail. It was all a lie! And there's more: we've risked our lives for huge sums of money of which I knew nothing about."

"And only now you tell me?" protested Júlia indignantly.

Aurélien told her what he had discovered. At the meeting at the Ministry of Justice, in Paris, the authorities started from the premise that the Frenchman of the NGO had not lied and that the tableau 75, located in Rio de Janeiro, was authentic. The curator used all of his rhetoric to convince his peers and senior treasury officials that, if the government did not take the lead, they would risk missing out on the unique opportunity to buy it. He exaggerated the loss of assets, if other individual buyers or companies acquired the valuable rug. He talked about American museums. He mentioned Sotheby's, which would make the price go through the roof. It was after the long meeting behind closed doors, during which he spent hours waiting in the hallway, that the French government made the ten million euro available and decided that he would be the person to bring the tableau to France. They didn't tell him anything about the high cost of the ransom, since it was secret.

He briefly told Júlia why the NGO's Frenchman was so anxious to meet him: he wanted to know if the money from the purchase was already in Brazil. He would get a large commission, promised by the curator. By then, Leonardo was already aware of everything, without the French government knowing that Big Head had taken the rug from the *babalorisha* from Bahia, killed him, and was anxious to receive the large sum of money — if possible, without handing over the Relic.

Aurélien admitted that, at first, he thought that the money to which the NGO's Frenchman was referring was related to an official request for financial aid to the institution. He only began to suspect the connection with the rug when Tinhão confirmed the story of the *babalorisha* negotiating a "lot of cash" for the rescue of the tapestry.

He recounted the successive unforeseen events after the fire in Rocinha. With the death of the owners of the NGO, Leonardo used the tapestry in the *giras*, imagining that the money made available by the French was already waiting in some bank and would be his with the arrival of the negotiator coming from France. He recalled that he was almost beaten to death just because Big Head had thought he knew where the French government's euro were.

When he came back from the beating and sent the photo of the Relic to the curator, the French authorities confirmed the authenticity of the discovery and automatically cleared the payment. A fair purchase price for the Relic had been negotiated by the French owners of the NGO before they died. When the money was criminally and electronically taken, leaving no trace, the French government had no alternative but to send two special GIGN agents to Brazil to invade the manor and bring back tableau 75 back to France, without being caught. A diabolical plot very well woven by white-collar criminals who took the French government's millions of euro, without leaving a trace.

The whole puzzle had been put together for the journalist.

"Unbelievable! Do you suspect someone in particular?" asked Júlia, dumbfounded with the unpublishable truth of the facts.

"With the exception of the consul, since he was under 'superior orders', I suspect everyone. I always remember my uncle at the Musée d'Orsay, when he mentioned the Apocalypse and compared the devil to money: 'It is the great lie of the universe in the service of exploiters and Satan'. It's a parable you can't forget."

"You're right. Now I understand why the French government had no way out. The Consul was correct," agreed Júlia, still not happy with the situation.

"They avoided an international scandal of great repercussion, and the best solution was to cover up the criminal ransom and immediately open a bank investigation. It is yet another great loss at this terrible time of the international financial crisis. It's crazy!"

"We all had to accept the official version without complaints," added Aurélien, indignantly. "We were forced to accept the fake discovery of the tapestry at Dois Irmãos headquarters in Rocinha, the lie that the two Frenchmen who owned the NGO had hid it under the bed, the thugs took the money, and came back to steal it and torture them. The forged 'receipts' prove the payment. The dead Frenchmen became the great martyrs of the saga of the tapestry's recovery. This was the version that was published by the press, without mentioning the missing money. It suited everyone. A very good plan, made by mischievous hands."

"Who helped you put all the pieces together?"

"I've put it all together yesterday, at the VIP lunch after the ceremony. I sat next to the representative of the Ministry of Economy. He confirmed to me that the millions of euro had been withdrawn and the government was investigating the theft. At dessert, as a compliment, he said that no one had ever suspected me. You can imagine how I felt when I heard that! Me, who was manipulated since the beginning in this Tintin's biblical adventure! Ah! He also told me that I was going to receive a medal for bravery and a promotion in my career as a librarian. A consolation prize!"

"We were really idiots," agreed Júlia.

Aurélien pointed to the "gardens of love", next to the balustrade of the lookout, divided into four equal squares of beds ornamented with boxwoods. The first one was called "Love Tenderness". The pruned shrubs were in the shape of hearts, flames of love and whispering masks. The second one was dedicated to "Passionate Love", made of intertwined hearts. It symbolized unbridled passion. The third one was "Volatile Love", with four fans with hollow horn-shaped angles, representing ephemeral love. The last square was "Tragic Love", made by blades of daggers and swords.

Aurélien was serious. He sensed that the unavoidable time had come to clear things up.

"Can I ask you something?"

"If you're going to ask me to help you recover the money, forget it. I had enough!"

"It's a question of love. I want you to come and move in with me."

Júlia looked at him with a serious look, pale with emotion. She looked deep into his restless eyes and finally managed to whisper:

"Let me think for a while, it's the only thing I ask…"

Júlia looked sad and caressed the medieval archer's suddenly stiff face with infinite tenderness.

"Think for a while?" reacted Aurélien astonished, his eyes angry under his thick eyebrows, incredulous of what he'd heard after the long romantic walks through the gardens of delight.

When she was invited to live in the City of Light, Júlia was afraid to make the biggest decision of her life. She would have the unique opportunity to be a Parisian, to immerse herself in the bathtub of the universal culture of knowledge and art. But she would have to forget her past on the mountains and the unique way of life of a Rio de Janeiro native, leave behind the roots of her childhood, her teenage memories, and the life with her family.

After a long silence, Júlia added:

"Why don't you come and live with me in Brazil?"

"Is that your answer?" asked Aurélien disappointed, but understanding her momentary indecision.

"It's not that. It is just an invitation of love," she replied, sneaking a kiss on his closed lips.

It was a difficult invitation to refuse, living in the Wonderful City. The golden opportunity with which he had dreamed for so long of becoming a Rio dweller, live with the sun shinning every morning, enjoy Carnival, swim in the ocean of the beautiful beaches and go to Maracanã stadium. But having to leave the *Petite France's* past, the dusty books from the libraries, the ancient culture, and his colleagues of the crossbow club. Having to leave the Paris lights, bridges, and air behind.

"I'll think about it, Júlia," said Aurélien with a half-smile.

At that moment, as if by a strange association of ideas, Júlia remembered her mother's interview in Mauá for a São Paulo magazine. Her voice echoing softly, through the gardens of love and the alleys of rose bushes: "You know, daughter, I think that in love, differences attract." All of a sudden, she saw the "little Frenchman" crossing her life and realized that very different worlds united them. She could never delay her decision to live in France, in an enchanted place like Villandry and with the man of her life declaring himself hopelessly in love with her.

There was a long silence. With a bit of sadness in their eyes, the two lovers looked out over the horizon at the maze garden, full of obstacles and shortcuts. Tears began to fall from the little aquamarine eyes.

"I wanted to…" whispered Aurélien in her ear, suddenly interrupted by Júlia's long, passionate kiss, witnessed by the four fancy gardens at their feet.

A gentle breeze caressed the alley of trees and the two lovers. Only the leaves that fell on the sandy floor could tell the rest of the sentence and the end of this comic book love story.

Chapter 30

IT WAS A SUNNY FRIDAY. The day before, the castle was the scene of a millenary war in the sky, which shook the Loire Valley. Now the grand day had come for the gallery to be opened to the general public.

The castle's curator, Ferdinand Rochemont de Sailly, could feel extremely happy and fulfilled in his office, located on the second floor of the castle. The largest tapestry in the world, out of its original headquarters for more than four centuries, now featured the famous scene of the devil imprisoned for a thousand years, which had never been publicly displayed before.

Curator Ferdinand had learned since he was a child that it's very difficult to see. All school education is geared towards writing and reading, seeing is not taken care of. Educators still insist that, in order to "understand" a work of art, it's necessary to read tons of books. They forget that it is useless to see a work of art, if the curious eye does not pause to meditate, analyze, and seek to understand for itself. Unlike his fellow curators, Ferdinand placed great value on looking, and avoided using long explanatory texts on the gallery walls. He knew that, if he used them, a circle of people would form in front of the tableaus, spending far more time to digest that information than trying to see, just see. With no texts, in the absolute silence of the semidarkness, people looked in awe, just seeing the scenes of the extraordinary secular tapestry.

Since it was one of the most important biblical scenes in the sacred book of Revelation, a day of great visitation was expected, largely due to the promotion of the media and the curiosity that the tapestry aroused in children, teenagers, and adults, from the first image, in which St. John is entrusted by Jesus Christ to write His message about the things that would soon happen to the *Seven Churches* in Asia Minor.

The day promised many emotions to visitors, for the unique opportunity to admire this extraordinary "comic book" up close, which helped to understand the prophetic and difficult interpretation of the Revelation, containing the divine secrets of Christ's struggle and victory against the Great Dragon, or Ancient Serpent, mere transfigurations of Satan, known as the great seducer of the universe. And in this fabulous biblical universe, the terrifying image of tableau 75 stood out, recently recovered in Brazil, which was only possible due to the fearless Aurélien and Júlia — authentic protagonists of Tintin's unpublished album.

The visitors arrived early and were already waiting in line, anxious and impatient, to enter the castle and access the three-hundred-and-forty feet of the Apocalypse tapestry. They counted the minutes to be dazzled by the realism and richness of the details of Flemish art, in perfect harmony with the concepts of ordering, clarity and simplicity of 13th century French art. An unforgettable display of all times for the eyes and the soul.

From early in the morning, a long line had formed at the castle gate that stretched across the drawbridge and continued across the Promenade du Bout du Monde. The guards checked their watches constantly. There were only ten minutes left until the opening of the ticket sales windows at 10 am, increased by one euro.

Most of the visitors were tourists. The others were from the city of Angers itself. They had read the exciting news reports that praised the biblical significance of the recovery of the seven-headed Dragon, finally caged.

It was also a journey to the past, as the booklets said, since the tapestry, next to the tableau, was the most expressive form of medieval art at a time when the Church encouraged kings to spread this art to teach the principles of the Catholic religion. And in that aspect, the valuable iconographic heritage of the Apocalypse surpassed, in interest, all biblical themes for its magnificent illustrations and prophecies about the end times.

A light mist covered the seventeen majestic towers of the castle and the flower garden in front of the gallery. There was the soft whisper of a morning breeze caressing the leaves of the trees along the main alley to the portal to the chapel. Everything was going on normally that morning for the reestablishment of public visitation.

All of a sudden, the old lame guard's anguished voice is heard, almost at the end of his round inside the gallery.

"Oh, my God! Oh, dear God!"

The accelerated and dragged steps of boots hammering the stone floor to reach the first phone in sight echoed, and then the guard's anguished words were heard:

"Call the police! Close the castle! Tell the curator to come immediately to the gallery! Hurry, hurry…"

"What's the matter? What's going on?" asked the girl that worked at the ticket box, nervous.

"There's been a tragedy, girl!"

The phone was abruptly hung and all the employees rushed toward the entrance of the gallery.

The guards in front of the gate did not comply with the ticket office's order to forbid the small crowd to enter.

Curator Ferdinand, panting a lot, was one of the first to arrive. Everyone huddled around the double doors and then, entering the lit room, accelerated their steps to where the guard who had called earlier and was now standing in front of the scenes of tableaus 74 and 76 with blue background of the Apocalypse.

"It's unbelievable! The tableau is gone!" said the old guard with a trembling voice, surrounded by the silence of the disbelievers.

"Oh, my God!" exclaimed the curator, his eyes stunned.

They all stood with their breath caught in their throats in the face of the immense void of the newly renovated and painted wall. The oldest employee of the castle, dressed in black, baffled, covered her open mouth with her hand, containing the astonishment in her small eyes. Nobody wanted to believe what they could no longer see.

The Beast of a thousand years was free again, with its golden trident turned to the sky, laughing somewhere on Earth.

***

font family Minion Pro
printed by Ingram
first edition October, 2020